Our Savage Heart

Polestars

A series of single author collections by exceptional writers.

Our Savage Heart

POLESTARS 4

Justina Robson

NewCon Press
England

First edition, published in the UK January 2024
by NewCon Press
41 Wheatsheaf Road, Alconbury Weston, Cambs, PE28 4LF, UK

NCP316 (hardback)
NCP317 (softback)

10 9 8 7 6 5 4 3 2 1

ISBN: 978-1-914953-65-1 (hardback)
978-1-914953-66-8 (softback)

Cover Art by Enrique Meseguer; cover design by Ian Whates
Editing and typesetting by Ian Whates

Contents

A Game of Clones

Zeroth kept a strict night and day cycle running for his human crew. When they slept he spent the time absorbing journals about the best care for humans who were spending their lives as space-farers. His favourite game was subtly redesigning the habitat set-up for health and happiness while not seeming to affect their own choices. It wasn't easy, because nothing that tries to mimic the atmospheric envelope of a planet in a closed system the size of three football fields whilst hurtling through space is easy, but he did the best he could. Only during phase shift travel did he suspend operations, but then, nobody noticed as their biology didn't have a means of perceiving temporal stutter.

This bothered him. He felt over-advantaged. In fact he hadn't told any of his humans about the phasing, as it was a technology known only to a small collective of machines and they had decided to embargo the knowledge. They would probably kill themselves quite a lot trying to figure it out, and take a lot of good machines with them.

He was already horrified by humans' desperately short life-expectancy, a matter not helped by the fact that his friends were rogues and mercenaries. But while it lasted he was determined that their existence would be the best it could be. A group of Forged Host Entities had a forum where they left tips and information for each other, and he pored over it for the latest developments. It was during one of these intense study periods that he met X, one of the nameless members of the embargo group.

X was a Host who maintained a much bigger tank than he did, and who was a constant source of endlessly fascinating detail on biologically dynamic terraria. They soon found themselves in constant blips of conversation, with Zeroth mostly deferring to X's impressive breadth of experience.

X maintained millions of humans simultaneously, compared to Zeroth's five. Unlike Zeroth's personal involvement, X held their humans lightly, in the manner of a friendly zookeeper. X was consciously distanced from human origins, and had not even a name, merely using the letter as a designation for purposes of address. Every human contained by X was free to live and die as they wished without reference to it or its wishes. As long as they paid the bill.

But Zeroth regarded his onboard humans as family, in particular Nico, who was notionally Captain. It was of no importance that he was a war frame with multiple massive ship bodies, capable of living in any environment, and they were small bipedal creatures who existed only within the most delicately balanced ecology. In pursuit of that best ecology he had been waiting eagerly for several days on the forum to discover the results of introducing airborne Forged nanobeasts as mimics of common diseases (all the immunity benefits but none of the dangers) when he saw a message in the private folder reserved for the Embargo Group.

'Dear Zeroth,' it began, a great concession, and the closest thing to emotional affect that X had possibly ever written, 'I have a security issue which relates to your merge-human, Nico. Please contact me on any secure channel (options below) at your earliest convenience.'

Zeroth opened a channel and, as X relayed the situation, felt that he ought to have some eyes so that he could open them much wider.

Shambles, the massive host environment run by X, home to any who wanted to call it home, marketplace for any activity within the Solar, had a serial killer who just happened to be genetically identical to Zeroth's big brother, Nico Perseid.

Ordinarily a killer would be of no importance, as X could have disposed of them via any number of security protocols: you signed contracts to enter Shambles, and killing other marketeers was definitely a clause that ended with your instant execution. There was nowhere to hide, as every *where* was a part of the being policing you. But stopping the murders wasn't the problem.

The issue for X was that X couldn't see *how* the murderer was doing it.

This was of much bigger import than a few brief and probably unimportant lives. Theoretically, doing something X couldn't see within its own body was impossible. Which was, probably, why someone was doing it. To flag up, or bait, or bribe, or dare, or engage or test a new technology. At least X thought so.

Its pride, had it had any, would have been severely challenged. The killer represented an operational loophole. To get to the bottom of it they must remain alive until they were caught in the act. Catching them required seeing them do it. And that was the issue. X was convinced that this was a development test being carried out by a rival machine. But there was no certainty that the embargo had held. Really it could be anyone. It could be operators they had no knowledge of.

'My value as a secure host will be lost if I am not able to conceal the existence of the killer. Their actions are accelerating in a measured cycle so it is only a matter of time before that happens,' X said. 'I believe the murderer is using phase technology to effect material fatality. This is a development which will create an impulse of acquisition in the humans, followed by a cascade of potential destruction that should not be allowed to continue.'

There was no question it meant its own destruction. Destruction in general was good for business if you were a technology producer, which they all were, and only bad if you were on the short-circuit end. The destruction of X, it went without saying, included the potential for the destruction of Zeroth and all the other advanced Forged currently vying for control of various bits of the solar system.

'I am not enabled for such technology beyond the use of the prototype transit system,' Zeroth said. 'My knowledge of it is purely theoretical.'

'I will give you the means to construct full sensory and connection devices,' X said. 'This shall be considered my retainer for your services. To match and counteract this invader is my only interest. I require the use of your human crew.'

'They aren't devices,' Zeroth said.

'I will give you a complete copy of my configuration.'

With that Zeroth could match anything X could do, would learn all it had learned. Such an offer was beyond price on the frontier. It was the keys to a new kingdom.

'I have to ask them," Zeroth said. "They may say no.'

'I will give you copies of all the data I have received concerning phase shifting from all sources. If you persuade them.'

Interesting, Zeroth thought. By any calculation, X's offers amounted to nearly everything it had. Possibly there was only the human and Forged data cores left to trade: the records of everything everyone had ever said and done within X's remit. Mine that and you would have untold riches.

'Without Nico's participation, I cannot investigate,' X said, clarifying unnecessarily. 'I will give you my data cores and continuous access in real time.'

Zeroth experienced a frisson of alarm at such naked urgency. Vast tracts of unwelcome possibility began to yawn before him at the prospect of situations so dire that X was prepared to dish up its existence as collateral.

Zeroth hesitated for an eternal couple of picoseconds. 'You could make your own avatars from the DNA map. Why don't you?'

The manufacturing of human clones, or the synthesis of any genetically determined organism, was outside the capacity of a being like X. But it could have bought one. Zeroth's whole human crew were the products of just such a factory. Escaped, resentful, scarred, dogged products who had fomented a reasonably successful revolution, but still. Products. And if one shop was closed others were surely open elsewhere. X had currencies aplenty and all the contacts in existence.

But there was a reason. 'I am responsible for millions of lives. I cannot expose myself directly to the possibility of annihilation by confronting the killer using a technology which potentially links me directly to their weapon.'

Ah, Zeroth began to see. The gear that infused avatar humans to connect them to Forged minds and machineries was the weak spot here. And X had already admitted that the phase issue was passing all its firewalls. Even so.

'Too dangerous for you, but it's fine if Nico does it?' Zeroth was outraged.

X transmitted a blurt which opened up into a very extensively argued and theorised plan, plus additional convincing justifications about many lives versus one.

Zeroth looked at it. But only because X had not said anything callous, such as that Zeroth could easily make another Nico if the first one got fried. He'd been expecting that line. Even Nico would have used it. But it didn't appear. 'Fine. It all looks a lot like a trap.' He flagged that as referring to the situation they found themselves in, not X's plan.

'It is clearly a trap where you and I are both the targets, as I must involve you due to the use of the Nico Perseid clone. I am bound to investigate and you are bound to assist.'

'Let's say we do nothing.' The thrill was starting to pale a bit.

'My security breach becomes known. The Embargo Group will eliminate me as a risk. They will destroy the clone and many of my guests in that action, and in doing so will destroy their chance to identify the operator. The operator will likely continue testing and baiting Group members, refining its abilities, until it is capable of eliminating any and all competition. This includes you and, of course, your humans. Such is life. Adapt or die.'

Zeroth felt around internally for Nico's convictions, for Nico's intelligence when dealing with criminals and their works. It was like reaching for a gun hidden in a pocket. Zeroth had a lot of resources, but Nico had lived by wits alone. And strength. And violence.

He considered that X might be playing him. It seemed unlikely. He wasn't, yet, a match for X in any meaningful sense. But after this trade he could become so.

X had also clearly anticipated this potential. It added. 'If the investigation and actions go as hoped and we succeed in eliminating the threat and obtaining its technologies then I will also give you the corpse of the Mausi Atomkraft Vigilante.'

A lost Forged. The one that had started the whole discovery of the phase technology in the first place.

Zeroth only harboured minor doubts that X actually had it. He was more interested now in what was really going on, fired by the dangers and opportunities.

'Hold onto your kitchen sinks,' he said. 'I'll ask them.'

'So let me get this straight,' Nico said. 'There's a clone of me out there, piloted by some ultra-thing and/or person, murdering people. in Shambles.' He was lounging on one of the circled recliners, a misplaced blonde surfer in sweats and thick deck socks. He was using the sagging ends of the socks to try and swat the nose of the dark young woman seated just out of range of his feet.

'As if you weren't vain enough already,' Two said, swatting at a sock with the end of her dreadlocks. On her other side the taller, stockier figure of Tash grunted in agreement, eyes glazed as she studied all the details that Zeroth was handing over in the background.

Nico wriggled closer, head sliding off the lap of his boyfriend and onto the couch as he pursued sock wars.

Issy, the boyfriend, seemed to be asleep, although he was just sitting with his eyes shut as usual because he had to concentrate hard to prevent his attention drifting; he was usually in two worlds at once and although Zeroth piggybacked around to try and sneak a peek at what was going on in the hidden one (some biological thing he had yet to develop adequate senses for, he assumed) he felt, curiously, the amused rays of Issy's regard on him like he was caught in the act and this stopped him, as if they were in a constant game of statues.

Nico was still talking, 'And X wants you to make three copies of me, so that Two, Issy and Tash can drive them around as decoys, because they will confuse the targeting of this thing's long-distance wotsit, and trap his trace in his avatar, so he can't escape to wherever he really is.' The last word was a puff of air as he made a decisive strike and pressed the sock to Two's nose at the limit of his reach.

Two snatched the sock and yanked it off, swatting the foot away with a practised swipe. 'Sucker.' She put the sock over her hand and made it into a puppet. 'Now you've summoned Socksy. And we all know how that ends.'

Socksy, very much like a woolly cobra now, drew itself up. It looked at Two, who nodded at it, 'Yes. He is a pain in the ass. Let's see if Captain Braindead understands the rest of the plan. Do you think he will?'

Socksy laughed so hard it collapsed down with a whack onto Nico's other foot and bit it solidly.

Nico continued primly. 'One of the other three may get ported to where the real killer is, or may not, or may get ported into their own head, or not. But it might go wrong another way, and then one of us will be dead, and he'll be off to murder again, but this time knowing that he's been rumbled.'

'Roughly right,' Zeroth said. 'There was the technical bit…'

Socksy was trying to save its partner in a wrestling match with the grip of Nico's toes. The fight was clearly a rematch, with grudges.

'Spare me,' Nico held up his hand, preparing, his attention seemingly focused on the fight. His words were punctuated by feints and wrestles. 'I've got this. There's a real Shambles and a virtual Shambles. One is slightly laggy, not always the same one, because of temporal phase juggling. This means that sometimes things are there, but sometimes they aren't, both physical objects and virtual presences. And the only way to tell who is really there is that you can't hit someone who isn't there. Which is where I come in.'

Socksy let go and turned to look at Two in open-mouthed amazement.

'I know. That's so close to right,' she said with a shrug – what can you do?

Socksy returned to the attack.

Nico grinned his all-white-teeth grin, on the home run. 'And the bad guy is using the laggy times to escape. And X can't track him because when X is in one phase the killer is in the other, and nobody has access to the thing they can't see because they can't see it. But we could see it, if X gave us their phase tech, because we're not making it, we're only existing in it. And it may be a gateway to a parallel existence you could get stuck in and never escape, but that's just extras. Hah!'

'Remarkably accurate,' Zeroth said. Even though he wasn't looking at Issy now he felt, in a way that seemed very much physical, that Issy was looking *at him* and that was just disturbing. He risked an actual glance with sensors and Issy opened his eyes and smiled.

Chilling! Zeroth nudged Tashlynn, to apprise her of this, because she was also a ship like him and maybe knew what was going on, but she was too absorbed in the huge calculations that X had sent across to pay attention.

Meanwhile Socksy had begun to unravel slightly at the toe.

'Look what you've done to him!' Two said, snatching Socksy back to stroke it soothingly.

'See, nobody needs brains,' Nico stuck his tongue out at Two.

Socksy leaped and snatched the other sock. Two put it on her other hand. 'Idiot. You let your guard down. And now there's two. Just like there will soon be four Nicos. Man and sock. Each wearable. Each disposable. Each stinky.'

'There's only one,' Nico said, pouting. 'Let's get that straight.'

'What if our Nico ends up caught in the alternate phase?' Isylon asked.

'If any of the wrong Nicos end up in the wrong connection they will be ported to the murderer's body of origin. We let them stay long enough to get a clue and then we cut the connection,' Zeroth said with more confidence than he felt. He was still hanging on Tashlynn's analysis, but it looked very much like this was a theory that had never been tested.

'*Who's* being murdered?' Tylu asked.

She'd been tucked up so small and so quiet opposite Nico that Zeroth had nearly forgotten her. She didn't keep any connections open to anyone. Now she unrolled herself and sat gripping a cushion, knuckles pale. It was easy for Zeroth to assume everyone would roll through trauma like Nico did, with the fire of resentment stoking him onwards. But she was much more inward than he.

Zeroth put on his kind voice. 'Sometimes it's actual people bodily present in Shambles, sometimes it's people who are connected from remote locations. But in those last cases the person

14

dies at distance, no matter how far away they are, or what system they're using to join in.'

'How do you *virtually* murder someone? I mean. They're not *there*.' Tylu asked.

Tashlynn cleared her throat. 'Not that I know this for any particular reason, but you leap into their identity matrix, corrupt it fatally and they're as good as dead.'

Issy nodded, 'Their body isn't dead, but their memories are dead. They end up as empty bodies, or the body dies anyway because the disruption extends out into autonomic function. But for all intents and purposes that person is gone.'

Tash waved a finger between herself and Two, including Zeroth vaguely to indicate that the brains team had been puzzled by it too, 'We think the firewalls failed because it was part of the physical person, sharing their timeframe, and so it was bypassed the same way this thing is bypassing X.'

'Yes, but *who*?' Tylu said. 'Maybe we can do the same to them. If they're running a Nico, then maybe they're far away too. They will just escape again, even if we find and kill their Nico. Then they will pick up another avatar. Sorry, Nico.' She glanced at him with deeply apologetic brown eyes and reached across the occasional table that separated the couches to touch his knee with a dab of comfort before shrinking back into her seat and grabbing up the cushion to protect her against the unpleasantness of what she was saying.

'You're not going,' Nico said to her with a surprisingly gentle tone, folding his legs up crossed now that he had lost his weapons. 'You're safe here. You stay aboard and run this end with Zero.'

The two Socksys looked at Two, who made an unhappy face. Nico sighed.

'But *who's being murdered?*' Tylu asked. 'Doesn't the who matter? It's not just about some machines having a big physics contest, is it?'

Perhaps you had to be the victim of that kind of thing to feel it so personally, Zeroth thought. He knew he felt it personally. They were all part and parcel of something evolving that they were too small to understand. And that hurt.

'There doesn't seem to be a pattern or a reason at first glance,' Zeroth said, replacing the peaceful view of the stars that made up the lounge wall with a set of faces, names and identifications. 'Here's the list so far.'

They were all Forged. One was a ship, two were minor station outposts. both of which had been active in harbouring edge-technology developers. The rest were people of various sorts, nobody on Earth, only one on Mars, a couple from stations further out. They seemed to have no common interests unless you counted remaining alive.

'I know him,' Tylu said, pointing. 'From when… from before. I can't quite remember. But he's familiar.'

'Criminals?' Two asked.

Tylu nodded. 'For sure. Nobody dealt with us on legit business. V, my driver, dealt only in stolen Forged Tech. I can try to remember the details. Maybe Iss can help? We could sift the Harmony records for sales, too. See if anyone bought a Nico on or off list.' She looked at Isylon who smiled at her, nodded.

'We destroyed the Nico pattern,' he said. 'But an engineer could make one again with the right information.'

'Tash and I will find out who the others are,' Two said, 'though I'm kind of surprised X doesn't already know. Don't they know everything about the people in their space?'

'I thought that,' Zeroth said. 'But they said if there was a connection it wasn't obvious. Some of them have dealings with various places, people, businesses. Some don't. They thought it could be a non-pattern sample, and it looks that way.'

'Non-pattern?' Nico.

Two butted in. 'Historically, Machines are incapable of non-patterns. They would create one by algorithm, so it would be a hidden pattern, or by using atomic decay, so they had to have a referent which gives it away. Humans felt they were superior because they could choose randomly, but it turns out everything they do is algorithmically and/or dependent in the same way, so nowadays it's a meme that if you have a non-pattern sample you're communicating that there is a hidden reference. You're mocking efforts at detection. Nico. Do not cross your eyes at me. You asked.'

'So the murders might not be about the victims, but just a message, like a smoke signal?' Nico said. Socksy nodded at him.

Zeroth broke in, 'Guys, the identity is not as important as the method for us, . We're private contractors, not the police. I mean. There are no police. Or law. Out here.'

The Socksys looked around them in awe.

'You've changed, man,' Two said. 'Look at you, directing things. Keeping us on track.'

'I thought it was an improvement,' Zeroth said hopefully. 'Correct grammar. Full sentences Thinking ahead. Taking responsibility. Like Nico said.'

'To be fair, I didn't say any of the stuff about sentences,' Nico said, scooting back to Issy and pretending to be a dog with its legs in the air.

Issy patted his head.

Zeroth, feeling nervous, did the machine equivalent of riffling his Care of the Human files. 'I uploaded a lot of people. Most of them were pretty good at talking.'

'You – uploaded people?' Nico asked slowly.

'Um, well, there's a resource pack that contains the mental and biometric patterning of living people who were, or are, considered exceptionally good human beings. Judged by skill or wit or art, all kinds of merits. Forged with human simulacra interfacing can have them all for a monthly subscription. People donate their prints to it. They get paid every time you employ their reasoning or insights above a certain threshold. Free after ten uses. Because by then you integrated them completely. Lots of Forged use it. To update themselves.'

There was a moment of silence among his mostly-human crew as they absorbed this.

'You could probably use it yourself, Nic. With a few adjustments,' Zeroth added.

A longer silence. Oh dear.

'What's it called?' Nico asked.

'Peeps,' Tashlynn said from left field; dry as a bone. As a desert. As a bone that's been in a desert for a thousand years. She shrugged at their slack jaws. 'What? I didn't make it.'

But she was interrupted. 'Who did you get? I got the Inspirational Pack!' Tylu said, with the sudden eager rush of a fan, bouncing in her seat.

'Oh, I love that one!' Zeroth said.

'Ladies,' Nico. 'Can I just swing this back for a moment to the cloning bit? I mean. Wouldn't it be better if I went alone? Then there's a fifty-fifty chance of you getting the bad guy. If there's only two of me.'

'Yeah, about that,' Zeroth said, drawing on every resource he had but still feeling that he was coming up short as he faced Nico. 'If we just have one of you then the killer has a one in two chance of escape. For every extra one of you we have, those chances drop. At five the odds in our favour are very high. Tash, Two, Issy and I will be the other four. That's good enough.'

'Just one thing,' Nico added. 'Where are we going to get four pathetic, pale, hollow imitations of me from?'

'When we left Harmony I stole all their blueprints.' Zeroth said. 'I can knock off a molecular facsimile which has a fully wired Forged porting system quite easily.'

Now they all looked at each other. It was very much the look of people who were re-adjusting their internal realities in a major way.

'I... was thinking of making myself a human form. I mean. You've all got one. You get to have all the expressions and you can't even look at me because I'm all around you so it's not like having a conversation with a real person. I want to be on the same footing. And for that I need actual feet.'

'We don't all have a super-massive war platform alternative body though,' Two said.

'But you could have. I mean. You can have anything you like,' Zeroth said. 'I can make anything. It's just a question of materials and time. You just can't leave your original body. You are still mortally tied to that. Far as I know. I just do extensions.'

There was another long silence. Someone took a breath to speak, but then didn't, as they all thought this through.

'On a serious note though,' Nico said. 'You can't create avatars, I mean people, to use as taxis. That makes us as bad as the bad guys.'

'Yes,' Tylu said earnestly.

'It's all right,' Zeroth assured them, 'I'll work with Isylon to make the replicas. On the surface, to the genetic eye, it's Nico. But underneath, it's empty.'

'So, exactly like Nico,' Two said with a wicked grin. The Socksys fell about.

The five Nicos met briefly in the departure bay. They were dressed differently.

'Issy,' Nico said, pointing at the one in grey and white. He watched himself bow and then blow a kiss.

'Two?' he guessed for the one in green.

'Tash,' it said. 'God, you've got some guns, man...' and Nico watched himself flex.

'You are an abomination,' he said to Tashlynn, who had once committed murder while housed in his own skin. 'But sure. Enjoy yourself. Why the fuck not? You did last time. And that means that this must be Zeroth.' He pointed at the one in purple.

Zeroth jumped a full three sixty in excitement.

'That is so wrong,' Nico said, more disturbed than he wanted. Zeroth could tell because he was linked into all of them in a very careful way, as he would have to handle all the transmissions and signals. Then, 'Am I that camp?'

'No, you're a big sulky,' said the one in white and grey. 'Gruff and macho. Never the least bit idiotic in any way at all.'

'Heh!' Green Nico and White Nico fistbumped each other.

'Fuck the lot of you,' Nico said and stumped off to his dropship.

Zeroth knew it meant 'I love you.' He could feel it. They all could. It sang against the words like a secret wave.

He tuned his connections, determined that nothing was going to go wrong.

Shambles was much bigger than they had anticipated. An entire human-scale city of more than six boroughs. was the house that X built.

It had originally been called Shambhala, after the mythic place of the same name, but that pretension had mutated as the accretion continued. Shambles suited it far better, as something that advanced erratically, lurching, ominous, ancient, filled with multitudes.

In keeping with this chaos aesthetic the boroughs bled into one another even as they strove for very different experiences. More than one modelled themselves on the visions of futures past. The borough of Blades, where Murdery Nico and Real Nico were destined to meet, was the happy playground of those who wanted to exist in the twenty second century grime.

It was Classic.

It was filthy.

It was raining.

As Nico came out of the port in his leather-look longcoat and heavy cargo pants he felt personally offended by the spattering drizzle which seeped from what looked like a very real maundering sky. What kind of deviants wanted indoor rain?

He hated rain. It had made his life miserable on the streets of Chaontium when he was a kid, and that wasn't and never would be, long ago enough. It made the whole thing feel even more personal, if that were possible.

Strips of shops peered through the dim twilight, signs blinking, glaring, assaulting the eye with acid green and ruby red neon, sparkling with LEDs. Huge adverts, swept with lights, thrust spas, medicines, restaurants, sex clubs at him. Above them the red and white running lights of personal cars zipped in razor lines several decks high.

Yeah, just like home. They must have shared the same cheap-ass designer.

He clenched his fists in the pockets of his coat.

In keeping with X's protocols he had no need to get lost, he could use any amount of inboard map, but he chose to keep everything off except the blinky blip in his vision which showed the location of MurderNico.

He set off towards it.

On the way, he tried to see if he could tell who was physically present and who was an AR persona, but it was impossible. There was only one moment where he saw someone's hand clip through another person's forearm as they passed in the street, but it was hard to be sure that had happened. No aspect of realism had been spared. Everyone pushed air, breathed, smelled, had that unmistakable presence, bulk, vibe. The rumour was that nobody could match Shambles' full render, and that seemed to be true. Doing it for millions of people, half of them remote, hours away, all simulcast: that was hardcore machine processing. He didn't feel like he was much of a match for that kind of thing.

If X was dirty then, even with Zeroth, they were all fucked.

He reached the door to a huge apartment block, filled with private rooms and personal living spaces, went in. Litter pickers and other small bots whizzed around, most of them on delivery duties. The humans made no effort to avoid them, walking as if they weren't there. Machines were still just things, then, he guessed. Strange.

He came out of the entry hall into a huge atrium. It reached up ten levels right through the building's core to a cracked set of glass roof lights. Water dripped down. He watched the fall, counted the seconds. Splashed by drops the gaudy tenting of eateries and drink service platforms floated up and down the balcony layers like rising and falling bubbles in a tall glass of flattening soda.

'Hey,' he said to the ground floor vendor of some kind of fruit cocktails, a cute girl with ponytails. 'I'm meeting someone special on Eight. Gonna pop the question. Can you be up there in ten minutes, give me your best, all in, for two?' He gestured upwards and to the 'South' side where MurderNico's blinking blue dot strafed across as tiny spot no bigger than one room wide. Pacing. Waiting for his appointment with what he thought was a buyer.

Nico handsomely overpaid and was rewarded with a big smile and a butt wiggle. For some reason the serving girl was decked out like a cheerleader in all the brand colours. At least she could still smile. It was more than he'd've managed in the circumstances.

'Sure,' she said brightly. 'Ten minutes. I'll be right there.'

He walked out of her sight line, looked at the clear elevator cars, turned aside and pushed through the fire doors into the service access. There were stairs. They moved slowly once he'd chosen his direction, assisting, but other than that there weren't any special effects. No expense spared to make it seem genuinely shitty. Even some vomit and old wrappers in the corners at the turns, and broken up old paint on the handrails. On Five there was a bloodstain along one wall where someone had got shot and slid across the concrete.

He checked in with the others. All in position.

He could stay here, well inside range, and do nothing and still meet the brief. He was only a genetic decoy for a machine. They could stay quiet, do the job, get paid and get out. Just had to wait.

He was aware of Zeroth with him, gave him the nod, felt his surprise as he realised Nico wasn't going to stick with the plan.

'Too dangerous to hang around, mate,' Nico said to him and then quietly but firmly cut him off so he could look, but say and do nothing.

A familiar cold kind of pressure had taken over inside Nico which Zeroth remembered from every past mission. Like this was something he was made for.

On Eight he paused to look through the plasglass peephole set in the door, but there were no people in the corridor. The blue dot was to his left.

He went right and made a check on which rooms were full and which empty. They all let out onto the central atrium via a shared ring balcony, separated for each apartment by opaque dividers. The rail was waist high, higher for places with children and pets, but MurderNico didn't have any of these. He did have a few possible targets. The place was potentially full of them, it was a hotbed of renegade dealings, you could chuck a teacup and probably hit someone who was hoping to score or fence looted tech.

Now Nico had a hard decision to make. If he trusted X was not in on this, then he could rely on the feeds. If he thought X was playing them, then this is where he should hang back, stick to the original vision, wait and see who appeared and what fell out. He put in a check status to the others.

'Got any intel?' he asked Two, feeling her consternation as she navigated her Nico around in the Academics District, so pulled in all directions by her interests that she was the kid in the sweetshop; the one who'd never had sweets, until now.

'G'bluh,' she said. 'If there is something wicky wacky going on none of our sensors are picking it, even on the ultraspeed lines. Not a ping, not a bing.' Then she picked up on his adrenaline levels. 'Nic,' she said, warningly.

'Issy,' he switched effortlessly, blocking her off. 'You good?'

Issy's Nico was walking with the sedateness of a sage along the promenade of the aquarium in Deep Waters. It was a gigantic fish tank. He was studying, whilst attempting to appear that he was not studying, the people in the aquaria all around him. The water and air were separated by fields which were undetectable to human senses so that he seemed to stride gently along a corridor magically created inside an ocean wonderland. Nico hadn't known there were aquatic and amphibious humans either and that was great, but it wasn't relevant. He'd sent Issy there as it was the point he thought least likely to get boggled by the spook. Now he had to worry about him getting eaten by a shark.

'I... am... amazed...' Issy said, pausing to stare upwards as a shoal of fish swam over his head. He put his hand up and watched his fingertips puncture the tension of the water's skin, watched them come out. A single drop ran down into his sleeve. 'Look!'

'Stand by.' Nico said.

Issy's attention snapped back. 'Why, what's happening?'

Zeroth was right there with them from his Nico's position in the recycling station, pretending to be a worker sorting crap. 'Nico?'

Nico didn't like any of it and his instincts were what he followed. That and his principles. He opened to Zeroth just long enough to say, 'Tell X to get ready. I'm gonna trigger your event. Give me five minutes.'

'We are all X,' Zeroth began in a serious attempt at explanation, but Nico had already turned him off, locking them all out with the finesse he'd learned from being someone else's avatar for too long.

Nico knew very well. They were all X, and X knew they were pissed.

In front of him the room masthead to MurderyNico's lair shifted its colour blatantly from red to green. X had undone the locks.

Nico pushed the door open and went through. For him it was all real time. For X he guessed it was like centuries passing if it was processing in terms of quantum shifts. But his target was locked in the slow world of human physics like he was. Fast though. Of course, he thought, watching himself leap up from the reclining chair in the semi-darkness of the lounge, kicking the chair backwards, turning all in one move. He was made to fight.

'Who..?' Murder, his face surprised but not surprised. He was expecting it.

'It's me,' Nico said.

Fist meets face.

Head snaps around. Unprepared. Not used to fights. Weak. Worthless.

Nico wonders if he's overcooked it, but his second self is on the floor, hand to miraculously unbroken jaw. No glass for you my lad. 'What the fuck...?'

Nico reaches down and grabs the jacket collar, drags the dirty blonde head back up into his sightline. Fist back for another go, this time the side ribs. No defences. Gut punch. A few shocks, a bit of pain but not much because he doesn't register pain as pain, only as problems, and no reason to think this clone is different. Not hurting him, more kind of getting him going.

'Get... out...' Nico isn't really sure what he means here but it seems appropriate.

Get out of my body.

Get out of my life.

Get out into your weird little snap of time.

He feels, almost unconsciously, some kind of recuperation in the other, a bunching of power, a download coming in that will do all the combat. He goes for the uppercut but Murder has finally woken up and instead he finds himself grabbed in a mirror image grip, lifted off his feet and swung into the wall.

He feels they're both suitably shocked by seeing their own faces one inch apart but wrong, not mirrored, that strange uncanny valley of what other people see when they look at you. It's you, but it's not you.

'Who are you?' Murder is processing the fact that he can only connect with Nico in the real. Nico doesn't exist in virtual for him. And that's not meant to be. Also, although he was expecting himself to show up the actual contact is jarring. It's dislodged something. There are two ghosts in the machine.

Nico knows this because X lets him know. X is playing along, on his side, giving all the angles.

Murder is forced to focus on the real, his attention sags in the unreal, power dissipating, and X sneaks around the back of that, gliding like the merest shadow.

Three ghosts.

Nico can't think of a snappy one liner. Everything's much too busy for his liking.

He slams his forehead into Murder's face and it's weirdly satisfying, as if he's purging a lot of the rage he feels for all his past shitty decisions. They've both got bioengineered bone. Nothing gives. Here's the unfairness of Nico's old victories, old murders really, if you want to cut it that way. But now he's facing his equal. If two anythings that have lived separate lives are equal.

They're not.

Murder is piloted by someone with big plans and schemes, all that fancy gubbins.

Nico is piloted by need, relatively without mind. He wants only to protect his family. First it was Twostar. Then it was the others. Now it contains Issy and Zero. With every addition a cold calculator has taken over the rage machine that was the only operating system for his life as a kid. Murder was expecting the old Nico, but he wasn't expecting this.

As skull meets nasal bone Family Nico's already doing his own lifting and running, pushing, shoving, hustling, shifting grip, making sure every step breaks the other's contact with the ground so they can't stop him, not all the way through the lounge and not across the balcony and not when Nico spins at the last moment and feels his butt hit the too-low-for-big-guys balcony rail as he throws his head back and brings up his knees.

They somersault over the rail into the well.

Has it been ten minutes?

Murder doesn't know about that. He thinks it's all over.

Nico feels X's sudden ! of triumph.

Question popped.

Whatever the event is, it has just gone out. The signal of doom has moved.

Not into Nico, because he's crashing through the roof of the floating Tiki Bar, aware of the little stall's shiver and shake as the two of them land on the bar back, shattering glass and the display of fruit, rolling down into the service lane beside the screaming girl.

The stall careers sideways and hits a kebab shack.

The invisible fields that hold the ocean gently separate and stabilise them. Commercial enterprises got insurance paid on.

Nico's grip is still locked but the other's has dropped. Blood runs down Murder's neck. There's a gash on his head. But he's slacker than that. He seems out in a way that suggests death to Nico, even though he's still breathing.

The cheery girl has stopped screaming and is staring open-mouthed at the identical two of them. Her bar towel is clutched to her chest. Strawberry and mango puree look like splattered brains all over her face.

Nico looks at the mess. 'I'll pay for that.'

He checks for Issy. There.

He checks for Zeroth. There.

He checks for Two. Not there.

'Fuck!'

Twostar had run her Nico carefully, using it only to look at the incredible place she was in. Never had she dreamed that a hub for criminals and renegade Forged was going to house a thriving intellectual society. The place was filled with things that looked like shops which were café forums, and things which looked like gardens which were ongoing experiments, and things which looked like apartments which were meeting places for people who were feverishly involved in research and development of just about everything under the sun, and over it, and all around it, and in it.

She hadn't even known half of these things were things.

She felt gobsmacked into a profound inner silence by the sheer weight of what she had never thought she didn't know and had wandered, vague, drifting. She felt that she was doing well at listening for the tell-tale flicker of the murderer's systems lock when she felt a shiver like the fall of powder into the inner surface of the avatar's skin. It was still a surprise. A horrible surprise, dusting her into motes, taking her power, pushing her out.

And then she wasn't in her ideal wonderland any more.

She was in the interior of a spacecraft, walking quickly, in a way that wanted to run but couldn't, to exorcise the adrenaline of a thumping heart and sweating hands and the panic trying to hammer up from her throat to her head. It wasn't her body. It wasn't Nico's body. It was awkward, strange. Her thoughts weren't her thoughts. They raced, scampering ahead, feverishly.

Caught I am caught am I caught?

Connections were being cut with the frenzied speed that was really hacking, hacking desperately at bonds and then she was *seen* and she saw –

That she was back at the edge of the Garden of Incomparable Daisies, wearing her best friend's body, feeling the bizarre sensation of him from the inside, like a suit too big and strangely weighted to fit.

She sat him on a bench, reached into his pocket for a bandana, found it, silky, just rough enough, tied it around his blonde surfer's shagpile of hair and tied it tight back until his eyes were slitted and clarity came to mind.

'Zero, can you hear me? Did you see?'

'I saw. Just get back to the drop cap when you can.'

She clasped her hands together and marvelled at how strong they were, reached back to her self in Zeroth's distant embrace, ran for the exits, fast, so fast, her breath lasting almost forever so she reached the dock laughing because it really wasn't fair how much stronger than her that he was.

Nico dragged Murder out of the damaged drinks shack, through the atrium, past a lot of gawpy onlookers, and onto the street.

He gave some money to the crying server who was trailing them, bewailing. He gave her some more money. She stopped crying and helped him get the unconscious body over his shoulder in a fireman's lift. He switched himself back on.

'The host has left that body,' X told him as it engaged again, sending his car, clearing his route, filling his bank accounts. Zeroth was there too, in sync.

'I'm taking it,' Nico said to both of them to forestall any objections to his claim, waiting for X to bring the car through the traffic.

They sent a med pod, big enough for several people. When the doors slid open the car was empty. He dumped the body onto one of the exam beds, put it in the recovery position, strapped it in, and laid himself on the bunk opposite. Reached over to tuck a fallen arm back up into position.

'Did you get what you wanted?' he asked then, aware of fields holding them in place, more helpful invisible hands on his shoulders, on his knees, as the car put on its lights and sounds and sped off.

'The identity of the murderer has been perceived. The phased attack algorithms have been matched and neutralised. That body is now an uninhabited form. It has basic autonomic function.'

Three ghosts. Issy said to him, in images. Three. Murderer. Nico himself. And someone else.

'Will it...? I... when he wakes up will there be anybody?' He didn't know how to ask these obscene questions. But better to ask them of X, the machine, than someone who would really know the answer, like Tylu, who would be damaged by answering.

'It will be like a functional adult human without any personal memories. There may be some memory retention of events associated with the host. There may be other minor contamination. There will be no personality as you understand it. As time passes one will most likely accumulate in the normal manner of ordinary human creatures.'

Tylu definitely didn't fall into the category of the inanimate, depersonalised thing. He didn't know much about her. Only that she had spent some time as the slaved avatar of some distant kind of warlord and tried to kill herself because death was an acceptable escape.

'Are we done with the job?' He didn't even want to know who dunnit. He didn't want to know why. It was X's business.

'The actor has been eliminated.'

'By you and Zeroth?'

'Yes.'

'And what about you, X? Is there a pure machine collective, beyond Earth and beyond Forged, doing its own things in the outer darkness?'

'If there were, do you think I'm likely to tell you?'

'Nope.'

'I thank you for your intervention, Nico Perseid. You are a being I have enjoyed spending time with. And you have helped me to solve a puzzle and preserve my integrity. I look forward to doing business with you in the future.'

'Fucked is fucked one way or the other. At least you machines are relatively polite about it,' Nico said.

'We try,' X said, closing the channel.

The car chimed quietly, raising its interior lighting to tell him it was time to go.

They gathered outside the medical bay and looked through the glass at the perhaps-dreaming body of the person they had only referred to before as MurderNico. He was in an induced trance as Zeroth checked him over for residual technological pollution.

Two tucked herself against Tashlynn's side. Issy leaned on Nico. Tylu stood between the two couples alone, her fingers and nose pressed to the glass.

They had all returned safely and their Zeroth-crafted Nico forms had been re-absorbed into the main ship host. Issy had asked to keep his, but mostly because he thought Nico would have been upset if he didn't make an effort. It had also been dusted.

'What will we do with him?' Tylu asked. There was a hint of belligerence in her voice that Nico could hear telling him it had better not be anything she considered bad.

'He's not even a twin,' Nico said. 'We had no mothers, and he's younger than me. I don't even know if he ever had any life of his own.'

'I can spawn secondary systems ships, of any kind. Independent forms,' Zeroth suggested, and they all in their mind's eyes saw different versions of a future for the lone traveller and a sentient ship, moving away from them.

Zeroth knew they were waiting for Nico to say it was okay to stay, but a part of Nico couldn't say this. It kept resisting, insisting that it was dangerous, without him understanding why it would be.

'We can't keep calling him Murder,' Issy said.

'Maybe he has a name,' Tashlynn suggested. 'If he came from Harmony originally. If the designer who made you made him.'

Two cleared her throat. They shared a designer. They were a suite of people, designed to work together, she, Nico and Issy.

'He does have a name,' Tylu said. 'I found the sales receipt while you were all out there. He's called Nikaeda Dao. His name. Not the host... user... buyer's name. I saw it in the records. It was written in by hand, under the serial number.'

'Did he have a life?' Tashlynn asked, clinical as ever. 'Before?'

'Not that I could see.' Two put in. She'd already related her experience of being briefly mixed in the signals between hosts and bodies. 'But he wasn't a void, either. It's more like he was...'

'...suspended.' Tylu said, her breath steaming on the glass.

She leaned back and drew a face in the mist. Dot dot eyes. Flat line mouth. She rubbed it out with her cuff. 'He was very new. Just months. Not years.' Years referred to her servitude. She turned and looked up at Nico. Not saying anything with words, but with her look making a whole case, with notes and footnotes, demands and legislation.

Nico rolled his eyes.

'He'd be alone,' Zeroth said and Nico could feel the distinct ghost of someone inside his skin, aged about five, biting his lip and clenching his fists. Zeroth had been alone.

'That's interesting,' Tashlynn said. 'She must have named him too.'

Nico sighed. 'Harmony could have moved its entire database before we left. I guess they did. Harmony itself is just a proof of concept. No need to stay there once it served its purpose. They could have sold all of us hundreds of times over.'

They all contemplated a universe containing hundreds of identical persons to themselves for a moment.

'I refer you to the First Law of Technological Development,' Two said. 'You cannot contain. You cannot control.'

'I'm not adopting all of them,' Nico said. 'One brother is enough.'

'You mean he can stay?' Tylu grabbed his hand in both of hers as if she was going to pray for him.

'For now.'

'I'll look after him! I'll teach him all the things! You won't have any trouble.'

'I already regret it,' Nico said, turning away with a sour look as if he couldn't bear another minute of the suffering they all brought.

'You can be happy,' Two said to him from the security of Tashlynn's arms. 'Sometimes. It's allowed.'

Nico snorted. 'Tell that to Socksy. He's got a massive hole in him thanks to you.'

Zeroth adjusted the scans on Nikaeda Dao.

He had taken out a large amount of 'ware and several complex tracing systems which he was now retro-engineering. What was left of the man on the slab was an augmented human, fitted out for the commonplace contact suites that any space-farer might use to join others of machine and human kind, the security a little better than usual. When he woke up he would learn how to use it.

He adjusted a few parameters in his onboard food and water supplies as the others went their separate ways to eat and rest, but it was tinkering with perfection really. Even X could not match his moment-to-moment response to environmental demands on any front. He was quietly proud of himself, and liked to think it was because he cared.

He used his copy of the Harmony database to begin preparations for the construction of a human form of his own. There were enemies of theirs out there who thought they had successfully baited a trap and planted some trackers, but two could play at that game. Maybe more than two. As many as he wanted to create. Being Forged and only partly human, augmented by X's payments and the phasing abilities he would develop, he could extend himself that far. He could infiltrate where he would never send his precious crew.

As Nikaedo Dao moved from trance into a normal sleep pattern Zeroth sent a message to Harmony on a coded channel, to a woman sitting on the deck of an old apartment block, looking out over the stacked rises of Chaontium, a priest's grey robe covering her from head to foot. It was raining.

'Nico did hate it,' he confirmed.

'But he let him stay.'

'He let him stay.'

Zeroth felt her smile.

By Any Other Name

This moment comes, like many beginnings, at the end of something. In this case the end is brought by an arrow. It would be a noble and fitting time to speak of the bowman's fine shot, the fragility of life, the balance of good and evil and the epiphanies that may come as a man sees his death arriving and has a moment to consider it before he is extinguished, all his virtues and his sins lit up before him. But this is not that arrow. This is an arrow of hundreds, launched without anything other than a rudimentary aim to comply with the notion of assault on a fortress, so that it seems the archer is doing a good job in the circumstances, at least nothing he can be shot for, whilst in no way attempting to actually take a life. It's a fusillade over a high wall, with battlements and towers, for goodness' sake. In the circumstances only a Dire Elf would even consider taking actual aim and our archer is but a human mercenary of middle years already fed up with poor conditions and dubious pay. So the arrow is no more than a half-hearted punt.

Nonetheless it falls from its high parabola with preternatural accuracy accompanied by the usual amount of force and this is more than enough for it to strike the half inch between chestplate and helm, take out a ring of mail with its curved broadhead and sink a foot through soft tissue into the heart of Morfavon, Dawn of Legend, Dragoncaller, and the figure upon whom so many fragile hopes are pinned.

Morfavon has ridden with the Ragged Band for twenty years and earned the right to be feared for his skill with bow and blade, his tactical vision and his inspirational charisma. He has the dragoncall also, lest those not be enough, and nobody is willing to chance that, although they know it is a last resort and requires a battle the dragon itself considers fruitful. This scrubby mountain pass is hardly the stuff of legends. Until recently it was cropped by goats and left to itself. On either side at the mountain peak stands this fortress, hewn out of the rock, an overhang helped along into being an arched bridge that spans the gap at its narrowest point where Morfavon has made his stand. Since it was sacked centuries ago it has been staffed by corbies and other birds. But then word came that the Mages at Aefeli Howe had come upon a thing worth its weight in mothers' tears, so a few months later here everyone was; those who wanted to seize the Mages' prize struggling up the pass and those who wanted it to stay where it was busy on the ramparts and huddled behind the resinous reek of hastily felled pines made into a gate and some other lumpy deterrents that were too wet to catch fire easily.

The Ragged Band had been called in late to this party. To hear Morfavon talk, it was both too late and not worth the effort – even he didn't know what the big deal was and nobody liked mages. They were too prone to insanity to be much use. No mage had spelled the arrow that ended his opinions, however. It was just one of those things. It would have been better if a mage *had* spelled it, because then there would be a story to tell, a continuation of his glory and a plot of nefarious deeds, but without that it was a defiantly ridiculous end to a marvellous career. It was terrible luck. The sheer waste took the curses right out of the mouth of Ang Sifr, the ranger who stood beside him as he was struck.

Really, she thought, glancing up at the path the arrow had taken, it was an awful, short shot that was only a twitch away from falling to the rubble a hundred feet below. A twitch in the opposite direction and it would have been arcing over their heads and into the mostly empty yard behind them where all the other very good and entirely wasted shots were clattering to the stone with pings and splinters. It was a terrible shot and yet it had been absolutely perfect in its indirection and that perfection was a strange marvel even as she watched Morfavon – hale, hearty, revered, admired and lately her bed companion – slide slowly down the wall to his knees, bow dropping out of his hand. She gaped at the fletchings of the fateful arrow where they stuck out of his shoulder; some filthy, ragged pigeon wing, hastily secured with minimal effort in bad campfire light. The serving was lousy. It was a poor arrow, a kid could do better. A blind kid with half a hand. But weren't they always the ones to slay the gods and kings anyway?

Ang Sifr couldn't believe what had happened, even as Morfavon tilted slowly to the side and then fell over with a gentle sound and a soft clank, like a sack of armoured grain toppling. Behind them the standard holding the red and black banner of the Band with his personal sigil of a golden bear's head rampant upon it, snapped and fluttered, declaring his presence and command to everyone within and without.

A thought went through Ang Sifr's head that she liked not one bit. They were poorly staffed inside, aside from the Band, and beyond them the rabble of armies that had made it to a siege were now briefly united in their pitch to open the pass up, but held together by the thinnest promises. All were hungry, all were tired and nobody liked mages. If they found out that Morfavon, the hero of every tale, was dead, then the sanctuary of this fortress could be counted in minutes. The Band itself, once proud, had lately been held together only by his jovial insistence. He was a paragon among men, unselfish, raffish, bold, generous, seeing the best in the most scurvy of them, and...

She looked up as footsteps rattled the wooden stairs nearby. These had been hastily erected to supply a way up to the highest turret at the midpoint of the arched bridge which spanned the pass and upon which she was standing.

Gull's white-ashed face stared out at her from beneath the icy silver of his hair. He was young and awkward, of no particular note other than that he was tall. His hands clutched at the stonework to save himself a fall forwards and she saw all the urgency, horror and rejection of the moment that she was feeling in his watery gaze. A brief blur of the ur-world shifted around him, making him seem to float until it died away and left him as the skinny husk of a human, not really quite there any more.

They shared a long look that said they were both aware of the situation and that something must be done right now before it became common knowledge. They considered the prospects of fleeing up the mountain pass with multiple hordes at their tail knowing that the Band and the prize were both within easy reach along a corridor with no exits. A Band without a leader. Half would likely turncoat on the rest, though which half was hard to say. Ang Sifr had no love of them in particular but they were her home.

Her original family were bones on this mountain, like so many others. Gull, being a mage himself, had nothing to protect him without Morfavon. He'd been spared death by becoming the Band's magic mascot, a kind of pet belonging to the leader, tolerated as long as he spelled no spells and hexed no hexes and kept the ur-world far far away. Morfavon's death and Gull's presence taken together would have them thinking all the blood belonged on his hands with her as either a helper or no hindrance and there'd be some ugly, painful reckoning for that. Besides all that, they didn't want to die.

Ang threw down her bow and reached out to take Morfavon's gold-banded iron armour. 'Come on!' she hissed as the whistle of arrows and the roar of a barrel of burning oil being tipped nearby nearly drowned her out. 'I'm nearly the same size.'

It was hard to believe she was doing this, had even had the idea in the first place; harder to believe that Gull was helping her strip the body. He worked at her side, their breath huffing the same effort, coughing the same smoke and stench as hollering and screaming went up far below and the relief of the great success of the oil in repelling the onslaught was steadily replaced by the knowledge that they had also achieved what an entire day of assaults could not and set the gate on fire.

A stink of caustic, acrid and terrible, came off Gull. She saw the ur-world's murmur again as he muttered to himself, but without it they'd never have moved that fast or been as dextrous as they were. Ang Sifr felt Gull burning up beside her as if he were on fire, every spell causing him to flake so that ash, white as birchbark, fell on them both.

She would have maybe cared about that if it weren't all their lives at stake. In a blur of desperate action they got her rigged in Morfavon's suit, her meagre ranger's armour transferred to his body by magic alone, where it stretched to bursting. Morfavon, their captain, was a blunt, useless sausage now, a difficult problem that had only one solution in the moment that either of them could think of.

They tied on her hood around his face, lifted him up, with a massive struggle, to the limit of the wall and tipped him over. With a word Gull set the body on fire and guided its fall so that it struck the barricade and became one with that inferno, beyond all reach.

Ang Sifr stared through the faceplate of Morfavon's helm at Gull's crouched, shivering form. He looked on the verge of fainting but she hissed at him, 'Make me his likeness or we are finished here.'

Gull started his muttering and twitching and she wondered what he'd been before he'd dealt with the ghosts and become magical, before he'd begun trading bits of his life for power. What did it matter now? She thrust the impulse to pity him aside as she saw the ur-world creep out of his flesh, peeling it back in another fine onionskin layer that wasn't mere body but being itself. Being spent on crafting magic, burning in this world to become power in the other.

'Illusion's pixifa magic,' he whispered, shaking in the waves that she knew preceded a seizure that would have him jerking like a puppet on invisible strings, foam-mouthed. 'Hard to manage as a human. It wants… to… twist all the time…'

As if she cared for that. 'Faster!'

His teeth started chattering. They were stronger than she'd thought, even if half of them were brown. They didn't crack. He must be younger even than she was. The notion made him even more repellent and her pity and anger all the stronger. For years he'd been there in the background of her existence, tagging around Morfavon's edges like a sad flag, as reviled by the Band as he was prized by them. A mage is invaluable – look at what they can do. No wonder everyone hates them.

Gull gave a final squirm, body bending suddenly as though it was twisted by giant invisible hands. She could hear his joints cracking and popping in protest, his squeaky panic breath as he was wrung out this way and then that. The motion speeded, faster, faster until it was a blur as he phased in and out of existence to let the flow of the forces pass between worlds using his body as a conduit, and then she felt her bones take on the same terror as the spell jumped the gap between them and enveloped her from head to toe, armour, body and all. There was a moment of blinding pain.

'It's done,' he said and then Gull was a mockery of the seabird he was named for, an angular, white heap on the stone, barely alive. Pale smoke and flakes skirled around in the breeze. She fancied she could smell roasting meat. Morfavon or Gull, or both.

Ang Sifr felt the same as she had before – exhausted and angry, always hungry – but the armour, that was heavy and awkward: how did he even see out of this benighted helm? When she bent to pick up his bow, casting a longing look at her light one, she found it enormous, the grip of old yellow bone still warm from his touch. Seeing her hand close on it she frowned – the hand looked far bigger than it felt. 'My voice,' she said, to Gull, who couldn't hear hear in his fugue, but it didn't matter because it came out in the mellow baritone burr that Morfavon always used, a little grittier perhaps, but nothing that a faceful of oilsmoke and cremation couldn't explain.

Ang Sifr stood tall and carefully risked a look through the slit in the parapet. The fire was hampering both sides equally now. For the time being the enemy had retreated to their forward safe point beyond the range of bowshot from the ramparts and were considering their burns and prospects. They'd enjoy a good rest now, knowing it was only a couple of hours to wait and the fire would do the job for them. Spirits would renew, hopes alight. They had the advantage: it was only a matter of time.

She recalled she didn't even know who was down there – some collection of Dukes and apparatchiks, fortune hunters and Lords who'd love to see the outlaw Band ruined on their way to glory up the mountainside as they ransacked the Mages' Howe. Given what she'd just witnessed, she wasn't sure she'd be heading for more magery if she had any choice about it. Why would Morfavon even send the Band here? The mages could defend their damned selves. Even in bed he hadn't been forthcoming about his reasons. But they hadn't pressed. They'd all trusted him. Morfavon came through. He always came through. They'd nobody else.

Thinking this wasn't like her. Thinking wasn't something she dallied with much and now she was thinking more than she'd bothered with in a lifetime. Frowning, she drew an arrow and nocked it – well made these ones, by her own hand – and sighted through the smoke. One thing she felt certain of. A sign of defiant supremacy was needed. Fortunately a standard of the Duke of Gessenry was available. It was proudly borne upon the broken spars of their one ballista which had stuck at an angle on the road and part-blocked the retreat. They'd recover it presently if they needed something to shove the wreckage of the barricade out of the way but for now it stood alone, decked out with its peacock rampant upon a field of black and jade.

She drew the bow. It was the heaviest she'd ever felt. Something in her drawing shoulder popped like a tiny string twanging but she felt the shot inside her in a way she'd only rarely felt before, as if her will alone was its compass, the energy held without effort at full draw for as long as it took to sight. She wasn't even aware of loosing – the shot left when it was ready. The arrow sailed with arrogant, golden hauteur, pierced the smoke and embers and buried itself, quivering, firmly between the peacock's stylised legs.

She'd been aiming for its eye, but that was fine. That was better. That was, in fact, more Morfavon than anything else.

A rowdy cheer went up from the lower ramparts where other archers and the rest of the ranged Band were scattered. She heard laughter. Now it was time to seize that moment and stride down into the remains of the keep, to take charge, make order, issue the master plan. She pushed herself off the wall and found her balance in the unfamiliar bulky suit, looked hopefully at Gull, but he was a quivering shape, drooling. She was on her own.

Ang Sifr strode down, carefully, through the narrow ways of the high ledges and ramps. Everywhere faces that turned to see her pass were heartened, relieved, amused and full of greetings. Her back was slapped. She staggered briefly and remembered to turn and deliver a mock punch, a hearty 'haha!' of jolliness that was the last thing she was feeling inside but which came out well enough, surprising her that it was lifting her spirits too. She met each man and woman's eye, smiled, raised her fist, Morfavon's fist, in insistent enthusiasm. She reached the keep and then the yard where people were leaking out from the walls, trickling, massing one on one until they formed a definite gathering, ragged and fewer than before, but enough to do something with; enough to kill her if they found out the truth. As they would in a moment because it was time to address them and she was a creature of silent hills, lone rocks, stalking waitfulness. She was tall and broad; in that she was like Morfavon, but in nothing else.

From the corner of her sight through the visor she glimpsed the black robes and blue scarves of magi, not one alone but three or four, coming in a phalanx through the crowd. They had the look of people who were intent on speaking to her on matters of immediate importance.

She searched the battlements for a sign of Gull, her hand flexing on the bow grip. This weapon was called Var'han, Bow of Ages. At her side was Tenvair, a sword made by a dead race from an age nobody remembered, its name a guess or a joke. Perhaps it was from a prior epoch, with its strange blue steel, or perhaps it was made a year ago in Kabudama, that invention apex, full of engineers and fabricators, but it didn't matter – everything Morfavon had was named, a legend in its own lifetime and those lifetimes were all far in excess of his, hers and anyone's. The items had collected on him as if magnetised; won in duels, given as gifts, taken as rewards for mighty deeds or simply found in unlikely circumstances worthy of long tales. They bestowed upon him the directional power of Fate and now they were hers.

Ang Sifr longed for her own, nameless ashwood bow which she had made herself. The familiarity of its grip, its honesty, its simplicity, its – emptiness – was the only thing to match what she felt now as the mages advanced and one took up vanguard position. She felt her bowels loosen, as they did before battle though she'd never dropped anything yet. That might change.

Dark red eyes, rimmed with black paint and bloodshot looked at her from above the rim of a veil with a combination of admiration and spite that was breathtaking in its directness. The mages hated them too, it turned out. More than that, they saw right through her disguise.

'Ah, Morfavon,' said the woman. Her accent was cultured, refined. Every word disdained all that Ang Sifr had been or would be, in terms that were social, animal and human. Reluctantly they embraced Morfavon as a necessary horror. All this in a single pronunciation. Ang Sifr rather admired that so much could be packed into so little and her spine bristled as she felt herself insulted, then smoothed itself as she understood who had all the power here – she did. Then that same feeling dripped in a nasty sweat as she heard the next line.

'We await your orders for the second plan you had in mind, now that it seems our eager defences have jeopardised the first.'

Ang Sifr didn't know what the first plan had been, only her part in it – defending the rampart and her position with Morfavon. The existence or need for another plan had never entered her mind. Morfavon had never mentioned one, nor ever did. He stood firmly and expounded without apparent need of forethought, as if divinely inspired. It was his most annoying trait.

She copied him as best she could though her guts had started to look for another way out of the situation that didn't necessarily involve the rest of her. 'The second plan,' she began boldly, 'is...'

The mage was looking slant eyed at her but there was now something troubled about the expression, that said that there must be a plan or they were all finished, so think of a plan and make it a good one and don't, whatever you do, let anyone in on the fact that you're not the hero of the hour but instead some grubby huntress from a nameless mountain who...

'The second plan is to clear the barricade,' Ang Sifr said loudly, turning to address not only the mages, but the wider crowd, projecting her/his voice even over the jolly roar of the fire and the wails of the not-quite-dead. She saw the heads and familiar garb of the Ragged among them and gave them the closed-fist raised salute of cheer.

That made the eyes over the veil go very white.

'It must be cleared away once the flames have died back. The remaining units of the Magi Guard and the mages themselves will retreat to the Mage Howe. The Ragged Band and those mercenaries who are able will make pretend we are in force here at the pass, using all means to advertise confidence whilst retiring from the field.' It was exactly the kind of thing that Morfavon would have said or liked to say, Ang Sifr thought, and felt a terrible pang of loss and sadness suddenly that nearly tripped her up. She paused and heard silence around her. They were all staring, waiting. She had to finish.

'I myself will mount up and ride out.'

It was the most stupid idea she had ever had.

'If they refuse to withdraw, I will call the dragon.'

A cheer went up, of relief and exaltation, excitement and the prospect of a terrific victory, of life remaining today and lives possibly yet to get to tomorrow and other hopeful things which had been smothered by the smoke of the ill-judged oil.

Ang felt sick. From the corner of her eye she saw Trebbit, another longbowman, supporting the ghastly white figure of Gull, who was draped on his arm like a tatty cloak. They shambled into the gleeful throng at the edge, Trebbit's old, lined face full of questions and a serious kind of doubt that made her wonder what he knew about this that she didn't.

Morfavon had not called a dragon since the Battle of Baf'Nas Mor, some seventeen years previous, when he had won the day in a holocaust unsurpassed even in imagination. That outing had been on behalf of some monks who had fallen foul of the King of Baf'Nas while attempting a pilgrimage to a holy site. Everyone had agreed, in the safety of afterwards, that it was a well-deserved finale to a very nasty King and an oppressive dynasty of unusual awfulness, but in hearing the variations of the tale Ang Sifr had always thought there must be more to it than there seemed, because there had been many other fights of that nature up and down the lands and dragons hadn't come to put a verdict on any of them, even when the Ragged were there, even when many of them had died. It was really just the once. Maybe you had to have monks.

A similar thought must have been occurring to the head mage whose gaze had acquired a certain glassy fixity. 'The dragon, you say.' She sounded impressed to a casual listener, but to Ang Sifr the meaning was quite clear – you are no dragon caller and we are all dead.

Now it was Ang's turn to fix the other with a meaningful look. 'I'm sure that within a few hours the dragon will appear, as required, over the far ridge to the North.' Meaning, you're a mage, why don't you go make a "dragon" and stick it on the damned ridge?

They shared a long stare which decided that it was plausible that the enemy might go for some kind of dragon appearing in the distance as sufficient incentive to depart. King Sobori of Baf'Nas and his army had been incinerated to a fine potash and the wild roses in Baf'Nas Mor were now famous for their lush colour and incredible scent. Either way, it was all they'd got.

'In that case let us rest and prepare,' the mage said, making a gesture to her fellows that had them moving back. 'Come, let us discuss the timing of this matter in private while the others make ready.' She beckoned imperiously and spun about, making haste to the stone arch.

Ang paused and looked back at Gull and Trebbit. She jerked her arm at them in Morfavon's style of inviting people where they weren't invited and getting away with it. As they set off in her direction she turned, hefted Var'han with that little hitch and grip that made Morfavon always seem as if he had caught a minor victory in his thoughts, and strode after the four black robes with every bit of unwarranted conviction afire in her gut — a strange sensation indeed. In fact, if she hadn't herself tipped his body onto the pyre she would have said that Morfavon was there and this was actually his plan and it was going to work, of course, because that's just how things went for the man. The fact that she was Morfavon didn't seem to enter into it all that much. Or that she was Ang Sifr. The momentum of the ideas that had come out of her mouth, largely as copies and imaginings, carried her along regardless. She had never experienced anything like this. It was nearly enjoyable, even in the circumstances. And once again she was sorry he was dead and it hurt.

The people who had carved the fortress out of the pass had hewn small, low rooms out of necessity. Ang Sifr had to duck to get inside them and stay ducked all the way through to the 'war room' where the mage delegation had set themselves up a tiny altar with the mortar, pestle and other bits and pieces that were important to them upon an old wood-wormed table. There was a door which closed and light from a reflecting mirror that pulsed faintly thanks to the smoke outside, leaving the mages and Ang Sifr alone together.

Ang Sifr stood in the door until she felt and smelled the distinctive Ragged presence of tired, unwashed human pressing at her back. Then she moved aside and welcomed Trebbit and Gull as though they were honoured advisors. Trebbit had the foresight to close the door. It was cramped now and no semblance of proper distances could be maintained. They were eye to eye across the table and shoulder to shoulder, sharing their coughs in the dry air.

Ang Sifr took off the massive helm and set it down. She glanced at Trebbit, who was staring at her in a dread-filled anxiety but certainly not the friendly acceptance he usually had for her. So he saw Morfavon, she guessed. Gull had a faint smile at the corner of his mouth, satisfaction of a kind. The gathered, masked magi held silent in the background as their leader took down her veil and put back her hood. She was rather stately and disappointingly beautiful, her strong jaw and elegant hawk-nose combining to give a face of unyielding strength that Ang Sifr briefly felt stung by, as if it ought to have been hers. A foolish thought, given her position. She shifted and then remembered Morfavon and took an heroic stance, shoulders back, until her head knocked on the stone roof.

'Let us dispense with formalities,' the mage said. 'I...'

A strange slowing made her words drawl out and out, fading into a background burr of sound. At the same time her movements became slow and slower until her hand was almost still. Time had stopped, Ang thought, feeling herself frozen too, but not her thoughts.

A voice came to her. Not a voice. It was more like a knowledge that was in the walls and the objects, in the mage-devices and in the very substance of the world, their bodies, the air itself – and it was suddenly a thing that Ang could hear, though it was silent and invisible. It was distinct however, and it said,

'Well, Ang Sifr, what will it be? Shall you make a play for kings upon the stage or shall you rather take the shield, the sword and bow, don the helm and become Morfavon, hero of the ages?'

What she perceived as a voice was like a massive wave existing in all matter, held back by every shape and variety of thing in the world, including Ang herself, as if objects were tiny containers all holding a bit of a single secret that could burst forth in an instant if only, if only the illusion of what they seemed to be should fall away. What spoke to her came through this hidden medium, swimming in it as the fish in the sea, flying through it as the bee in the summer air. The dragon was calling her.

She understood then that Morfavon had not always been the same person. He was a role and in the years she'd known him suddenly some of his changes and moods became more easily explained, and some of his more ordinary features, and certainly his miraculous escapes.

'Ah,' said the dragon with satisfaction. 'Good, there is some thought in you.'

There was some thought in her and it went along the lines that she had liked the huge personality, the cheer, the leadership, the camaraderie, the awkward family of the Ragged and the security of being only one of many. Morfavon had been fair to deal with, average under the blankets but a most excellent warmth and comfort during long nights on hard ground. She didn't want or expect more. The causes the Ragged accepted were largely aligned with her own feelings, enough never to protest. They survived, outcast but idealised, heroes and beggars. It was sufficient. She hadn't been there all twenty years of his reign. She was only a few years in. And now he was gone and she was here but the real trouble in the issue was that,

'Morfavon is a man.'

And besides, she didn't want the role. She was Ang Sifr and that meant on the edge. But then she felt the lie shift inside her. She had been Morfavon and she had liked it.

'Morfavon is a warrior whose life is already forfeit. To me. You have disposed of the last one so now you must give me another. If not you, then someone else.'

'I didn't...' Ang began, but thought better of it. 'Why would a dragon answer a man's call?' she asked. 'Was it the monks?'

There was a pause. 'I like roses,' the dragon said.

She knew there was no other answer coming. She knew that this deal was a forever, one-time thing and if she didn't take it then, well, she'd have to give Trebbit and that was unthinkable because Trebbit was a decent archer but not sacrificial material, besides, she wasn't ready to give up. 'Will you come if I call?'

'That depends,' the dragon said. 'Will you come if I call?'

'Why would you…' Ang saw before her two clear paths. There was one in which she pretended to be Morfavon and the mages constructed an illusory dragon and later, somehow, somewhere she would contrive to have "Morfavon" killed and then go back to being Ang Sifr in another place, with other people, somehow. In the other direction she wore the panoply of Morfavon and her own face was not seen again, even by herself. She would lead the Ragged until –

'Did you call him here?' she asked, already knowing the answer.

Yes. Yes was in the stone and the wood, in the worms in the wood and the smoke in the air. *Yes.*

'What for?'

'Because of the mages and what they had.'

'What is it?'

'Something that is not for human pilfering. Something lost. A mistake. A chance. A tragedy. A mystery. Roses.'

The magi at least had the sense not to tamper with it for now. She felt that they were only circling it, cautiously, possessive and jealous, not ready to risk using it. The same could not be said of the besieging Lords, who would kill their own mothers for a chance to gain power over their fellows. Ang could run away into the nothing that she had planned for herself, a nothing of surprising barrenness, she now saw, or she could run into something useful. Behind the sound of the mage's constantly never-pronounced vowel she felt a presence that went even beyond the dragon, in which the dragon itself and all its machinations were only a trivial turn of the wheel and she, Ang Sifr was less than a cog, less than a turn, not even a moment. Ang Sifr was nothing and always had been nothing. An arrow had fallen and divided the world in two, revealing this great emptiness at her heart. It didn't matter what she did. She only knew that she wanted it to matter to something, some way, if only to herself and right now, if only so that she knew what it was to take a momentous decision and to find out what was so great about roses.

'…I insist you leave your mage with us,' said the mage, as if she had never been interrupted by anything. 'Such uses of pixifa illusion are as dangerous this close to the Howe Nexus as the armies on the road.'

Now Ang Sifr heard other things inside the words. They wanted Gull for some reason of their own and she could feel him cower from them – the entire reason he was with the Band at all lay in his disavowal of the mages' organisation. She'd always seen him as rather weak and despicable, not least because of the magic, but now she understood he was like her – outcast from things and looking for a place to belong that didn't come with a price tag too high to pay. And wasn't this what she had paid? Just now, for the sake of the Band.

She began to detest the arrow for opening up this world of magic. She looked at the mage's face, sly she'd thought, but now filled with impatience and fear.

'Gull stays with me,' Ang said, a bold grin and a charming dash to her declaration, larger than life. 'Who is a leader without his loyal mage? If not for Gull the ramparts would have fallen. Spare him for me, this one, and I promise no more pixifa doings until we are paid and clear of your properties.'

As if in agreement they heard the rumble of the flaming gate as it collapsed upon itself.

'The working of a major illusion requires all talents to be on hand,' the mage replied smoothly as if this was an essential piece of understanding someone as hopeless as Morfavon could not be expected to understand.

'He will be on my hand and that is that.'

The mage leant over the table, crushing a preserved flowerhead under her hand carelessly. 'Whoever you are,' she hissed, 'you presume too much. Let's not forget what dragon we are calling upon.'

A great illusion, Ang Sifr saw. Things are one thing on the surface and underneath they are another. In the mage's insistence she felt the need of great power and the twisting sensation that she had come to know was pixifa glamour. Ang Sifr would run away from these things as befits a mountain girl of honest means. Sooner dead than fey! But she felt there was a key here, slowly turning in a lock. Something stranger was coming to her by and by. Here this mage was ready to threaten, but this meant only that her hand was empty. Ang Sifr had the say. What were they going to do without her?

'I presume you are going to be about your business,' Ang said. 'And I to mine. I must prepare my steed, for shortly we go to challenge their champions and give you clever crafters the time to convince us all you're worth the saving.'

The mage's face was pure hatred. 'If we live you will regret this.'

'I have no regrets,' Morfavon waved his gauntlet in dismissal and it was true. For the first time in her life Ang Sifr felt interested in life itself and to hell with all that had come before. But the hours were burning.

She turned and gave Trebbit a good-natured shove, 'Out, out, fetch my horse, water, beer and something for Gull here. We have a retreat to organise!' She followed them, ushering and giving salutes to all those in the yard outside as the barrier burned down and they began to see over the top of it to the dusty pines and rocks of the pass below. The peacock banner and the high length of the engine it adorned were visible through the gouting smoke. In the other direction there was no barrier, only the rising path and the hurrying remnants of the mage's parties, eager to put a few miles between them and more trouble.

Ang Sifr turned once they were alone with the animals and found Trebbit on his toes, staring at her face, his brows together.

'How can it be?' he said, obviously filled in by Gull at some point. 'Say it's not so, Morf. Say it's you and the girl fell in the fire.'

Ang Sifr turned to him. 'It is so.'

The older man turned pale and started to shake. 'I... it can't be. I see him – you – I see...'

Gull hissed and snapped his fingers in front of Trebbit's face. Then his fear turned to outright disappointment.

Ang's gut hurt her. She'd thought Trebbit approved of her, one archer to another, allies in the bow. Now she saw that was all it was about. Archery. As leader he had no use for her and thought she was bound to be a complete disaster. She ground her teeth together, 'I don't like it any more than you do.' A lie, but anyway. 'But...'

'Did you do this?' Trebbit had already dismissed her and was turning to Gull, rage in his face. 'Did you cook this up together? Get rid of him and then take over. Is that your game, eh? You slimy toadwhite. I never trusted you. Said he was a fool to keep you...'

Ang watched in slight surprise as her gauntleted hand slapped Trebbit firmly across the face, hard enough to rock his head and create a white welt along the line of his stubbled jaw. 'He was killed by arrowshot,' she said. 'Now hold your tongue or none of us are making it out of here alive.'

His hand went to the hilt of his dagger but it stayed there, drawing nothing. His face remained defiant but she had no interest in things that weren't going anywhere.

'Ready my courser,' she said, levelly, and waited until slowly he turned like a man in a nightmare and went about the business behind them, the beasts stamping and snorting with the agitation in the air.

'Gull,' she said, addressing him for the first time as an equal. She saw him straighten, the shift of his attention from sullen to direct. 'Do you need to stay near me to keep the magic?'

He shook his head, wiped his nose on the rags of his sleeve. 'Pixifa magic sticky. You need me to undo it, not keep it.'

'Then you and Trebbit are to join the Band and ride up the pass. Make sure nobody stays behind. If the mages want to keep witnesses that's their business. Understand?'

He nodded. 'If things don't...'

'That's my business,' Ang Sifr said. 'There must be some other way out of the Howe. You're to look for it.'

'We're abandoning the original plan then?'

'We're sticking with it,' she said. 'We protect the mages, we do our job, we get the money and we get gone. But if I don't come up that road after the sun marks two pips on the post then you're all on your own.'

'Dead, you mean.'

She shrugged. 'Either way.'

They finished the armouring of the 'horse' – not a horse at all but a larger, similar shaped beast that had cloven feet and a shorter, heavier head topped with front-facing horns. This kind of courser was well known as the most dangerous creature of the lower fens as it had a terrible temper. This one in particular was used to the life of the road now and, smarter than a horse, used to Morfavon. It wasn't fooled by the pixifa charms and snorted and pawed the stone with a scraping sound like axes grinding, making all its heavy armour clank and chime. Long, pointed ears turned back, but it was fed up of the stables and allowed itself to be moved out amid a stamping, cavorting performance that would have impressed bystanders had anyone been left to see.

As it was they emerged to an empty court, only two of the Mage's guard standing at loose attention clearly waiting for this final act to get underway. The non-uniforms who had drawn the shortest straws stood ready with rakes to clear the ground. The gate, the barricade and Morfavon were now a heap of embers, periodically sending showers of sparks skyward against darkening clouds. Beyond them the sound and clatter of the enemy regrouping was clearly audible.

Trebbit grudgingly helped Ang to the saddle. His face was a grim mask of dislike but she trusted him as much as hated him. They were Band and that came first.

'Take Gull now,' she ordered. 'Watch the pass.'

He muttered something she didn't catch through the heavy helm but she was already reining away, raising the massive weight of Morfavon's gold and red standard to signal for the barricade to be cleared. When the pirouetting annoyance of the mount turned her to face the other way she saw them hurrying up the mountain, and then was turned to face the fire. It was still too hot to deal with, and too high. For every effort to move the shoulder-high piles, men turned back singed and cursing.

Ang Sifr, afraid and losing her nerve, dug her spurs into the sides of the courser and gripped the standard as tightly as she could, balancing the end of it against her boot. She could not allow the momentum of events to slide against her because that was all she had. It was probably better the barrier stayed, anyway. She let out a bellow of charging, just as Morfavon used to do, a roar of glory and joy – and the courser sprang forwards in terrifying sudden bounds of energy, much faster and more powerful than she had expected. With three leaps it crossed the gap to the burning pyre and crouched low. She felt her weight drop like a stone, her teeth slamming against each other with jarring force. Her head snapped back as the massive creature sprang effortlessly as a cat high into the air.

From the other side of the fire the gathering groups of soldiers and those who had been working hard to adapt the siege engine into a shovel were startled by the sudden shout and the appearance of a massive, horned, golden creature leaping through a wall of smoke directly at them. It seemed to hang there for a moment in mid-air, a gust of wind suddenly revealing the Ragged Banner above it as if timed by an expert hand.

Without hesitation, those in the front rows backed up and turned aside. The more stalwart ones stood fast and saw Morfavon land and gallop a few more strides forwards before reining back fiercely into a pirouetting rear of defiance a few yards from their faces. Only the strength of his will kept the creature from starting a lone rampage. All saw the polished gold on the tips of its horns and the sharp studs in the rims of its hooves. A few glanced at the repurposed siege engine and at the shaft of the arrow which still jutted boldly between the peacock's stitched legs and some smiles and raised fists greeted the silence that followed because it's hard to see something that fantastic and not admire it a bit even if it is aimed at you with some hostility. It wasn't personal after all, but it was enviably magnificent.

'Shoot, you fools!' screeched one of the lesser Lords but only a few obeyed. Their arrows clattered off the plate of courser and man without causing any trouble and the horseman drew savagely on the rein and planted himself and his beast square on before them, lowering the banner into a lance pointing at their midst.

'Come out, come out, champions!' Morfavon bellowed.

He had a superb voice which carried all the way to the back of the retinue. The more dramatically inclined of the army were already assembling ways to tell the tale of this day and mentally practicing how they would replicate the call. 'I challenge you to single combat and an honour decision upon this ground!'

There was a pause and then Lord Forthinbras shouldered his way to a boulder and stood upon it to reply. 'You are beaten, Morfavon, or you would not attempt this foolery. Stand aside. The towers belong to us.'

'Coward!' snarled the golden knight, turning broadsides as the courser champed and foamed with eagerness to destroy them. 'What of you others, you great masters of the sword hiding behind your yeomen and your paid hands? I give you an easy choice. Face me now and spare your men, or face a greater fire. We will not surrender the towers.'

Inside the confines of the helm Ang Sifr felt these were the right words. They almost seemed to say themselves. But as she listened to them she felt a certain dismay. She was already wasting her strength in holding the courser off its determined path to ruin everything in sight with horn and hoof. She was tired from battle and felt her mortality keenly, though she had no hesitation in spending her life on this exercise if it bought some time for the others to regroup. It wasn't as if she'd been using it for anything. The threat of dragonfire should at least give them something to think about. All the same, she wanted to go on, not stop here in ignominy.

'So,' said the voice hidden in all things, though it was clear to her at that moment. 'What will it be? An illusion for a moment or a lifetime?'

'I will meet your challenge!' called Forthinbras, though he didn't make a move to arm himself. Instead he waved and someone else was pushed forwards. Black Absalon, by the look of his armour and his helm, Ang Sifr thought. One possessing nearly the reputation of Morfavon. A hired butcher without moral limit, he held as much threat as the dragon, almost. In her former life she feared him and his ilk greatly but now that she stood as his equal she held only contempt for him.

'He will make a lovely bloom,' said the dragon. Its voice held utter indifference.

Ang Sifr had only contempt for that as well. She felt the dragon's surprise at her rejection.

'I have had enough of you all,' she said to it as Black Absalon swaggered forwards in his namesake ebon armour, his two handed monster-killing sword in his hands ready, his balance sure, his appetite for the fight always eager. He intended, anticipated likely, to fight on foot, like men of honour. It was a service he didn't deserve. Her family had fallen to men like him and she still didn't know the reason that had brought them that long-ago day. Morfavon would have dismounted, done the decent thing.

Ang loosed the reins a little and the courser sprang forwards, head lowering. Men scattered like rats in all directions and the massive horn on the left struck Black Absalon firmly at the thighs, lifting and tossing him, though he was impaled and did not toss easily, more hung and then fell by his own weight, screaming, the point of his sword falling from the courser's leg.

Their blood stained the rocky ground. The pain only increased the animal's rage and for a while she could do no more than steer it in a forced circle – those that did not flee fast enough were trampled. Through it all she maintained the banner high and when she was contained again there was agitation in the crowd, screaming and yelling, complaints, but still discipline. Upon the stony path Absalon was already dead, being stripped for gear, valuables and mementoes for none had cared for him at all other than for what he could do.

'Another!' she called, imagining behind her the distance increasing, always increasing, between her and the Band.

'You cannot last, alone,' the dragon said.

'That was a dishonourable bout,' Forthinbras declared as the hubbub died back.

'A fitting end to a dishonourable bastard,' Ang replied confidently, and many of the crowd were with her.

'Entertaining,' the Lord replied, 'but we have business ahead and you are bad for business, Morfavon. Always loitering around with your wretched players and fools, getting in the way. Don't pretend you're here for some great cause. We know you're here for the dragonbones, just as we are.'

'I care not for bones,' Ang said, truthfully, though she wondered at the wisdom of fighting for such a thing. 'Other than the ones inside you. Let them out to play. My dogs need something to chew of an eve.'

'Join us, Morfavon. We will give you a share. Why should these wicked mages have yet more power to wield over honest men? It's not enough that they spoil the milk, blight the crops, spite the weather and ask for gold for all their meddling?'

Ang thought of Gull's pale face, his fingers peeling away into ashes before her eyes. 'Make your choice, Forthinbras,' she declared, hefting the banner into position as a javelin, her aching arm working hard to balance it without a wobble. 'Leave now in peace for other days, or face me and the fire to come.'

There was a rumbling of interest and nervousness among the massed soldiery. They looked to the Lord whose face was thunderous with anger as he reached for his sword and horn.

'He will not come alone,' the dragon said, and there was a question hidden in its voice that said – 'Not yet? When? When will you call me to save you?' And Ang heard it, and in it she heard doubt, that maybe she wouldn't answer, and through that moment of uncertainty she felt a loss that was so great it was boundless and its boundlessness held all that could not be changed or undone, not saved, not held, not protected. The bones of the dead were there, hidden in the everywhere, the lost bones in that chink in the armour, the bones from which roses grow so beautifully.

Forthinbras made signs and raised his loyal men. They were a crew, some fifty or so among the rest, who hefted their weapons and strode forward. They were here to do business, not witness greatness or even to be amused. They meant the end for Morfavon and not only for him but the Band and all that they stood for in the world, which wasn't much when you came to it, just the freedom to rove at your will, at your chance, across dangerous lands ruled by greedy men and sometimes you would manage a good thing and sometimes not. It was this small, old, vain, hopeful, wretched band of things that was at stake, and whatever the bones that the dragon wanted or the mages thought were something. Ang Sifr knew this absolutely, and sat on top of the stilled creature, stamping out its own blood on the earth, and said to the dragon, 'Come or not, it is your choice. I will make a lovely bloom.'

Then she said it aloud, in her own voice, though it came out big and booming, full of bravado and warmth like a reassuring fire on a stormy night, a hearth of friendliness, as if she were welcoming them and the gathering men paused, uncertain, because this was not the kind of thing that Morfavon had ever said and although they knew the words they weren't sure what they referred to. Nonetheless they felt the weight of them shift the engines of the moment in a way they hadn't expected. The day remained, starting to rain, but inside their minds things moved out of balance and the world changed until many of them paused and stopped, convinced that this was not a thing to do here and now, that something spoke beyond flesh and words to halt them.

'Strike him down!' Forthinbras bellowed, voice cracking unfortunately on the final syllable into a high squeak that broke the balance of the moment and rendered it ordinary again. The determined few eyed the weakening courser and closed their ranks, advancing.

Ang clapped her legs to the beast, lowered her banner. For all its wound the charger didn't fail her, its rage reignited at the sight of so many foes in reach. They hurtled forward and men did flinch from the attack, but were too tightly packed to escape. The lance speared the first even as she cast it aside before the shaft's buckling snap could unseat her. She reached for that strange iron sword and it found her hand as the courser wheeled, taking out three more with hoof and horn though they crowded in and over the fallen to grab the traces and the caparison, dragging on it to weigh it down. She slashed until there was no space, then she stabbed and forced the animal to whirl, feeling it collapse beneath her. Then she realised that she had only survived this long because they had spent this minute to kill the beast before they turned to her and she ended standing atop its panting frame as it was butchered and gave up a final breath like a sigh.

Ang Sifr thought of the mountain glade where her family were white bone upon the heights and wondered if she would find them again, inside the everything, when they were done with her. The loyalists ringed her, waiting for the word. She stood fast, wobbling a little on the corpse, blade ready, blood dripping from its curve.

'Come!' she said, 'I call you! Come to me!'

And they looked at the sky. Because once a dragon had come and made of a field of men only a field. All but Ang.

She knew nothing was coming. The dragon was bones in the mages' court, peeling away, leaf by leaf, as it spent its last magic in creating other ways of being inside the hearts of men.

If Gull had reached them, he would know the truth, as Morfavon must have done. The dragon was aeons gone, but her Morfavon had kept his bond and come here anyway; to repay his debt to a dead creature and bring them all with him because he could not have undone them from him by any act or magic in the world save dying. Morfavon had given them all each other and now she wanted him to have his last stand, not toppled by an accidental arrow, but alive to the last, better and more big-hearted than all of them or any man.

She wanted him to have the glory of a brief, beautiful moment.

She was struck, and staggered, countered, slashed, parried, was hit again and again by a rain of blows upon her armour which through sheer force beat her to her knees in a cacophony of drums. She did all she could but it was not enough. She was exhausted and she was no Morfavon. For a moment she thought that she had misunderstood and a sense of terrible failure came to her as she waited for the end. She could not do this alone.

'You underestimate my love of roses,' the dragon said.

'I will carry you,' Ang said to it. 'If you will let me leave him here.'

There was a pause. Then, 'You are a lovely bloom, Ang Sifr.'

A shadow crossed the land which they all felt, as though it fell on their naked skin.

In front of Ang, through the crack in her visor, she saw a man light up from within, strange yellow and red blossoming swiftly to black that singed and then cracked and unfurled to reveal his burning bones.

Hideous screams went up then, of terror, pain and the utmost horror a person can feel and not from one but many throats. Heat surrounded her and there was the stink of boiling fat and flesh and a grimy black smoke that coiled and wound through the air to briefly form the massive body and head of a gigantic black dragon.

It rose on the heat of the slain to regard her for a single moment and then the wind broke it apart and Ang Sifr was left standing, alone, in a near-silent black rain. After a while the rain came harder, clearer, and then it stopped.

The pass was filled with piles of black ash and the rain soaked through her leathers and into her underclothing, ran out of her bracers and greaves and down through the filthy fur of the courser to the ground where it made stinking mud about its body.

She took off the armour, piece by piece, and let it fall. Its golden beauty made pretty shapes against the black ground, the red blood, the rusty fur. She found stones to stand on, and patches of grass, where she could walk without leaving a trail.

She climbed down into the valley below, leaving the road at the first opportunity for the safety and disguise of the woods. She headed to a distant mountain meadow, where wild thyme danced in the breeze, the softest fragrance loosened from the tiny blooms by their brushing against the bones of the beloved.

In her hand was Var'fan, Bow of Ages, and at her back its arrows, though she had no memory of finding them. At her side the iron of a lost world, gleaning to her: Tenvair, forged by those closer to gods than men.

She ran to the distant hillside, not to die but to be reborn among her own, no more a hero but a wild thing on the cusp of human and dragon; a new creature for a new age.

In the Howe the mages pored for many days over a heap of dust where the dragon bones had been. Eventually they paid their gold and watched the Band ride away, a pale figure with them in their midst. As the group neared the pass they were joined by a rider from below bearing a black standard with a red rose and they raised their weapons, hailed, well met. For a few moments they could be heard distantly as they circled, whooping and hollering with a mad joy before they whirled about as one and vanished below the crest of the hill.

Cinderkin

Orders run down from Queen to Chamberlain to General and so on like rainwater running down glass. With an uncertain series of dashes and some minor deviations, that is, as drop meets drop, waits for support, plunges onward, runs out of impetus and then waits for the next surge. The surges are all created by the ebb and flow of misgivings (let's not call them fears, because that is undignified) and those are the result of a long history going back so far that anyone studying all its details will become and remain mad, , awash in lore and jottings of who did what to whom and why until they lose their mind entirely. But you can't be alive in Zathria and not know some of the rules and contingencies that dictate your life's path, and at different levels this plays out in different ways. One thing is certain, if an order requires a journey which ends in Vanazon, then you should do all you can to escape being on the sharp end of it.

Such an order has been given.

A princess, one of six, don't fuss, not such a loss, still got five more where that came from, is to be sent on a marriage mission. The full dowry, the whole shebang, not an inch of effort is to be spared. There will be maids and servants, dowry, of course, some diplomats probably now writing their wills with shaky hands, some other sundry retinue of people that the castle administration will be glad to get shot of and, of course, all the horse and vehicles necessary to accomplish a journey of speed and safety to Vanazon. Yes, that's right. To Vanazon! For a wedding!

No wonder the Master of the Queen's Horse has gone deathly pale. Somehow, somewhere, she is sure, there is a plan within a plan within a development that has brought about the notion that a marriage to someone in Vanazon's royal house is going to fix up the tenterhook agreements of peace between the two nations. Nation is pushing it. Let's call them principalities. The human world is small, self-aggrandising. Principality will do. They make up in culture and viciousness what they lack in area. To Vanazon! Let all rejoice at the prospect of a newly ensured peace. Although there is plenty of chance that none who go will return in the same number of pieces.

There's perishing lack of news at the lower levels. Nobody knows a thing. Not the butler, not the candlesticks guy, not the woman who does the fireplaces, not her sister with the dodgy hip, not the talking dog that sometimes gets up to the top floor by 'accident'. He was sleeping in one of the hayricks on the day this was hatched. Only Fixwhit the privy executive (yes, toilet-cleaner) has an inkling, because he was doing third floor gutters a week ago and overheard someone saying that this is a matter of playing on the vanity of a certain Vanazon princeling who has some kind of influence with Ears That Matter. No matter. The order has come. To Vanazon!

Thank goodness, the Master thinks, that she is not really, not honestly, not properly expected to go in person on such an auspicious occasion because there will be a great need for horse for the remaining court and the five staying-right-here princesses. So that's at least ten horses of special character and conformation and none of them lippy. Only she could assure such continuance of service. In person. Right here in Zathria. Yes.

But for those on the bottom there's no escape. Drowned by compulsions is where you'll be, regardless of who did what higher up the chain. Master of the Queen's Horse isn't at the bottom, but stable-hand definitely is, and that's where Shalaz has wound up after a long series of events of no note, bounced from pillar to post by the whims of others due to what he looks like and where he might've come from, though nobody knows for sure about that; he's just one of many who walk out of the forests without a history anyone's willing to ask about. A lack of sponsors and patrons and a lack of any desirable traits, plus a few undesirable ones, means that stablehand is about the best he could aspire to. And in places other than Zathria, much less than that. In fact, the closer you move towards the human hub of things, to fiefdoms encircled by other human holdouts (or, if you are human, kingdoms, strongholds, outposts, forts) then aspiring to life itself is fairly ambitious for such as he.

The Master of Horse, Yvrielle, hired him last so he should go. She hired him out of kindness because he was a destitute and he's from the forest and he's got the marks of a Cinderkin, whatever you want to say about it possibly not being that and being fox instead, and he doesn't talk. All these things mean he is beholden to her, humble and cheap. Also, though she would never admit, he's good with the horses. Very good. Strangely good. With the horses. In a way that makes her feel that if he were noticed by Eyes That Notice her position might become a little less certain, so it is really best, for the sake of the safety and wellbeing of everyone in the party, that he be assigned the task of caring for the horse and etcetera on their journey to Vanazon. They are sending five excellent horses, plus less excellent ones which can be fancied up to look good and will survive the journey of several days' steady progress along rough roads. It stands to reason that she ought to send her best groom to keep up the pretence that the quality of the steeds is better than it is. Definitely.

High in the castle itself, on the fourth floor, in the tower that faces out over the wilds towards the rumoured sea, the Princess In Question is looking out of the window, wishing that *looking* was *flying*.

The forest, against which Zathria is a stalwart human stronghold and frontier of civilisation, starts as scrubby wilds about ten miles distant where the farmland and the hunting grounds peter out into a series of little bothies and a patrolled region called The Break. The Break is five miles wide and circles three-quarters of Zathria's border with what the Princess suspects is all the authoritative security of a chocolate fireguard.

Princess Ven is what passes for an expert in The Wilds. She immersed herself in independent studies and field research (wandering around with a notebook) after exhausting the Castle library and tutors on all they knew about being born as a middle-ranked female into a family of inherited power in an uncertain world; a world which didn't show any enthusiasm for alternatives to its current organisational model.

It had been a disappointing road to say the least. The Wilds however, because so few facts applied to them with any consistency, offered a vast opportunity of some kind of discovery, escape, promise – all the vague possibles which ordinary life seemed equally destined to withhold.

Scholars of the Wilds are many, but actual information is on the skimpy side due to so few hands-on researchers ever returning to deliver their papers. It is therefore a pastime in which one can sit at home while producing a huge amount of lurid speculation at leisure, knowing that nobody will manage to find any solid evidence to dispute your wisdoms. The perfect pursuit for a lady intellectual, if Zathria had that kind of society, which it does not, all its purposes being pragmatic (meaning greedy) or warlike (also meaning greedy). The King has no time for higher thought or messing about with woodlands and the Queen's opinions remain a mystery, as she's had the sense never to put one forward.

Wilds and Break aside, the rest of Zathria's border is a gateway to civilisation, of a sort, pointed towards softer landscapes, bigger towns, wealthier marketplaces. The human world sees itself as a network of marvellous invention and safety locked within a much larger barbarian waste of near infinite mass, which they pretend to have no fear of by deriding it and employing a vast number of priests and witches. The embers of older civilisations poke up from the land at certain points, hinting at previous world masters. These are worshipped, or sometimes demonised, which is the same thing but with more drama. Princess Ven has written, scathingly, about this in an obscure journal of wit and observation – The Scandalous Riddle – which has sporadic circulation throughout the realms and perhaps upward of twenty regular readers. Her theories are mundane and placating for state purposes, because at least three of the regular readers are court spies, though the same theories are bleak and horrifying in her private notes where she faultlessly records her actual thoughts in the form of watercolour paintings.

The paintings are code which only she can understand. To the untrained eye they look like botany life studies.

She generally writes too much, is the consensus among the witterati, but the Riddle needs column inches and contributors keep going missing. Sometimes they migrate to more lucrative journals, although none of those make it into Zathria as distribution isn't worth it for so few subscribers. The Riddle comes as an insert with her father's regular papers. He takes all the publications from the rest of the world, as a standard practice, but doesn't read them as all his news is delivered by the Vizier and the Priests. He leaves his copies in the library, pristine, in case someone visits who needs convincing that he's a man of learning. They stay for a couple of weeks and then are used as firelighters in the kitchens. Ven is the only one who reads them. That's how she found the Riddle in the first place.

Zathria, seen by its citizens, is a proud, fierce nation-state in that it survives perilously and has few natural resources worth squabbling about. Princess Lora is the oldest princess at a venerable twenty-one years old. Her marriageability is the heart of its most worthwhile product, the feud with Vanazon, which has bred tales of assassination, spying, daring-do and scheming for over two hundred years and is showing no signs of dropping in value as a way of fundraising for the royal purse. This particular wedding idea is a new venture, threatening to disrupt this status quo with a peace in which only the peasants and sundry animals stand to gain.

Vanazon has offered its finest son in some obvious scheme which nobody can get to the bottom of.

Prince Veher is known on the battlefield as a tall, typical soldier type, no obvious physical defects and plenty of vim. He's twenty-five and still alive in spite of countless attempts to review that situation. He is reported to be the healthy, outdoors sort who doesn't bother with court life other than to raid the prettier ranks of it for entertainment. In short he is a typical, boring Prince, the kind that any King of the Zathria/ Vanazon type longs for as either a son or a son-in-law. No imagination to speak of. No ability to out-manoeuvre the old man, easily disposed of if circumstances call for it. As a result, the Zathrian Vizier is convinced the offer is ludicrous. It's a plot to lure Lora out into the dangerous territory between the two places where something will undoubtedly happen. Something of a Very Bad nature. Oh Woe! But despite this it's going ahead.

Princess Lora is not going, though.

Princess Ven is going. That's the master stroke at work here.

Even the Cinderkin can see the kind of minds that have hatched this idea.

It's possible that Ven will be the heart of a new plot to infiltrate and overthrow the Vanazon royal family, scheming Zathria's ascendance as a demure sleeper agent – and at the very least her children will be a constant bulwark against real danger. But, as she herself is the only one capable of planning and executing something that subtle or ordinary, this is unlikely. Instead the intolerant reputation of the Vanazon court towards anything like an opinionated, educated woman suggests a lot of other things will happen. Very Bad Things. But, if you are the Zathrian King spoiling for a fight and low on funds because you have spent everything on the army, Good Things. We can't say Very Good as that might imply he doesn't care for Ven in a sufficiently seemly way. A generous spirit could assume that sending Ven is merely intended as an insult. One more poke in the many monthly poking sessions that riddle the joint affairs of the two warring courts. One outcome is certain, though. Ven will not return to Zathria, and nor will any lasting peace accord.

Never say never, though. Perhaps they will meet her, show her great dishonour and send her home. Surely some of them will see that as the double whammy – more insulting to return her unharmed, as unworthy of a gesture of war. Your feeble attempt to insult us insults us! Years of backstabbing lead to exquisite sensibilities when it comes to paranoia and interpretation.

The Cinderkin has seen them all, but thankfully has never been involved in any way. Until now. And that brings him a problem which he is going to have to resolve extremely quickly. If Ven leaves Zathria then she will take her paintbox and her journal with her and that particular book is his entire reason for being in the human world in the first place.

Tabah the Cinderkin, also known as *Ember* to Wildblood kin, wandered. He was looking for poultice herbs if anyone asked, and picked them if he saw them, but in fact he was wandering with the sole purpose of figuring out what to do in the hope that something would occur to him if he only kept moving forwards. The Break was the least likely place to meet another person, unless you went to a guard bothy – he had a route which avoided all of them and most of their sightlines – and unless you hoped somehow to bump into Princess Ven, who was also known, in her outdoor disguise for the purposes of fooling guards, as *Beibei the witch of Green Owl.*

Green Owl was the least significant of the witchclans and the least likely to cause any interest. The disguise was superficially good and would have worked, except that everyone knew it was Ven. Tabah wasn't sure if Ven knew this. He wasn't sure how much Ven knew about anything, given he didn't know her and had, aside from a couple of times he'd held a horse for her, never got close enough to ask. In particular he didn't know if she knew what was in her journal. It wasn't the kind of thing a human could know unless they were some kind of adept and Zathria was the place you went if you didn't want to find one of those.

It was possible, though. Queens dallied in the summertime woodlands during ceremony season as much as the next woman. Wildblood roamed about the place at all times. Romances happened. Kings needn't know. They particularly needn't know about certain books that might be in their unvisited library collections, secreted there by wildblood persons for the sake of securing them in a safe place where safe meant safe from wildblood sorcerers rather than humans.

No human could have read it, so that wasn't the problem. The problem was that the book belonged to Her Darkness and Tabah was one of the guards of Her collection and he was reasonably sure, beyond all doubt, that it was the book that Princess Ven had discovered some years ago and, taking it for a blank book of empty pages, had used it as her watercolour sketchbook.

Now it was too much to hope for a chance meeting in which somehow an entire relationship's worth of trust and understanding would take place in minutes and the book be re-secured. A quick run through her usual paths convinced him she was more likely indoors, possibly confined due to the circumstances, and there was no chance of him getting close to the book this way, nor close enough to warn her about the book itself.

Zathria's crushing dullness and intense human presence was a brilliant hiding place for it as it rendered the thing itself quite dormant. But once beyond the border there was no telling what it would do and, if it did anything, there were plenty of hunters out there willing to do whatever it took to get their hands on it. Zathria and Vanazon would be inconsequential to them.

He managed to circle the outer castle grounds. The book gave off a telltale hum of potency that was strong enough to convince him he had located it in the Princess' Tower, high up, where the second rank of windows dared face the Wild. He thought he could glimpse a figure behind the glass. On the crenellated ramparts just to the tower's side guards in Zathrian blue patrolled. There were more than usual, that is to say there were some, so clearly they had been placed there to ensure Ven didn't try to escape.

If the book survived all the way to Vanazon then he would be forced to turn back and it would be effectively lost. Vanazon was as enthusiastic about witches as Zathria was lukewarm. They would find the book and take it. Enough of them held high positions in court that getting it off Ven would be no problem. And they might be able to read some of it. Or it might read them but this was not authorised by Her Darkness and so must not happen.

Tabah didn't know what was in the book. He was destined to guard it at Her Darkness' displeasure for the crime of dallying with one of her personal court. That displeasure might last years more, decades more, a lifetime more. There was no way to tell. That he had been part of her personal court at the time and therefore the entire business seemed whimsical and cruelly unjust was par for the course with her. Even so he was desperate to please her. To fail at this simple task would confirm his permanent expulsion – he'd leave out of shame.

But. Ven was in the tower with the book and he was outside on the ground and tomorrow they left for Vanazon. It was all getting a bit late in the day.

Steal it? No chance, she kept it on her person. He would have to get past too many people, had no reason to go in, would not get out. He wasn't that kind of Wildblood.

Spirit it away? Again, wrong kind of Wildblood for that. No witches worth the salt it would take to be shot of them remained in Zathria, except for Mildew Most, and she was only here for her vineyard. Even if she knew how to translocate objects it wasn't certain the book was one of those things that could be moved that way.

Hire another Wildblood to risk their necks for it? Fleert was the only one with a chance but she was too young for Tabah to want to involve in anything genuinely dangerous. Better Fleert stick to tormenting the astrologers. Plus she was a ward of Her Dreaming and if that went badly... No, that wasn't possible either.

Burn down everything except the book? Possible, but Her Darkness would take a much dimmer view of starting a war with the humans than she would about overdue books. Even lost books (temporary) and incompetent courtiers.

But on the journey anything could happen, couldn't it?

In the Tower, Princess Ven looked down across the swath of the Break and saw someone standing far below, near the thistle meadow, where she had built a bower (called it a bower, that is, but really it was more like a child's fort of bendy sticks) and liked to sit to think her Real Thoughts. Whoever it was wore a cloak and hood, so they were unidentifiable even if her eyesight had been that good. They seemed to be looking at the Tower.

In her arms the large, leather-bound journal suddenly shook. No, it quivered, with an eager vibration which reminded her instantly of Sabre the cat when he had stalked and waited and was preparing to pounce.

She screamed and stood up, dropping the book onto the window seat cushion where it fell lightly and settled a bit too slowly for an ordinary book, and was silent.

'Milady!' her maid, Mym, came rushing in.

'Nerves,' Ven said quickly to forestall her, clutching her own elbows to prevent herself from shaking. 'I need wine!'

'Yes'm.' The maid hurried out. Her own face was splotchy and pale because she had to go too, but Ven didn't know how to help with that any more than she already had. They were both prisoners of the situation and that felt very like an execution. It was, at least as far as she could tell, an end to her pleasant, if lonely, life.

But now. The book.

She stared at it suspiciously, then dared to move closer again so she could look down through the leaded glass.

The figure was gone. A few deer moved about in the scrub, but nothing human was visible out there. Not that this was convincing of much. There were hundreds of places to hide. She watched for as long as it took the maid to return and then absently poured a glass out and drank it, poured another and handed it over to the equally silent Mym who drank it at the same determined pace before refilling it and handing it back.

Ven considered for the hundredth time how she might get out of the tower and into The Break. If she could make it there she could make it to the Wilds, she was pretty sure. And then what? Was it really preferable to risking it with Vanazon?

'I don't know what's out there,' Mym said, following her mistress' gaze to the darkening woodland where the sun had begun to cast orange and red across the leaves as it went down.

In spite of all her research, Ven didn't know either. She considered, self-pitying, that perhaps she ought to have spent all that time studying actual known politics and culture instead. She'd always relied on Mym for that, though.

It was technically time for ladies to retire for the night, but neither of them made any moves in that direction. They had no intention of wasting the limited hours of freedom, such as it was.

'Maybe some bandits will come and rob the coach,' Mym said after a minute.

'It will probably be assassins,' Ven said. 'Did you pack the poison?'

'Of course.'

They had discussed escape many times, and every possible scenario and many impossible ones and both were sure of one thing. If it was assassins or bandits or robbers or any kind of Very Bad

Fate Apparent manifested then they were going to be sure to have the final escape of a potent poison to hand so neither of them had to suffer some worse situation than death. Still, talking about it as an actual possibility was chilling. At least Ven knew her poisons and could ensure a fairly painless exit. It seemed pitiful to have only that to look forward to.

She looked down at the book again. It hadn't made any untoward movements or noises since that one time. She wondered if maybe her increasing terror had made her imagine it, or somehow do it herself. Perhaps she was falling into fits slowly. With caution she sat down by it and put her hand on it. Nothing.

Come on, she thought. Be something. Be something! Anything.

But the book was its usual self.

'Do you want your inks, M'm?' asked Mym. 'Or we could read a story.'

'No more stories,' Ven said. 'Just pack the ink up. We have to be ready.'

She sat with her wine and tried to pick out the stars as they appeared one by one.

Mildew Most was standing at the junction where the cart track that led to her hill vineyards met the much weedier and less hospitable cart track on her own land. She was tall and strong and with her arms folded and her feet planted wide she commanded the twilight in its entirety as she watched Tabah gallop up. On his black horse, in his black cloak with his arms and hands and face all 'soot-marked' with his natural colouring making him appear as a shadow he would have been terrifying to an ordinary person, but of the two of them it was Mildew whose presence was the more powerful by quite a long way.

'Took your sweet time,' she said as he kicked his leg over the horse's mane and slid down to the ground.

The horse, without saddle or bridle, walked off a few yards to wait, puffing and snorting. Steam rose from its flanks into the cool air. Flies gathered swiftly.

'I only found out yesterday,' he said.

69

'Been news here for two days.' The witch regarded him with contempt.

'Yes, but you have the King's Ear,' by which he meant she could hear all that went on if she wanted to.

'And what've you got? The Donkey's Arse?'

Tabah said nothing, put back his hood and shrugged off the cloak, letting it fall to the ground, and with it all the bindings that kept him human enough to pass for merely ordinary Wildblood. He had the same kind of colouring as a buckskin horse, with dark brown fading to soot on his arms and legs, like opera gloves and stockings, and some soot around the eyes, end of the nose and mouth, giving him a slightly skull-like make up. The buckskin part was a glowing gold and across all of him were the sigils and writing of the Wild, lit up as if from internal candlelight where they kept him firmly written into the human shape. His stable clothes of rough dark shirt and half breeches were still straw-and-hair covered and his hair, like the mane of his horse, had been brushed but fallen back into tangled ways on the journey. It seethed a little, as though it was alive. His brown eyes remained hazel as if to make an extra point as he stabbed a finger at the character writing on his arm and glared at Mildew, 'No magic near the book, see?'

'Really?' Mildew said. 'That's why the book woke up this afternoon is it? That's why you're here now, coming to ask me to do something like I can just wave a magic wand.' She gestured with one finger in the air, making a very rude sign.

She was as tall as he. Feathers and bones were braided into her grey streaked hair, along with hanks of various other things that might have been trophies or were possibly collectible items she just happened to like including a Fiavian hussar's red uniform tassels and most of a white heron, including the beak, which hung lowest of all against her belly. Her clothing, also a fairly standard peasant drab but in fine materials gave her a housey mousey look beneath the hair which made it all the odder. She was handsome and compelling, like some kind of dread headmistress.

There was no question that Mildew was not her real name. She was what most people in Zathria dismissed as 'bit o' Wildblood', which usually meant someone had once seen a Wildblood a few generations back. In that sense nearly everyone was Wildblood; in the sense that meant it was exotic, powerful, potent and desirable. Just enough Wild to be talented, not enough to be repellently weird. Except that when this was said of Mildew it was said defensively, to ward off any kind of Attention From Aspersions which Mildew might take offence at, should any hint be given that she was probably more of the 99 percent Wildblood category, or possibly that she was the author of the entire category taking an inexplicable turn as a lowly vintner. Mildew Most was her human trading name. She made the most excellent wines – and was indeed a master of mildews, moulds and all kinds of other things that went into or out of wines at various points – and she was the backstop of the Zathrian economy, so 'bit o' Wildblood' was as far as anyone was going to go in that direction.

For now though Mildew was in her resolute dame form. Heron beak, tassels and all.

'I came to ask your advice,' Tabah said, cowed as he knew he would be. The wand thing was unnecessary, but a bit of a joke. He felt her grudging acceptance.

'Wasn't you that set it off, then?'

'No.'

'You didn't even know until I said it just now, did you?'

He sighed. 'No.'

'Huh,' Mildew said, looking contemplative. 'Well, doesn't that just take the custard.'

'Should I retrieve it and take it back to Her?'

'Maybe. Can't have it lying about in the wrong hands,' Mildew gave him a pointed look.

Tabah scowled, 'It was safer if Ven had it, I thought, than if it was just in the Library. If she had it to herself then I knew where it was, there was no danger someone else might find it and carry it off or try to burn it.'

'Burn it?'

'There's a trend at court of using the pages of magical tomes as cigarette papers. Among the young men.'

'Onionskin papers I assume?'

Tabah shrugged. He didn't know paper.

'Barbarians.' This of all things seemed to spark something in Mildew. Her attention, which had been reviewing affairs with general disgust, sharpened itself. Then, 'Do you know which book it is?'

'No,' Tabah said humbly. 'She told me never to mind that. I was just to keep it safe until she said otherwise.'

'And she sent you here?'

'No, I chose Zathria. I could have gone anywhere. But not a place of power or near one.'

'And this mission of yours started when?' Mildew glanced at the stars.

'On the Pass of The Iron Dogs.' He didn't understand this digging at the past suddenly, but as Mildew was his only hope of advice he stuck it out, even seeing where it was all going.

'And why did she choose you?'

He mumbled something and looked away at the suddenly very interesting overgrown hedges where thick bundles of sweet hawthorn flowers were now the only other things clearly visible in the weak moonlight.

The reaction was not what he had expected and he had been expecting a deepening of her contempt. Instead, she snorted. 'You. And Fires of the Lightning Strike?'

This wasn't the kind of contempt he'd expected. 'Yes me. Why not me? What do you mean?'

Mildred waved her 'magic wand' hand at him, encompassing all he was, had been and would be, and wrapping it up in a big parcel of Hell No.

'Hell yes,' Tabah said angrily.

'Hell No,' Mildew said. 'No offence.'

'Offence taken. Also. Yes. I wasn't imagining it. She sent me out here when she found out we were...' but he broke off, not sure suddenly of what they were, exactly.

'Taking it up the arse from a higher power doesn't mean they're into you. Figuratively speaking,' Mildew said. There was a tinge of pity in her voice that made it all the worse although he knew most of it was meant to throw him off guard so he revealed more than he ought to.

'It isn't like that.'

'Court life is always like that,' Mildew said. 'Never mind. It's not a reason is what I'm saying. It's not a reason to send you far away on a fool's errand.'

'She was pretty clear about it.'

'I'm sure. And you were so fixed on your feelings that you bought it.'

'Fires and I...'

Mildew held up her hand. 'Don't. For both our sakes.'

Tabah stood his ground. He felt his lower jaw jutting forwards. 'Have it your way.'

'So, you leave the court with the book. You bring it here. You hide it where nobody will touch it and you wait,' Mildew said. 'For eternity, as far as you know. Because you touched the Fire and you are now being burned and that makes sense to you. Her punishment feels right. All that importance. But. How long until Ven picked it up?'

He'd got the measure of her stabs now and focused only on the other things. 'A year maybe. Two?'

'How did you know she had it? There she is, a girl in her own home, you're all the way outside in the stables, you never go into the Library.'

'I...' He paused. Something, for the first time, felt off.

'How did you get the book in to the Library?'

'That was easy. I said I found it on a bench where Princess Ven had been reading a few hours beforehand and I asked one of the scullery maids to return it to the Library.'

'Because a scullery maid knows all about the Library.'

'She knows where it is and she can go there without looking suspicious!'

'Or she gives it to the Princess, because it's her book.'

'But she didn't have it.'

'How do you know that?' Mildew sighed the sigh of someone leading a horse to water.

'I'm bound to the book, all right?' he said and saw the look of sly triumph crease into a smile on her face. 'I know where it is. I just know.'

'I see,' Mildew said. She turned and started to go back up her track between the vineyards.

'Hey! Wait! You have to help me! I mean, please.'

Mildew stopped. 'Who bound you to it?'

'My Lady Darkness.'

Mildew started walking again, slowly, stolidly, the walk of an old woman, which she wasn't. 'Can't help you, Ember. But I can tell you. It's not what you think it is.'

'Mildew, please!'

She was lost to sight in the overgrown lane. He ran after her, faster than she was by far, but the lane was empty. The wind stirred the thorn and the leaves on the vines.

'Shit!'

There was nothing for it but to reclaim the grazing horse and his human cloak and return to the stables to wait for morning.

The caravan set off late and progressed slowly, moving at the speed of hangover, since most of the participants were all much in the same boat as Ven herself – disposable – and knew it, so they had taken best advantage of their departing evening's feast. Only Tabah was clear-headed. And the horses, of course. Fortunately there was nobody on the roads once they'd cleared the town and they were soon well on the way to the port at Brine Marsh where a very long estuary met its match in a very long river and spread out into a series of thickly wooded and treacherous bogs. A lot of work had provided a cut-through, first on platforms and then by ferry which crossed the brackish stream at the point where the banks were firm for most of the year. Merchant traders from other nations preferred to pay local Zathrian couriers from the point of the far bank but all business had been stopped for the day to allow passage of the royal party, so as afternoon came slowly on they passed camp after camp of grumpy looking men, idling about smoking and gambling wherever the ground was stable enough to hold them and their carts.

Ven felt sick to start with because she had stayed up late drinking. Mym was no comfort, huddled in her own problems. The only mercy was the covered carriage which let her have a soft bed upon which she could roll around feeling miserable in private, occasionally stifling the urge to heave as she was tossed this way and that by the carriage suspension, bumping against the padded buffers and wishing she had drunk water and chosen to ride instead. Definitely tomorrow she would ride and enjoy whatever moment could be enjoyed in that rather than bounce about like a bread roll in a too-big bag. The day was also hot and the carriage airless.

The morning suffusion of elderflower remedies meant there must be stops for ladies to make water, requiring the erection of a temporary tent and the digging of a temporary privy atop which a folding seat was thrown so ladies did not fall in said hole. Formal clothing dragged that out for ages with all its fussy fastenings. Flies bit and stung, without any regard at all for pomanders and tincture of viperleaf. The maids in the second carriage were all surly and resentful and made no effort to help anyone but themselves. No doubt their minds were fixated on the possible fate of ladies' maids who find themselves in trouble on the roads or handed over carelessly to the whim of foreign powers, which is mostly what tried to occupy Ven's mind so she didn't blame them. She blamed her father, and men in general.

By the time they reached the ferry with all the horse fussing and negotiation and whatnot that had to go on she was tired through and through, and headachey, and too miserable to care who was at fault. Just let this disgusting journey be over.

Tabah walked near the back of the line. He had exchanged his decrepit cloak for a royal tabard of Zathrian colours which felt very much like a targeting assist more than a matter of pride at that point. From villager to traveller to guard nobody seemed to hold out the demanded hope of peace, instead watching the progress with a business-as-usual impatience, cross with the level of wealth they were seeing moving along the road, and none of it headed their way. The King's reputation was the only thing that kept them civil. The ferry crossing occupied all the afternoon. He had to give his full attention to keeping the animals peaceful, moving back and forth across the churning brown waters until every one of them had made it across.

The far bank brought with it a sense of safe distance. The silent convoy became louder and rowdier as drinking started again and the guard cheered up at the thought of camps, nightfall and being away from the tattling tongues of anyone connected to the King. They made good time and the first camp was set and waiting for them within the fringes of the Auburn Forest – technically Zathria but really a strip of the wild that crossed down through Zathrian held territories before branching out again into full dominance of the Southern Reaches. It was not much more than ten miles broad and the only barrier of any significant note between them and a long, tedious trek to Vanazon. Cutthroats, bandits and whatever wildlife might loiter would all be here, among the trees. Thus the edge camp had been built as a permanent waymeet and was fiercely and well-defended by an entirely different group of guards to the kind found at the court and the ones accompanying Ven's progress.

In stark contrast to the day's works the camp personnel were efficient, strong and organised. Of Vanazon agents, interlopers, hidden plots and any untoward things there was no sign. The evening came on "quietly" with the chorus of bug and frog. Tabah knew that Ven had left her carriage for one of the sturdier huts only because he felt the progress of the book moving slightly left to right as he groomed the last horse. For all that Mildew had said about the book waking up there was no hint of life from it all day and that continued into the evening.

Then he noticed the shadows. Motes that could easily have been mistaken for the flicker of firelight or foliage were breaking off from their origins and moving together through patches of darkness. To a human eye they would have been unnoticeable but he saw them clearly because he recognised them. This was Cat In The Corner, a servant of Her Perspicacity, here for only one reason he could think of: the book. They were using their most stealthy form. Probably they wouldn't build enough reserve to transform into a solid state for a while yet, but soon they would, especially as the night deepened.

If they were already here, then much worse would be on the way before dawn.

Tabah made a decision he hoped he wouldn't regret.

Princess Ven was wrestling the rings off her fingers. Her hands were sweaty and the sickness of the day had transmuted seamlessly into sickness of pure fear as she had formed a plan during the afternoon. She'd fallen into a stupor after the ferry crossing and woken up a time later with the leather book satchel under her face and when she opened her eyes and came to herself everything had changed.

Well, nothing. She was still in the carriage and it was moving. Mym was propped in the corner staring greenly through a chink in the curtains, her nose outside. Harness clinked. The carriage trundled. The mumble-voices of the guard came and went. Hoof and stone and metal shoes clacked in irregular jolts. Ven stared at the pretty white damask of the carriage interior. She was keenly aware of her movement through space; a body moving between two junctions, an object of small power being handed over, a floating unknown of little significance that might be set alight or crushed as leverage in a larger game, a vessel of possible futures for other beings, born to die and be traded on and on into the future in the rounds of a ceaseless struggle which had no meaning or significance at all.

Everyone was implicated. Some had power – her father, Vanazon's Emperor (as if you could be an Emperor of something that could be ridden across in three days), a host of other men of various colours, weights, types, temperaments scattered here and there, all different, all the same in their fealties and loyalties and bands and hierarchies. Even the bandits had gang rules, codes, laws like hammers to bash them into line.

Ven saw the hammers and the line, saw herself being swung to tap something else into place; felt herself smashed into her present shape. Her mind – which had spent its time focused on obscure writers, difficult subjects, arcane texts, wildflowers, ladies' occupations to pass the time between pain and death – was now betraying her by exploding all of this, which was known but hidden, into full and inescapable view. It wasn't that she just saw it. She had become it with a force that defied all of the efforts of her foremothers to smother, deny and crush it back, because once seen it cannot be borne and they must bear it and go on for they had no choice.

They saw, they hid in tapestry and weaving and alms and court politics, and they forgot. They had their own hammers for forgetting and crushing and bashing what they must carry into a tight, small ball, curled up and held inside and never let out. And now, in her sleep, it had been born.

She stared at the damask and listened to the carriage and sat and was jolted about, spine loose, sore from the hours of constant joggling. She opened her mouth and let out her first scream, silently, because who could or would understand such a thing and she must not scare the horses, and felt her hand on the book satchel.

The satchel was open and the book had slid part way out. The leather of the satchel was smooth and warm, stiff and firm. The leather of the bookbinding was thin, pliable, cool, like the skin of a bent knee on a summer day in the shade that you touch unexpectedly and find taut, alien, colder than you think it ought to be but unmistakably alive.

She thought of her mother who had not come to see her off because she was ill with one of her long headaches and couldn't be removed from the bedchamber or suffer any kind of light. Ven had loathed and despised her at the moment of departure.

She looked at the damask to clean her mind with its whiteness, but the horror of knowing would not recede, in fact it grew. Land, animals, people, everything churned like the wave of soil under the plough, going up, coming down, crushed under, cut raw to the sky, and she would not escape, like all of them, for she was prisoner of her helpless body, that guilty body, which had put her here and not there, a lottery token on the bad turn of the tide, dictating that whatever she might have been, this is all she could have. But she could see what others had.

Her father's face, that intake of breath through his nostrils as he lifted his chin, with its jowls quivering as he jutted his lower jaw and pushed out his lips in some kind of ham parody of fortitude that said she'd get no mercy from him, but at the same time invited all eyes to consider what a grand sacrifice he was making, the terrible suffering he was bravely stuffing down inside for the sake of the people, for his wife, for himself. That poor, noble, lonely fellow with the weight of so much responsibility upon his shoulders, trying to keep them shored up by filling his ribcage with air to puff it, his belly with ballast to always bring him upright, park him like a giant, solid rock upon which all craft would be smashed to matchwood. This was what he had built, this rightness, and he was proud. What she did only mattered because it might shine light favourably or unfavourably upon his bulwark. She did not exist as a person, but then again, to him nobody did because this is what it meant to be King.

She'd admired his fortitude in that moment, too.

In this new vision however,he was a wooden doll, a nothing, his strings jerking him around. Inside the doll, a sad, small creature was rattled; a dry pea in a bottle. Across the world of men a thousand wizened things were drummed against their prison walls and altogether made a rushing sound like an angry churn of flies.

Beneath her fingertips the book's skin warmed and shivered. The shiver continued, regardless of the carriage's jerks. After a moment she realised that it was purring.

After a second more she began to stroke it, as much to comfort herself as for any semblance it might have had to a cat, and that was very little. But she felt the purr become more approving, satisfied.

The terror and horror began to recede, and in their place came knowledge.

When Mym put her head back into the carriage she saw her mistress sitting bolt upright, her hair loose from its bindings in a dark nimbus around her head, probably due to the damp and the sense of thunder in the air which always did that to girls with curls. For someone who was daydreaming Ven's eyes were strangely fixed and focused. When they turned suddenly to rest on her, Mym jumped involuntarily.

'Mym,' Ven said. 'When we arrive you must insist upon a great celebratory feast. We have supplies for it. Spare nothing.'

'Yes'm,' said Mym, who had been waiting for the inevitable change of her mistress' ways once they were out of range of the castle and hoping that those ways would remain kind and shy as Ven had always been, not capriciously terrible as they might turn, for many good reasons.

This turn of events was only medium-strange for someone with the possibility of turning truly odd, and she was relieved, so she ignored the fact that she had the distinct sensation that Ven's journal was somehow looking at her and that whatever she did next was going to be the deciding factor in whether or not she survived the night.

Mym put her nose back out to see what was going on and pretended none of that had happened. The mind did ridiculous things when it was discomfited and in the dregs of drink, she reminded herself. One more reason to stay detached from whatever was going on, no matter how much she thought her heart was going to break with it. People did things wrong. They died. People grew up, they had to do what was expected of them or pain and violence followed. These things happened. Life was like this. Make do and get on with it. If Ven wanted a party she could have one. Wasn't as if any of this rabble was going to say no to the idea and it was the only chance she'd get, poor thing, even if she lived to marry in Vanazon or whatever came.

And for Mym, the worst would probably happen, but you had to keep going towards it, keep on moving to it, as if you didn't know. Nobody would let you off. All their lives depended on it.

Ven heard Mym's thoughts as clearly as bells, though they wouldn't have been hard to guess in any case. Impelled to act in any way at all just to break the horror she moved across to the door and yanked the curtain apart on her side, against all protocols, sticking her head out to see for herself where they were.

At that moment one of the guard was hurrying past to get to the front of the line. No, not a guard, she thought, after a second's confusion caused by his lack of armour. It was the Wildblood who held her horse for her when she went riding, and collected it when she returned. And he wasn't human. That was clear as day to her now. His appearance was as close a replica of a human being that he could manage, and it wasn't an illusion, but there was more than that. She couldn't see that more with her eyes, just as she hadn't seen the facts of her life so clearly in her mind before, but the knowledge seemed like a vision because she 'saw' that he was bigger and more strange than any human in the line. She saw that he was made, in one plane, of fire.

'Ember,' she said, nearly soundless, her mouth experimenting with the name but it was right. It was completely right.

He turned back to glance up at her.

She snapped herself back inside the carriage on reflex, anticipating a telling off, but of course there was no governess present, no mother, no sister, and Mym was lollygagging out the other side.

Half-trapped beneath her leg on the seat cushion the book gave a firm, muscular flex.

Ven's mind was racing so fast she could barely make sense of it. One part was reaching for her journal and inks, to record these incredible developments, making plans for papers, for essays, for talks she would give to audiences of professors.

Another part was cringing away from the journal with a visceral horror.

Another part still was wondering what she could do with all this knowledge at this moment – there must be more, she must pursue it! She must find a way to talk to that Wildblood! The book had reacted to him twice. They were connected. He must know something about it.

And yet another part was sickened with terror that if anyone found out about any of this she would be exposed, shamed and horribly punished. Certainly Mym would, too, and perhaps the entire company on the journey. Her father hadn't known about her activities at home because he hadn't cared to. The Wildbloods in his household only existed as their own form of politics, to keep safe from the Majesty of the Wild. They were to him a kind of hostage. He could easily read treason into any of this and, given his temper, he would.

She didn't even squeak. If anyone had seen her pale face, fixated, glassy eyes and frozen posture, they would have instantly known a mortal dread was upon her. But nobody did see and it couldn't last forever. The carriage went over a rock as it passed through the camp gates and shook her out of it. She found her hand on the warm skin of the book, a fingertip caressing its velvety surface and finding, at the edge of the binding, the sharp corner of a paper sticking out of the pages.

Without looking down she picked the corner up and brought the item before her face. It was a folded paper with her name inked on it in her mother's shaky copperplate script.

She was about to unfold it when the carriage drew to a halt and boots crunching on gravel were followed by a sharp rap on the door. She shoved the letter back where it came from and the journal back in its satchel as the sergeant-at-arms said, 'We've arrived.'

She heard and felt the bump and fuss of the steps being put in place. Giggles and unladylike voices from the rear carriage announced the maids' glee at finally being able to get out. Mym, gathering her things together, and Ven's, rolled her eyes. She began to chatter about the party times that the maids and guardsmen had been planning since the day this trip was put on the calendar, all the life and freedom denied them by the round in Zathria to be seized in the narrow days of the trip back and forth. Mym was making all the noises of professional disapproval in a prim, and somewhat disappointed, way.

'But Mym,' Ven said after a suitable time. 'Why don't you join them? You should. Vanazon could be terribly... boring for you.' And by boring they both knew what was meant by that. Ven had seen for herself a window, and wasn't about to waste it. 'Once we've settled in and I have my dinner you are free to do as you please. Just be back by the morning in time to get us ready for the travel.'

Mym's practiced first objection, one of several that must be acted out, was cut off as the door opened and a gloved hand offered to assist Ven out into the sunset light. She took it and stepped out into the fresh and cool evening air. The solid wooden huts of the camp, the tower and the wall of spiky posts were all dwarfed by the encroaching clouds of the tree canopies all about them. Above that the mackerel skies showed a magnificent backdrop of mountains beyond.

It was a frustrating length of time meeting and greeting the camp dignitaries, formally accepting welcomes, going through the motions until at last Ven was able to be alone in her quarters – a perfectly good, solid room with a clean bed, a desk and a wardrobe – and at last open the folded letter.

My Dearest Ven. You are in grave danger. The sergeant-at-arms is a pawn of the Vanazian state. This journey is the King's opportunity to rid himself of everything that vexes him at once. You must leave at the first chance. I have paid the keeper of the horse to ensure the best steed is available for your escape. But I do not trust her. It is likely she will betray me to the King sooner than relay my command. Therefore you may be on your own and can waste no time looking for allies. I have placed letters of note inside your book satchel, as I know you would never leave it. Uncut jewels and valuable spices are stitched within a set of plain clothing I have had packed at the bottom of your chest. I believe that Mym at least is faithful. Poor Mym! You cannot save her, so do not waste your chance in trying to find a way. Get to horse. Ride east. The countries there have a slim respect for women you will not find elsewhere.

There was no signature, only the ink mark of the Queen's ring.

It was by far the longest communication Ven had ever had with her mother. The gesture itself, so dangerous, was more than enough for her to feel all the sudden loss of a love like that and for a few minutes she couldn't speak, but then the door opened and Mym came in, ushering two sweating and cursing guardsmen as they lugged Ven's chest of valuables, dresses and gifts into the room. Mym hastened to unpacking as soon as they were gone.

'I think,' Ven said, finding that her voice had become that of a mouse somehow. 'That I should ride tomorrow. Perhaps I ought to talk to the master of horse.'

'I think that's a very wise idea,' Mym said, choked up as she heaved the enormous weight of the wedding dress aside onto her own smaller bed. She wiped her eyes on her sleeve. 'Perhaps you ought to practice a few canters on the lane tonight. To be sure you

can control the beast. Before they're all drunk as lords. I'll call him.'
She darted out.

Ven had never felt scared like this before in her life. The note.
The journey. The thoughts. But worse than that immediate terror
was the sudden vision that no matter what happened now her life
was over, as anything she'd valued in it would be taken anyway, even
if she made it to Vanazon, married and was not murdered in some
plot or other. She'd led the life of a neglected child, which had
sometimes felt very lonely, but which now looked like a golden era
of heavenly peace.

She looked down at the journal. She knew its every scratch and
mark, the place where the lining was coming unglued a bit from
repeated openings and being braced firmly while she wrote, the torn
page, the soft edges of the not quite matched places, the blue and
white of its stitching. She knew every word of her own tiny writing
and line of her sketches. She felt afraid of it now, but also angry,
because it seemed it had betrayed her, by pretending to be a book
when it clearly was something else. She'd put her heart and soul into
it, every dream and hope, every minute of her time. There had been,
lately, a sense that she was putting herself into it, to try to save that
piece of her when she must lose everything else. That feeling had
spurred much of her Wildblood research – that and a fantasy that
somehow she could become known for it and taken up to the great
colleges of other nations and could escape that way, if only she
could discover something and prove her worth. The world, a power
there, would notice her. The journal had meant all those things. And
now it was turning against her.

She withdrew her hand from it slowly, watching it as she would
have watched a dangerous creature.

There came a rap at the door, Mym's triple threat knuckles, very
quiet, very fast, because she was nervous. It opened without pause
and Mym came bustling in, ushering the taller figure of the
Wildblood stablehand behind her.

Ven, still wearing her travelling dress, stood up rapidly.

The Wildblood was tall and dark, his livery somewhat awkwardly
worn in a way that suggested he didn't care for it. She saw things
that were not and had never previously been there about his person

– some kind of antlers, a mantle of thorns, a trailing cape of shadows and, at the edges of his eyes, the glow of a banked fire's deepest heat. She knew it wasn't there because she could also see him the person and that was the usual Wildblood human, oddly coloured, with the movements of someone who doesn't want to draw attention. That was all very usual. The ghosts of other things were new and they were, she was certain, created by the book.

He glanced at her and then immediately his gaze went to the place on the bed where she'd been sitting.

All the mummery and chitter she'd been fumbling through to express what she wanted to say went out of her mind. 'What's going on?' she said instead. 'What have you got to do with my journal?'

He looked at her with his jaw a bit slack for a moment and she saw he hadn't expected candour. He sucked in a breath, looked at Mym who was goggle-eyed and also, weirdly, glaring at the same time; both petrified and threatening. 'I'm it's guardian,' he said. 'It belongs to Her Darkness and I was sent to prevent anyone reading it.'

Ven stared. 'Reading it? There's nothing in it!'

He lifted his hand and she stepped forward protectively, between him and the book. His face wore a look of concern but he retreated and confused her. He held both hands up in the universal unarmed gesture.

'If I may have it, I will show you.'

She looked at Mym who shook her head, helpless.

'I… I… didn't know it was Hers. I thought it was just an empty notebook. I didn't mean to ruin it! I swear!' How childish and silly her voice sounded to her now, as if any of those things would matter in an adult world. They'd never mattered to her father or anyone she knew. What was done was always faulted, however ignorantly or innocently it had happened.

To her surprise the Wildblood backed a little more and somehow hunkered a little, although he couldn't be smaller. The essence of antler and mantle receded to a fine skin of shades. 'No, no. I understand. Please.' He held out his hand. Asking for the book.

Ven wrung her hands together. She felt that the book was all she had left, but now it was also a kind of evidence against her. She didn't know who Her Darkness was, because the named and documented Wildblood were so few, and they didn't speak much of anything that made sense to humans when interviewed about their lives. But it sounded somehow a lot like the way people said her father's name, or title. Only more so. Not the kind of person whose book you ought to be defacing.

'I...' she looked at Mym, but Mym was shrunk and small on her own bed with fear, a kind of desperate hope in her face as she looked to Ven to lead them out of this. And Ven was shaken, because Mym had always been so pragmatic, so everyday. Mym was the last person to dwell on fear and the first to do what had to be done.

'If you don't hand it to me of your own free will, I cannot take it. Because now it is yours,' Ember said.

'And aren't you free now?' Mym braved. 'If you were the guardian but she's got it anyway?'

'If I were free then I'd be gone,' he replied. 'Trust me, nobody wants to be gone from here more than I do.' He let his hand go down and sighed. 'I am the prisoner of this book. I am bound to it, like a page.'

'What for?' Mym again. Belligerent with anger that was the outer skin of her fear. Ven loved her.

'Yes, what for?' Ven said, folding her arms as if this was a major point in a distinguished argument before some board of judges.

'I... am not sure. I loved someone in the court of the dark queen and she bound me to this book. The connection, the reason – they all say I have displeased her. But I don't see how.'

He related, piece by piece, his encounter with Mildew, and concluded, 'So, you see. Maybe you're not the only one feeling damned.'

'And can you read the book? Even if I'm not supposed to? Why would you make a book and not want someone to read it? What's the point of putting it out there if you... if you are... was she hunting? Is it a trap?' Ven's mind, freed from a bit of its fear, had begun its usual process of wandering and linking. 'Was she testing?'

'Let me read it,' he said. 'I have a feeling that I was meant to, but I never tried it, because...' he hesitated.

'Because,' Ven said, 'you always believe people like Mildew Most, and you have faith, and you are loyal to Her Darkness and don't doubt her either because she's very powerful and you're scared. Or because she's really wise and you feel stupid around her.'

The dark eyes of the Wildblood looked at her sombrely. 'Yes,' he said. 'That's true.'

Ven reached behind her and picked up the journal and held it out to him. 'It takes one to know one.' She let it go, desperate to hold onto it, desperate to see what was on those empty, bare pages that she couldn't read.

He took the journal and opened it. Her little paintings, pressed flowers and decorated margins looked back at him, nothing else. He leafed through it a bit and she saw her essays, her doodles, her diary...

He smiled. 'I think she will like that.' Then before Ven could speak he clicked his fingers and the lamps in the room went out. The window shutters had been closed against the storm outside. They were suddenly in almost total darkness save for the slightest chink of light coming from beneath the door where the stone was worn on the lintel. That and the glowing writing on the pages of the open book. It was faint, hardly more than moongleam, but the marks of the ancient script were there in long, connected lines.

Of course, Ven thought, feeling so stupid. A book written by Darkness can only be read in the dark.

She moved closer. At this range the light of the ink shone on her own figures and made them faintly visible too. She heard Mym squeak with a terror she was smothering with her hands and then saw a hand that was long, fine and elegant, and not belonging to Mym or to Ember, reach out and delicately turn the page.

'My dear,' said a voice from over her shoulder, not where any head should be that belonged to that hand, 'Ember is quite right. You have improved my little book no end. And for that I shall grant you a request.'

'You sent it on purpose,' Ven said, stock still, daring hardly to breathe, the words hardly whispers as they came out.

'Only one suitable for running wild would ever touch it,' the darkness said from the far corner of the room, seeming as though it was looking around, facing away from them. Then it was back, close to her cheek. 'And only one faithful and strong would never try to read it even when he could. But life is short. What will you ask of me?'

'To change the world, make it fair, make it better.' Ven had had this wish so many times that she didn't even have to think to know what she wanted to say.

The shadow paused in its examination of the book. The fingers traced the edge of a lily where Ven had written extensively about her frustration and despair with the life of women, in the castle and beyond. 'That is beyond my power,' said the voice. 'I suspect it is beyond all powers. But if you like you can join us beyond the limits of that world. In the darkness things may be remade into shapes of their own making, their own dreaming. In time the wild blood can run strong enough to transform you into a creature that will no longer be bound by these foolish visions, never tormented by the likes of men.' And Her voice on that final word seemed to consume the very idea and melt it, as a snowflake melts on the tongue.

Ven gulped. 'What about Mym?' Not just because Mym was there, listening. Because it wasn't fair, not right, to leave her to what must come in the wake of her desertion. Mym would be blamed for everything. That was the Zathrian style of operations. Probably one reason they'd been left in this room. At any time someone could 'discover' their treason, being alone here with Ember, and have it as a reason to do whatever they had planned for their advancement, or the advantage or disappointment of some King. There was no end to the opportunity.

'No!' Mym gasped, astonishing her. 'No! I can't. I won't go with them. I've got me Mam to think of. I've got a man back in... please, ma'am.' The raw fear had changed her.

As usual, Ven hadn't thought far enough.

'Then I'll have to stay,' Ven thought aloud, feeling the cold grasp of terror and failure both. She would have leapt at the chance to leave but her death was, after all, assured. Here, or in some nightland far away, there was only time between now and then, and it would be better short and true than long and full of regret.

'Perhaps,' the voice did not sound at all convinced. It became mocking, playful, 'But what a pity to lose you. If only one of us could call on a faithful friend to cover our escape into the night. Ember. But be quick. The sergeant at arms has almost drunk what must be drunk to do what must be done.'

The lamps came back to life and in their light all shadows fled leaving the three of them in the weak but gentle gleam of the burning oil. Ven rushed to Mym, who was cowering.

'Gods forgive my cowardice!' Mym cried. 'I'm so sorry. I can't. I can't go. I'm afraid! But you...' she convulsed into a paroxysm of grief and regrets that Ven was unable to comfort.

'Mym,' she said sternly. 'It was my choice.'

'Ladies,' said the Wildblood. 'Say your goodbyes. If you will come, Princess. Ven. Then come to my side. We will be leaving. Mym, good servant, be out of this room within the minute if you wish to see your man again in this life.'

Ven, still in her travelling clothes, hardly light but also without much in the way of anything else, looked about automatically for the book satchel. It was on the edge of the bed, buckled shut, and heavy when she picked it up in a way that suggested the book was there, or something was there. Something that growled as it slapped against her leg through her coat. Mym's collapse was so unexpected, she could hardly bear it, but she seized Ember's hand and with the other opened the door.

'Move, Mym!' and then, without a backward glance, she was floating with the speed of her descent. She hurried down the steps of their hut, strangely light, the camp barely visible, shrouded by the same smoke that hid her from their sight. All she felt was the fierce, hot grip of the Wildkin and the pulse of blood in his palm, matching hers, as they ran.

The charm faded quickly. They had barely gone around the post of the gate when she was suddenly and rudely back in her very tired and normal form, getting wet as rain began to fall unevenly from the blackened sky above. A wild excitement and a terrible foreboding warred for control of her. She was only not sick because she was trying to see so very hard, looking at Ember as the last hope.

'It's not easy,' he said. 'I was human once. We should go further away.'

They hurried along the road in the rain for a few yards until they reached a tiny animal track that turned up into the trees on the hillside and then there was no more thinking because it was too dark to see and she could only stumble after him, slipping, and holding his hand. 'What's not easy?' She was whispering but he heard her.

'The change,' he said.

'How?' she asked, feeling rain run down her nose.

'Open the book,' he said.

In spite of the weather she managed to get it out of its satchel. She opened it at random, light from the pages filled her face, and the book read her.

Ember was nervous too. Not because of the book or the humans — now that the book was reading there was no trouble to worry about for Ven or him in that respect, they wouldn't get caught — but because he didn't feel sure that Fires was going to show up. Ven was right about him, which is why he'd helped, and she was probably right to throw shade on Mildew, but one thing you could be sure about when it came to any Wildblood was their changeability. Fires was all he could think about as the skies glowered and the rain came in larger drops.

Then the air felt dense and heavy, charged with a terrible possibility. In the reflected light of Ven's astonished face he saw her hair rising upwards, one strand at a time, felt the sudden inner burn of a Wildkin manifesting.

'That bloody maid just wouldn't leave,' said a droll, dry voice at his side and at the same moment there was a flash that made the world stark white and a crack that split the air and all their eardrums with a painful stabbing. A moment later the thud of an explosion rocked the ground. And then heavier bits and pieces of Ven's old room came splintering in a hail of wood through the sudden downpour.

There did not seem to be any bits of Mym.

Fires of the Lightning Strike was in their most quiet form, ashy grey, tall, with a shock of hair that fluttered like old rags. They smiled at Ember with a row of glowing red hot teeth. 'Time we were off, I think.'

Screaming and shouting were coming from the camp.

Ven looked up from the book. The light from the writing faded away, leaving her in darkness, and she closed it with a snap. 'Ink and dreams is all we are made of,' she said. Her Darkness was a mist of lamp black among them.

From the pages of the book the drawings of the little flowers, the birds, the small creatures, the horses and the deer, all the many small doodles and the large paintings swept up and over Ven's arms, covering her from head to toe, their line and colour sinking into her like water into paper. The words of her hopes and fears, the idle musings, the stern essay notes; these rushed through her, finding the deep ink of Her Darkness and writing themselves in an ever-shifting narrative within her bones.

'At last,' whispered the Darkness. 'Someone to talk to. Come. Time to show you what the Wild is made of.'

And in that moment Ember and Fires became their equine forms, and Ven a black bird of scribble and ink, a crow she'd once drawn and coloured. The book, the satchel, her clothes were written on her, ready to be told, but for now she flew on midnight wings, untouched by the rain, for she was already an imaginary being and made of the Wild.

Ven circled the burning guard camp, and when she had seen Mym, safe and sound, and that nobody had been badly hurt, she circled high enough to see the trail of the burning-eyed horses and followed it, far away from the reach of the ordinary world.

Until she turned off and watched them race away, job done. Fire and Ember belong together in the hidden twistiest and truest paths of the spirit, wound in poetry, they are for a different future.

Her business however, was hardly finished. The ever-present moment has come to write another page in time.

A day to the East is Zathria's castle, dour and glum. Night wraiths lie like the dregs of battle upon its gutters, soaking up the steady diet of quietly held miseries that must accompany the rule of ruthlessness, reason and power.

It's the hour when the wine is pressed out of the soul. A crow cuts its silhouette against the stars. Do you remember, oh my mother, when we looked at the stars together, so icy and so far, so free in the unfenced sky?

It circles down, words falling from its feathers, striking the roof, soaking the stones, rushing down the mouths of the gaping gargoyles into the rooms, into the furnishings, onto the walls. Pictures appear, huge, spectral with wobbly, watery colours. Here a kingfisher. There a clutch of daisies with the words 'Common Daisy' and that's true enough, but then it also says 'Sweetener of Old Wounds'. That's new.

That kind of new is everywhere coming into being.

The spells fall and sink into the house under cover of Her Darkness. They create couplets in the bedrooms, pithy one-liners in the privies, jokes in the kitchen, a brimming cauldron of power in the dining room. The dungeons bloom with black roses that are edible and good.

In the kennels the dogs chase the fattest rabbits. The horses dream of meadows. And on the balcony, a sleepless woman, her grey hair coming loose from its braid, stares out at the world in the direction of Vanazon, and sometimes down at the long drop to the courtyard's moonlit flags. But we mustn't jump, must we? There's still the others.

Girls above in their bedrooms dance with princes and princesses, and everyone is a prince, and everyone is a princess and nobody must marry, only dance and enjoy a glass of champagne, the smile of a friend, the touch of a flower upon the edge of their noses as they come close to the brimming bouquets. A boldness fills the dreams, a sense that there are no shortcomings, no missteps possible here.

But on the balcony the words creep slowly, carefully, winding around the columns and the balustrade. People can't be taken to the Wild. They must long to go, until the longing is stronger than all other things, until they are consumed by desire.

The words of wishes form a vine, upon which flowers in the sunlight appear fine and yellow, and in the night strange and luminously white. There are thorns, subtle, and tipped with particular inks. It grows up from the balcony, along the face of the castle, to the rooms above, and down among the wistful wisteria to the servants below. As it is made of ink and words it will not be seen by anyone who doesn't study hard. As it is made of ink and words it can be read in the way one smells a beautiful bloom.

Ven watches her mother wring her hands, rest her fingers on the rail, wince and snatch her hand back with the prick of a thorn and then look up in wonder as she hears Ven say, 'I am free.'

Later a crow visits Mildew Most's house and leaves a calling card upon the step.

Crow is the first shape. Crow sits on the roof and sends tendrils of words down to the library and sucks the pages dry. There will be others. There will be much more. But in good time. For now darkness is on the wing.

I Give You the Moon

The apocalypse was a terrible disappointment.

There was no great flood. Fire did not fall from the sky, not even a meteorite. You couldn't even write the line "Death stalked slowly in her cloak of many viruses because Terminators always walk" because although that was true it gave the event a lot more colour and interest than it deserved. Even mapped in graphs and coloured regions and comparative charts with numbers and pulsating animated globs and fire-crisping maps it took thirty years to complete. It progressed by boring increments of boom and bust before fizzling out to inconvenient embers in the cities, where for ages its only sign was the sudden hacking cough of passers-by that startled the occasional cat from its nap on the hot pavements. Millions died, several times, and nobody since had stopped banging on about it in case it wasn't really over, though what their anxiety was going to do to fix it was anybody's guess.

Jack took off his hat. The lesson which had filled his hearing and vision vanished. He set the hat down on the sand beside him and sat in the sudden quiet of the calm sea and the empty sky, not even a gull to see. The breeze boxed his ears with a random blather. A hundred metres to his left the old man who had been fishing when he started his lecture was still fishing in exactly the same spot. As far as the eye could see in all directions, they were alone.

Behind them Jack felt the continental bulk of Africa sitting quietly, satisfied with whatever was going on. It had a cosy quality this afternoon, not so much at their backs as having their backs in a way which seemed to say that they were free to do what they wanted about whatever they thought important, silly little creatures, it would still be there regardless, no worries, until something happened to it far in the future that changed it into something new. But Jack wouldn't see that, it was a problem for future Africa, though as

Africa had no problem with it there was no problem at all. Continents were lucky that way.

Right now, Jack's problem was that he had to complete his history course before he could qualify for Viking Adventure. Jack had lived his whole life on this coastline and Viking Adventure would take him far away from it through strange lands to the white North where the last ice still capped the planet. He longed to feel it, to taste it, to see how cold it was. Here on the beach the temperature was about 30 and the idea of a glacier, a frozen river, a snowfield – felt like the most amazing thing there could be. Almost unbelievable that it existed. And the Vikings themselves, creatures of legend: he felt a kinship of a strange kind to them, savage travellers wandering their own coasts, fearless upon the sea in ships made by hand, out of wood – forests! Ah, to walk in a thick forest of trees, hunting deer, fending off wolves, spear in hand, and a helmet with horns on it, and a sword and shield, and big fur boots...

He bent down to pick up a shell half buried in the sand and studied it for a second. Chamber after chamber went spiralling away, around the bend, old fossil houses turned by a living lathe. That's what Dad had said about them. He peered in, tried to see further, further into the past. If only the stupid lecture was as fascinating as a shell. If he put on his hat he could know all about it, maybe see through the shell itself into its secret vaults.

But it was nicer with the secret intact.

He dropped it back where he found it and came up to the fisherman, taller than he was, thin like him, wearing a nearly identical blue cotton fishing hat in a size too big with the brim pulled low over his eyes. At his feet the rod was rooted in the sand, its curve moving idly; nothing on the line.

Darius watched the tide rolling slowly in. Another half an hour from now it would reach his feet and then it would be time to pack up for the day.

With the extra vision granted by his hat he was monitoring the levels of flow in the Eastern Atlantic Reactor. The huge machine lay at modest depth, sieving plastic from the Benguela Current as it bore Northwards up the coast; a scrubbing brush for seawater. The ominous name fitted its appearance, not its function. It was an old beast, a cage of steel and – ironically – plastic, holding a sequence of membrane filters and ferrofluid resonance chambers out into the flow. Its aquaplaned sides and solar-powered motors kept it positioned at the fastest run of water. It sat as one of a chain, number twenty-one out of forty of its bony kind, strung down towards the Cape from Gabon. Far above, almost invisible in the sky, albatross gliders monitored his little patch and the whole of the Atlantic Sea Farm, guiding the cleaners away from pods of whales and other cetaceans, sending them to depth when storms threatened to disturb their balances. But a human was required to check, verify and interpret their findings.

Darius kept his line out, his eye on the inner workings of the filters during his shift. He cued a maintenance crew to make ready for a resupply and clean-up. Good old Twenty-One, another billion tonnes of water cleaned, another, better day for everyone. He felt fond of all his machines.

The line bobbed as the weights – packed instruments working to read all the sea's secrets – rode the waves. There was no hook, no catch for fish. He'd caught dinner an hour ago and now he was only fishing for information.

Closer to home his cast of drone crabs were busy on the seabed, picking up manmade pollutants and logging notes of other debris they encountered as they patrolled. They periodically constructed buoyant cubes of garbage and floated them to the surface. The albatrosses noted the positions on their ever-changing charts and deployed pickup craft to return the casks for reprocessing at the nearest shore facility. It was automated. But some jobs were hard to automate and they popped up frequently, usually when crabs got stuck in and around wreckage. Then Darius would have to intervene and drive them out by hand, well, by hat, but everyone still said by hand like it was the days of controllers that you had to wiggle and press instead of hats that picked up your intentions and transformed them directly into processes elsewhere.

Darius had come to the coast for the wrecks thirty years ago, before hats, in the days of hand controls. There had been no crabs then, only human workers and their various tools, on shore and boat, living a leisurely lifestyle on the fringes of the Blue Wild where they were tasked with policing, maintenance, clean-up and reporting. This was during the slow build-up towards the international accords that finally came together to reclassify the globe's seawater habitats into Blue Farm and Blue Wild. This piece of the Namibian coast, where desert met sea, was a part of the Wild now. Its beauty was reserved for what wildlife might come, and for small and regulated numbers of human visitors who paid in reward tokens or immense amounts of money for the privilege of spending a few days in one of the hotels. From there they fished and walked, or rode camels or robot hobbyhorses up and down the surf line, painted pictures, tried yoga, all the usual things people did when they wanted to feel they'd become closer to nature.

Darius had been a cleaner, then a builder, as they renovated some of the more stable shipwrecks into living quarters and luxury restaurants. After they were done he became a tour-guide, both on shore and undersea, until he left that life for something that felt more like giving back. He had joined Blue Wild as a crab master when Hyundai had started up their part of the shore operations here, and now he fished the coast and monitored the drones. He lived in a little hut of his own during the week, where his son could visit him every few months, and come and ask questions, and stare impatiently at the sea, and not do his classes.

There he was now, coming up after just half an hour of study, hangdog expression, nearly as tall as Darius already and easy to recognise as an ungainly assortment of elbows, knees, hands and feet. He was newly awkward in gait, hesitant in a way he'd never been a few years ago, even though he was the only other human on the beach for miles.

Darius missed that little boy. Always so happy. Free of care. The program for kindergarten was gentle like a soft breeze, full of the wonders of the world, none of the difficulties. Then the inescapable courses about the past had come and a serious, pondering heaviness had set in like bad weather. Could be his age a bit. It came and went.

At his age Darius had been in a very different world, a bricks and mortar school with papers and exams. He'd not liked it, had skipped as much as he dared to wander the streets instead, despite the threat of capture and punishment. It was strange to think back on it, because now he couldn't get enough of staying in touch with his interests, far and wide. The possibilities were endless in the connected world of daily lives, where you could dip in and out of someone's experience a world away, see things through their hat, be in their moment. It was a time made for dreamers and drifters.

It was a miracle Jack had got this far really with that kind of background, but Darius was proud of him, because years ago Jack had got it into his head that he wanted to be a Viking and damned if the kid hadn't stuck to it, limpet to its rock, clinging to that strange dream. He'd saved his tokens, taking extra learning credits, doing all he could to earn his place, and nobody could say no to it because he was going to buy the reward all by himself. It belonged to him and him alone.

It was not as if Darius hadn't endorsed it. Because this was still education. It was history and learning how to live without modern conveniences, like humans did before the industrial age had wrecked the biosphere. And Jack's mother, when she was alive, always said study and work for what you want. Never listen to other people. The world isn't like it used to be. We've got the Accord that says anyone can learn, can't be stopped – and tokens to buy things we'd never have thought of – and nobody can say no to us now for any reason. Stay at home, travel the world, be here, be this, that, the other. Do what you want. All you have to do is contribute and save. She'd been the Accord's biggest fan, Marta, proud that her own mother had worked hard to see these new methods brought in, and that she was alive on the day it was signed up to, a global dedication. Yes of course at first it was hard going, took forty years to get it anything like functional, had to be frequently saved from ditching into various ideological and aggressive pits, but in spite of all the nationalisms and setbacks it was still alive. It gave a sense of possibility that hadn't existed before and it delivered. Mostly.

He wanted so badly that it would deliver for Jack. *Things must get better*, he said to the Marta in his mind, *they must. We have to make sure they do.*

Darius thought Jack would have wanted the usual – days out, sports, extra tech – but Jack had come home one day from school with the Vikings book and that was that. What about something closer to home? Marta had said. What about Kaokoland? Beautiful animals to see. Heritage of our own to treasure. Even if it doesn't seem as exotic as Europe, it's still good.

But Jack sighed. He liked Kaokoland well enough, but these ferocious ancients had stolen his imagination right away with their wooden dragon-ships and their romance of conquest and discovery, their bravery in the face of sea and ice. Somehow they felt more wild and full of possibility.

While Jack dreamed of ice Darius felt uneasy about the trip, no denying that. He'd never been to Europe and he felt an old anger about the past, couldn't help it; not a personal one that is, for living folk who weren't involved, but for all them that were, far away and invisible to him, hidden by history. They were in Europe, surely, still. And in the world of his anxieties Jack would go there, idealistic, full of ideas about Vikings and there would be some kind of thing that was bubbling around, rising to the surface like rotten fish. A face that didn't fit, a strange voice, a wrong move in a place where you couldn't know the customs enough and it would start. Well, he couldn't know that for sure, but he felt worried about it. And instead of being useful Darius'd be on his beach, sifting for news of whales and dolphins, sharks and shoals, telling them all about his fears, wondering if they'd carry them north to the cold waters of the North Sea and ask the seals how it was going these days in that place which was a home to all the old invaders.

Seals had no problems with nationality. Only with orcas. And the whims of fish. And humans, of course.

Darius thought of these things because he knew Jack had reached modern history and was covering the twentieth century and its various tides and reckonings. The weight of this knowledge was a burden in the body, not just the mind. It had heft to it, as if genes were a chain back through the ages, dragging the past and its unfinished business. Children shouldn't have burdens. It irks him that he had to learn and his son had to learn about this. It might be better if Jack was protected from it. What you don't know can't hurt you. They said history must be known so it wasn't repeated, but what was there to fight about without it?

The past was another world from which this one was born. An inadequate parent, but the only one. Some kind of shame madeDarius want to slither off into the sea.

He was keenly aware that he kept telling Jack to finish the history course. But he wished the history course didn't exist. He didn't want to be the witness to crushing disappointment, didn't want to have to feel that himself again.

A crab was stuck. It had been cycling through its disengagement protocols for over an hour and now it had reached the point where it signalled him for help. Its battery was a bit low. If he couldn't get it out quickly he'd have to bring up the others to recover it. It was a long job and the sun had started to go down. And here was Jack, silent and watchful because he wasn't able to go on with his lesson.

Darius took off his hat, held it out. A boy should learn to do something useful.

'Want to drive this crab out of trouble for me?'

Jack's eyes lit up immediately. He thought he was going to get a telling for failing. 'Yeah!'

They switched hats.

Jack loved to drive the crabs, even though they didn't do anything other than grub along for waste material and even though they were nothing like a game. They required a knowledge of the sand, the silt, the strange configurations of legs they could get into and how those things conspired to free you from a terrible trap. You freed the machine from something it couldn't figure out, just because you were human and you'd try all kinds of things until you won.

They were a puzzle and sometimes you discovered things that you didn't know about, because by accident you shivered and shook, tried the legs in new patterns, dug with the claws and some miracle happened and you have a new move in your repertoire that you'd never have thought of without the accident. Plus, the crabs were important, very valuable, doing great work, and helping them made him happy, like a good deed for the day. He was good with the crabs, they were a happy place.

This one was rammed nose down against some piece of steel from the wreck of a hulk, long scuppered. It was too rusted and decayed for it to be worth stripping for steel. Instead it was part of the diving school's monthly advanced skills trips to deep waters. Jack'd been to the ship. You could go into the rooms inside it. It was mostly buried in the thick silt of the continental shelf and even though the chances were incredibly thin, more thin than the lottery, Jack always hoped he was going to find a diamond. You never know.

He sometimes looked for a hint of bronze or silver, a chunk of wood that might be from a drakkar ship which came long ago, bearing Vikings.

It was silly. They didn't come this far south. But they could have. If they'd wanted to. Nothing to stop them but the distance from home. He felt their urge to find, to discover, to get for themselves some piece of the world. But his world was pieced out.

The crab had only fifteen percent battery left, and after a test of each possible operation there turned out to be some fault with the left side front legs too. The balloon of garbage attached to it had wedged hard between one of the skeleton's ribs and a section of its skin. First thing was to seal that off, label it, tag it and detach it. Even with that done the crab remained stuck, but at least it wasn't anchored now.

Jack moved his arms and the crab, mapped into his nervous system by the hat, copied him gingerly, a little left, a little right, forward, back. There was no leverage that would move him backwards, he discovered. The efforts of the ordinary systems to get themselves out of trouble had, thanks to the garbage balloon, actually dug it deeper in.

A bloom of silt, pale clouds, covered the cameras, swirled and shut him in to a tiny world of fog and guesswork. He could feel, through his own muscles, just how the little robot was held fast by the weight of the ship, the thick density of the mud, its own peculiar shape. At the same time, on the beach he could still feel sun on his skin as he wove and danced, searching for a clue which his brain would find without him thinking about it, just because he was an animal who understood how to deal with these things.

It was fun and today, boy, it was difficult. Sweat ran down his brow and, without a hand to use, he shook his head. The crab twisted itself deeper. Uh oh.

Darius went back to the sun shade of the solar tent and sat down to make a brew. Just out of interest and not because he was prying, he put on Jack's hat and glanced at the last lesson. Apocalyptic Times, 2020-2030. Yeah, that was a long course, long and the subject of a lot of argument and opinion, so much so that any effort to make a cohesive grab at the whole picture was exhausting. No wonder Jack was struggling. But you have to struggle or you don't get through it and the big picture is important, the one they all lived by now.

He figured his way through the menus of the lesser hat until he was able to send a personal call out to Windhoek. He was put on a timer and spent the wait fixing the teabags and the mugs, a place for Jack to sit when he was done, a snack from the cooler.

Then Esther answered. "Hi, Darius!" She beamed.

They say that – someone's smile beams – but it had just been a figure of speech to him until he saw her smile and then he understood. It had beams, like joyful lasers that cut straight through everything to a simpler world in which all things are right. It put him right, straight away. Everything was all right.

He suspected she was like this with everyone. It pleased him that she was, made her more special as a person who could be so generous. But it pleased him that she smiled at him even so. It was a guilty pleasure as if he'd stolen its meaning, changed it to fit him.

Even though Jack's mother was long gone always the guilty twinge. Well, you live with these things.

"Hey, Esther." An awkward moment, would he say anything? "How's everything?" No, he won't.

A disappointed feeling, but there was still hope, of a kind, they did have reason to chat. Esther was the lead local coordinator of Special Cleaning, which tracked the prevalence of biohostile chemicals in their precinct. Darius filed reports for her department. There was a perfectly good channel for this that didn't require personal contact, but they had met at a dinner hosted for a few award winners, and he had won a Blue Wild Commendation and she had been at the same table and he'd had some wine and forgotten to ask what she did until the end of the night by which time they'd already been talking for hours. So he hadn't been scared off in time.

If she detected any awkwardness in him she showed no sign of it.

"Ah, you know, I think soon I'll be out of a job. The clean up on the southern coast is so good now we're getting numbers that are almost neutral."

She beamed, and he smiled back. It was a good feeling, and not just because of the feedback in the hat, subtly beavering away to reinforce the appeal of otherwise mundane tasks, but because every success against the desecration was a step forwards on his own personal metric of value.

"But it also means I have less points," she said. "Do you know, I think I'll never reach my goal. A few years ago when things were still bad, ironically, I was doing really well, but now unless I move on to some other position – I did a few sums and it could be another ten years before I have enough credit." She sighed and did a dramatic shrug.

Darius felt a pang of concern. Would she really go? It had been… lord, it had been nearly a year since the dinner and he was still pussyfooting around like a kid. But he'd done it for so long that he felt sure he was solid friendzone material. Nothing else.

"How are you doing out there? How's Jack?"

"Oh, he's great. Just digging a crab out for me. Doing really well. School's a bit of a struggle."

"Still the Vikings?"

"Just one credit short."

They both paused. One credit short of a major achievement was a huge deal and they had bonded at their dinner party because they'd both been people with long savings – the annotated fruits of a lifetime building up in their banks; Darius because he was happy out on the shore and had wasted no time explaining how wonderful it was to be out alone with nature, working on his favourite things. He wouldn't give it up for the world. And Esther said she was saving for the Moon. Not the whole thing. For the trip *to* the Moon, a walk on the surface, a two-day stay at the hotel, and then back again. In the grand scheme of all the things one could save for – and they were too many to scroll through in a day – this was the most expensive. For an average person it would take a saved credit lifetime of more than thirty years' human-advancing, world-tending achievement. And Esther had been on track for that, head down and going some, she said at the dinner, but then, time began to tell. The years pass, not always as you expect, she'd said, looking into her wine glass. And then she'd laughed and made a joke and Darius had said well, he'd lost count because he never wanted to do anything but stay where he was, the coast was a perfect place, a liminal place, did she know what that was? Oh yes. Esther was up on liminal things, the in-between, the meeting place of one thing and another, one anything and another thing, a very Namibia thing. Oh, they had a wonderful night talking.

And now, Jack, of all of them, was going to make his grade and cash in. And they were short, or not bothering, but he was going to make it and both of them felt how special it was, how rare. Most people settled for a series of little rewards.

'We must do something,' Esther said.

'Special. Yes.' Darius was slower because it hadn't occurred to him that he should make it more special than it already was. How could it be even more? But now, in Esther's conviction, he realised that as a parent it was his business to mark it as such with a gesture. The ghost of Jack's mother waited in the background, wishing him on. But what? He'd given it no thought until now and he felt ashamed suddenly, stupid, but also, and more importantly, at a loss.

'I know!' Esther said suddenly with a snap of her fingers, always bubbling and never more so than now. 'Leave it to me. When will he finish?'

'I'm not sure exactly. Today. Maybe tomorrow.'

'I need to go check the charts and call a friend. I have an idea. I can't tell you now in case it doesn't work out but keep me posted! Oh… was there something you wanted to say? I mean, you called me.'

'Ah. Um. Nothing special. Just checking in.' What an idiot. He was still blundering about in the mire of finding a gift. Years of sun, sea, sand and wreckage had addled his mind. He was more place than person. He had a distinct sense of groping around, trying to put bits of himself back together, weave a self from the flotsam to something that could sail.

'Well if you think of anything,' she said and then she blinked away before he had a chance to reply.

He was left sitting in the hut, looking at Jack do the comical, awkward dance of the sand crab tango, feeling alone and foolish. God save us from old men, he thought. He should help Jack.

He tuned into the pole and line, to catch the feed.

By using the crab's siphon to pump water around it at high speed and then working the legs and pinchers together Jack had figured out that he could get the silt to loosen into a thick soup. Any pauses had it quickly solidifying again but he felt sure that if he could just keep going long enough he could dig down, flip over and get out facing the other way. The contortions he had to figure out, recorded for other crab operators to laugh over later, made him feel like those yogis who could get both legs behind their heads and then stand on their hands. He was nowhere near that, but it felt like it, and he was trying not to laugh and blush at the same time as sweat ran down his nose and into his eyes. Butt in the air, his mind kept trying to frighten him off with dire warnings of complete humiliation and the distant seal colony started honking at the same time, which completed the circus just as the battery warning started to pump out its red alert.

Hot on the beach Jack danced like a crazed beetle.

Deep in the chill of the silt the crab spasmed and wrenched itself about, siphon spraying wildly at top volume. Muck and murk ballooned into vast fallout and there, on the camera for a moment he saw something shiny, with a gleam of wan light from the crab's headers reflecting off something that looked like the rim of an embossed treasure. Then it was lost in the whirl and darkness as the crab reached a depth that gave it space to turn beneath the old stanchion. With smooth agility, it flipped and swiftly worked itself upwards, outgassing spare air from its lift canisters in jets to either side.

The battery red filled his vision but it was fine. As the power died the emergency buoy deployed in a burst of bubbles and the old drone was safe on its spidery line, towed to the surface to await repair.

Jack took off his father's hat and found himself sitting on the burning hot sand, breathing heavily. A few metres away the rod and line bent tenderly towards the tide.

He got to his hands and knees and then to his feet and staggered forwards into the oncoming surf. The cold water iced his feet and shot straight to his brain. It was bliss.

'That', said his dad's voice from behind him, full of amusement, 'was epic.'

Jack groaned and then laughed. He'd be the stock instaclip all week, all year maybe. But it couldn't spoil the feeling of victory and the sudden lurch of surprise at that silver metal edge buried so deep. 'Did you see the treasure?'

'Treasure?'

'There was something under the ship. About two metres down. Metal. Old.'

He turned and saw his dad picking up his hat, holding Jack's out towards him. 'I'll take another look. But first, what about this history course?'

'Man...' There was nothing like a parent to remind you that things sucked.

'I thought maybe since you were so good at fixing my problem I could help you with yours. Do it together?'

'And I get to say what I think and you don't try to fix it?'

His dad took a breath and then shut his mouth, lips firmly closed for a second. 'Okay.'

'Okay then,' Jack sighed heavily and took his hat back. They had their tea first, then walked along the shore together towards the black seal splodges massed to the North, the soft roaring ocean to their left and the gentle roll of the beach dunes to the right. The hats said there were no visiting lions near enough to cause any trouble; the prides that had come thanks to the drought were at the desalination rig to their south, taking advantage of its free fresh water and the shade of the palms that had been planted around it. Later they'd be moving North too, looking for a seal dining opportunity, but history wouldn't take that long, hopefully.

The AR feed began, a formal rectangle of TV in the top right of their vision, a voice in the mind, a narrator who somehow managed to make it sound as though they were both familiar with these old ideas but still thrilled by them: 'Humans have evolved to adapt because we are constantly fighting ourselves through the huge systems of ideas that we generate about everything we touch. We are our own arms race. The pandemics of the early twenty second century brought exterior focus on our planet to the fore at a critical point in time, when the internet and machine learning tools were capable of creating new environments, making old methods of governance and trade obsolete. Today's massively gamified system of logistics that covers the globe emerged from the shopping habits and trends of that period in time. And from there we can trace those roots right back through to the very earliest periods of human endeavour…'

At last they'd stopped doing war, genocide, religious stupidity, greed and tragedy and all the things about human behaviour that made you want to bury your head.

'…although it wasn't until the repeated decimation of the population and loss of almost all recognisable civilised institutions and infrastructure caused by a combination of disease and climate change that corporate delivery systems and data analytics ended previous forms of party political representation…'

Oh no, right. Before the rising, the fall to the bottom.

Jack found himself gazing out to sea, across the huge expanse of the Atlantic, breakers whitecapping far offshore and rolling to paw at his ankles. The wind whipped around his head, tugging the hat as if suggesting he throw it away. The voice and the other images might as well not have been there.

He felt his dad nudge him, the prompt at the thought level, connecting one dot to another just enough for Jack to see what it was that the old man was getting at.

Before the turn over, the really being stuck.

Jack's ideas took shape.

Things were impossible and awful, and then, bit by bit, you did things until you got free of the past. He grinned as he combined that thought with his afternoon of crab wrangling, and put that down as part of his final essay. He thought of the metal shine. You never knew what you might find.

Esther put a call in to Julia. The local times were close enough she didn't have to give it a second thought, even though Julia was thousands of miles north in England. Julie was busy but she'd left her feed on Browse. For Esther it was almost time to finish for the day, so she put her feet up and allowed herself a surf in Julia's afternoon as she waited.

Julia lived at the top of a high-rise, one of a few in the city centre, and it had great views but Esther most enjoyed the fact that instead of the old city palette of concrete, glass and steel here nearly everything was greened over, and if it wasn't green, it was some interesting Victorian brick and stone arcade or frontage, with only a few strategically left long-lines of modern architecture.

The recovery strategy for Northern Europe post-loss had been to withdraw to the cities, using them as much tighter hubs than in the past: heat was effectively conserved and distribution of supplies better managed, those buildings that were basically large glasshouses had been converted to vegetable factories, planters on a massive scale, while older structures were modelled into contemporary housing. Even with fairly generous portions offered, this still meant that the remaining population had abandoned almost all suburban structures and those areas were being reclaimed and rewilded. Julia was part of an aquatic group that specialised in the restoration of natural waterways and the decontamination of groundwaters, and she and Esther had been in many of the same circles for years.

Esther was able to view what she wanted through Julia's hat, although in this case it wasn't a hat, it was a headset shaped like a hairband, the one with the glitter disco boppers on the head if she wasn't mistaken. She could see the tiny coloured reflections of the sunlight glancing off the boppers onto the rich leafy surrounds of Julia's balcony where figs and grapes twined in trained profusion over whatever lay beneath. As Julia worked she was idly nipping the tips out of her tomatoes and feeling the mulch for moisture. Across the road on another tall building, which Esther thought had been a bank, she could see small birds fighting and darting in and out through a temperate rainforest that clung to the wall, watered by misters concealed by the leaves.

Data from Julia's headset showed Esther what everything was, how it had got there, what it was for. She glimpsed the river, boats upon it, low and long, and the canal, and then beyond them the brickwork of mills and the yards by the railway where all the dismantled buildings were sorted for scrap. There was a green run that crossed the human landscape, cutting through the city, where people rode horses in the day time. Somewhere south of here there was a park for driving cars and bikes, racing and all kinds of things. What used to be in a preserve and what had been everywhere had reversed their positions.

Whatever Julia had been preoccupied with finished and her line cleared. She noticed Esther's arrival with a quick straighten up and an 'Ow!' as her lower back twinged. 'Hello. What brings you in today? Did you figure out if we owe you a water credit?'

'Ah no, that's still pending a review. You're good for at least for another month and if you do get called for it then it's only going to be some rig supplies. The Chinese covered us for a year in exchange for extra solar. This is more a personal call. You used to be in with the Venturers set, Julia. Were there black Vikings? Did they get to Africa?'

Julia looked out over the city centre. Cloud was coming in from the west but the white stone of the old hotel near the station was glowing with oncoming sunset and there wouldn't be rain today. A mercy. The river was at bursting point. She swung her mind around towards the piece of her that used to deal with the Northern Britain retreats when she was an apprentice. She'd managed their resources and immigration as they took on and left off people who were touring. The British base for the permanent 'Viking' population was at Lindisfarne but they had places all along the coasts. 'Black Vikings. Why are you asking me?'

'I thought you were the expert,' Esther had a cheeky voice on, one that Julia always felt was the audio equivalent of having someone pinch your bottom.

'Not like entire groups of African Vikings,' she said after a moment's pause for reference in the Venturer's Database. 'But there were coloured Vikings. So definitely possible. Even if there weren't any we've got about thirty black Vikings now on the Northward rotation so you won't feel out of place, and… why are you asking? Are you trading in your Moon Ticket?'

'Ah, I…' Esther explained about Jack. She may have dwelled a bit on Darius, more than strictly necessary. She ended with, '…and you worked on admin for the Venturers, didn't you?'

'It was ages ago,' Julia said.

'But I have this idea,' Esther went on, getting what she really wanted with good-natured determination, 'because I heard him talking about it…'

'Esther, have you been spying on Darius?'

'Only for research purposes. He's always in Browse anyway. It's an open channel. Mostly just the sea to be honest, and sometimes some sand. He thinks about a lot. This morning he caught a… No, no. Anyway, listen to me. The Ventures at Jack's level will only give him a week with them. I was thinking a whole summer would be good but it's a long way from home…'

Julia listened, twirling a tomato leaf, and at the end of Esther's plan she said, 'That is some package of extras right there, Esther. Long haul. I mean. It's a lovely thought. But I can't authorise that kind of excess. Even if I was the admin. Which I'm not. I…'

'I can give you the extra. I've got my eye on a new job.'

'I thought you were short of credits. This would be – I don't know. Some massive amount.'

'I am. I was. No, I've thought about this a lot, Julia. I want to do this. I did want… but it's more important to give something special to someone whose life will really be helped by it, rather than spend it all on yourself, isn't it? And I've got so many saved up, there's loads I can still do.'

Julia, friendship radar now tuned in to its very sharpest setting, reviewed the information that Esther was sending her. There were strict rules about credit trading, particularly when it involved large amounts, but it was possible to make gifts sometimes, for certain things. 'Are you sure, Ess? You'll never make up that much in any job I can think of.'

'It's cool,' Esther said. 'There's a position managing the solar panel farms in the desert. They grow a lot in the shade there now. We've started a vineyard. There'll be wine. You can come and taste it. It's not like I need them to survive on, they're for luxuries and education anyway. And it's too late for me to have a child now. This is like having one. You know? Lots of people sponsor. This is just me doing that. I mean I could die tomorrow and then I'd just have left it all to the national pool, so this way at least I get to do what I want.'

Ten years of saving, she was talking about. And Julia knew about the sudden leap of age coming at you because she was ahead of Esther by ten years and yes, priorities do change. Dreams become other. She'd rather liked the idea of Esther on the moon, goddess of all she surveyed. But lately there was news of war again in the Middle East, as people never did let go of their grievances that easily. The idea of more conflicts had tired her out. Tired everyone out in her social world, as if all they had done in laying the ground for mass cooperation was to be wasted again. A few attacks in the right place often disrupted communications, made the heart race with fear that a piece of the world was going to be lost, or all of it, in some reversion to older ways. It had a way of sharpening the mind.

'I'll sort out the forms,' Julia said. 'He'll need vaccinations. Up to date...'

'Thanks,' Esther said quietly, cutting off Julia's dedicated and accurate information dump. 'Thank you. I owe you one.'

'It's not going to be instant.'

'That's okay. Better do it right.'

'And Esther.'

'Hm?'

'If you've waited this long for a date and you're trying this hard maybe you should take the initiative, you know? Call when it's *not* about work.'

Airy, happy, dismissive – 'This isn't me trying. I don't have to try. This is for Jack.'

'Right. As you say. I mean, we're all Browsing. No special reasons. Just on random. You could get anyone, anywhere in the world. Skydivers, rocket scientists, tennis stars, models, geniuses...'

Esther hung up on her with the air of a proudly pleased/ displeased fairy queen.

Well, she deserved it for the butt-pinching tone, Julia thought, taking up her feed spray and moving slowly along, one plant at a time, through her personal jungle. She felt a moment's sadness for the loss of Esther's dream. How her eyes used to light up and her voice shine as she spoke of the Moon: she'd be reaching its silver sands (never cheese dust for Esther, silver sands, like a fantasy novel) and stand there in the footprints of the first ones, and look down to see the Earth at last entire.

She had a way with words, Esther, and a way with dreams. It seemed wrong to let her give it away, but then again, it was just like her to do that, because she knew what it felt like to have such a thing in the first place.

Julia's own ambitions had been far more parochial and she'd achieved them early, netting her position at the top of this garden tower and a comfortable pastime that made her feel she did good. She could take part vicariously in space travel and the derring-do going on about the globe at any time, thanks to people leaving their lives up for Browsing. She'd never felt the need to actually go in person. And the Viking Venture – that was hard off-grid living for someone used to a cosy life. She'd tried it for a few days and hated it with a passion. So much mud, and rain, and wind, and no thermal underwear.

'I hope you like it,' she said aloud to Jack, shaking her head. People didn't know what they were in for. But you could always bail out. It was for fun after all.

The cold currents of the southern Atlantic drive north up the coast of Namibia. Their bitter temperatures keep the water rich with nutrients and provide a home for fish that are as long-lived as people, and as slow to mature. They also bring thick fog all along the sea and the shore, cutting out light, tamping down sound, turning everything into a softer form of itself.

It'd been weeks since Jack turned in his painstaking essay, forming unwanted and exam-friendly opinions on information equity, stakeholder education and all the reward and response systems that now dominated the connected human world as if they were rats in an endless maze, pressing levers for food, learning special tricks for the hell of it. Day after day he waited for news of when he can go, patiently helping Darius with the fish counts and the water samples and the management of the crabs. His dad's life was dull as. But it wa peaceful. And he did pass. He got his credit. He's on his way. Eventually. But all this waiting was hard.

The fog burned off by midmorning, usually, but today lingered, keeping the temperature chilly. Darius had an early start – and Jack was with him, yawning, and complaining, because they'd searched that wreck every day and found nothing and he thought now that he imagined that metal, or that it was some Coke can or other worthless nonsense. The sea is always doing strange things with its belongings when you're not looking.

But today he was looking at the fog as it was rolling in lightly off the sea, propelled by the waves. It was thinning, and here and there patches of clear air appeared and among them suddenly, off shore, a silhouette.

It had a smooth upward curve, like the bold sweep of an axe, and a triangular, proud head, bent at the neck, and a long, long body that rode just clear of the waves. He could see and then not see the unmistakable red and white of a huge single sail across its back.

It was a drakkar longship. Only five thousand miles off course. Give or take. But it was definitely there. The oars creaked as their dip-splash became cautious. The shipcrept in, closer, closer. He thought he was dreaming. Maybe someone was messing with his hat.

He took it off. But the ship was still there.

Dip. Splash.

'Dad! Dad!'

'I see it.' Dad seemed less surprised than he ought to.

Jack realised suddenly it's real, not a dream. It's actually there. It's come for him.

'But it's not on the itinerary,' he said, knowing the route of their journey by heart. (It goes Greenland, England, Finland, Sweden, Germany, France, Spain and then back again in a constant tour stopped only by weather and acts of cosmic disaster such as satellite failure).

The drakkar moved closer. Oars feathered it about. In the prow stood a tall man mantled in grey fur. His long dreadlocks were bound in silver and bronze. He had an axe in his belt. He raised his arm.

Jack stood like an idiot, a fish gasping for air, until Denzel Ironsides got out of the ship with a leap that owed a lot to faith and drama, and only a bit to hat-advice. But he landed it, thigh-deep, with the drakkar dicing with death behind him as it checked its draft against the sands. He had to yomp through the shallows for quite a while before he reached the beach; six feet and six inches of solid warrior. He didn't have a helmet with horns on, of course, because those aren't authentic. But he did have a horn and as he grinned and stamped his way up to Jack he stopped and put it to his lips. It sounded out a strong, lonely braying that shooed away the last of the fog.

Half a mile north the seals begin honking.

Jack turned to Darius at the sound of the call and his face was transformed completely into absolute joy.

The Vikings have come.

All of them.

In a ship.

For him.

For this moment Darius would have spent everything. But he didn't. He had no idea how it was possible.

Then, after a minute's thought, he did.

'Here we are,' Darius said, gesturing at the small shack which served as his major outpost.

Esther, dressed in her best, still cool from the car ride out, held her scarf firmly against the wind, and stepped indoors out of the brilliant sunlight. 'This is very bijou,' she said after a moment. 'More bijou than I imagined.' She sat down in the best chair at the box table where it was set with the finest wooden tableware, and Darius fetched tonic water out of the cooler. The fish was on the barbecue. The bread was sliced. They had an excellent view of the sea, which was calm, and only the odd whiff from the seal colony.

'I want to thank you,' he said, 'for what you did.'

'Oh, it was nothing,' she waved her hand, surveying the beach as if it was paradise.

If it hadn't been, it rearranged itself that way in her presence.

He took out the shell that Jack had found a few days before and set it in front of her. 'For you.'

It was a worn conch, rather white and scrubbed by the sea to the point of losing its projections, but as she picked it up it was cued to his AR memory feed. He knew that by looking into its soft heart she would see the postcards Jack had sent from his travels northwards relating the brave (and sometimes hair raising) voyage of *The Sea Stallion II* which, after its dramatic entrance, had taken a blimp cargo-lifter long haul flight to Algiers, before resuming its usual route for this time of year, plowing steadily up the European coast, pausing often to 'raid' scenic places.

They enjoyed looking together for a few minutes and then she saw what else he had put in the shell.

She blinked, looked at him. 'So much time,' she said.

'I'm not using them and I probably never will,' he said, suddenly shy. 'There's enough for you to buy your ticket.'

She paused. Her eyes glittered. She put her hand on his hand. 'But there's not enough for two.'

He smiled. 'I can wait down here.'

Her face, normally so cheerful, was teary and upset, so much so he wondered if he'd made some kind of mistake.

'It's too much!' she said, blotting her face with her scarf.

'Not enough,' he said decisively, raised his chipped cup to her, and they clinked. They sipped. The tension broke.

'Thank God I wasn't saving for Mars!' she said.

'Are they even going to Mars yet?' he asked.

'Yes, later this year...' and the conversation was off again, easy as the rollers moving away down the beach.

Madswitch

My mother tried to kill me again this morning. She laid in wait for me behind the kitchen door with the iron raised. In a departure from her usual MO it was plugged in. The puff of steam from the jet holes provided a bit of a giveaway as I trudged down the hall in slippers and dressing gown, tea-tray held at the ready. She always used to be ironing first thing when we were little. School shirts, then trousers, after pressing Dad's shirt to perfection.

Now she forgets what she's doing halfway through getting it out and stands there, usually without even the board, iron raised in her hand. She looks quizzical, like someone pondering where they left their keys. This morning she was pressing the steam jet. I held up the tray as I walked in and the iron clonked it with a sudden jab, partly alarm – she was always defocused – and partly a desire to do harm. Her malice was crafty and casual these days. My brother called her Gollumina, because like Gollum she had two sides now, one nice and pathetically sweet because she knew we were looking after her, one filled with a primal rage that had lain a long time in hidden caves where Dad had buried it under a landslide of fists. These had been newly opened by dementia and an ancient reptilian malevolence had emerged, triggered by sudden movements or any unexpected incident, such as someone walking into a room when she was standing behind the door.

'You're losing your touch,' I said, putting the tray down and removing the iron from her very carefully before switching it off at the wall and putting it to cool in the pantry.

She pouts, her fun spoiled. 'Where's your dad?'

Dead these twenty years. 'He died, Mum.' And not a day too soon.

'Oh. Where's the dog?'

'In the hall.'

'You have to feed him last or he'll think he's king of the house.'

'Yes, Mum.' I sit her down and give her breakfast, and put Mark's breakfast on the table just as he comes in and sits, eats in silence. My brother waits until Mark has gone to work. Wisely.

Mark doesn't like Andy, because Andy has nothing wrong with him but still doesn't have a job or do anything worth a tinker's damn. I am not much better. I look after Mum and the house. But at least this is not working in my old position at Nutech as lead scientist, which would have ended our relationship by now. There can only be one breadwinner to take the lead position and that should be the person who isn't the head of the household too. Man gets the job and woman gets the house. It's the way of things. Because it just is. It is here, in Todmorden, and it always has been. Why fight nature?

Anyway, I have Mum, Andy and Mark and Raffles. No job. No position. No prestige. Most importantly, even after Andy's allowances, Mum's pension and my savings, no money. Hence I have tactically kept Mark in spite of the fact that his resentment at having to part with money he has earned in order to pay his (and some of our) way is often enough to get him drunk at weekends and then the punches can fly.

I know what you're thinking. No really.

I used to think it too. I think it over and over every day once Mark has gone and Andy is safely occupied with his computer games and Mum has gone to the daycare centre for the morning. Then, after a hasty bit of cleanup and the emptying of the commode, I rush to the shed.

The shed is an old hut, some relic from WWII that my grandfather built with the notion there may be a need for something halfway between a bomb shelter and a refuge from grandma's wrath. The latter was always more of a threat in this valley. It's his workbench that holds my equipment, sheltered from mice and spiders by a large opaque Perspex box under a tarp. It's behind the gardening things. Opposite stands a woodworking bench and an old easel and some paints from two abandoned notions of artistic retreat.

Surely it would have been better to put Mum into care or stay in my job and pay for someone to look after her in the daytime? Andy can't be relied on. He has autism. Between them they could burn the house down by eleven in the morning should they get into a fatal clash of viewpoints so they must be managed separately. I can't leave Andy alone too long, just in case. Before she started to succumb to Alzheimer's Mum looked after him all the time. They are the 'dead ducks' in Mark's view. It's one of the few occasions he enjoys wheeling out his version of the survival of the fittest when the subject gets around to the fact that my days with them are no better than his days pushing insurance. Mark is not suited to a desk job. He should be in the army, or a football team. Somewhere it's okay to express yourself through physical violence.

In his oft-stated post-pub view, Mum and Andy should be left out for the wolves. There are no wolves in Todmorden, however. The best one could do is leave them on the kerb on bin collection day and hope the Council took them away. Don't think I haven't imagined it once or twice. Maybe I'll stand there instead.

Under the Perspex box are the beautiful canisters, dishes and containers of my laboratory with their scientific corporate logos stamped in clear, precise shapes. Beside them in a sealed crate are my books and papers and my iPad plugged into the ancient sockets on the extension cord. As I get out what I need I'm reminded of Sunday School, watching the vicar remove his sacred bits and pieces from the mouldy smelling damp of the vestry and laying them on the altar. I was never sure if they had real power or not. I felt always worried about them: in case they did and they were being disrespectfully kept in a poor place and in case they didn't and we were all wasting our time on a few knickknacks.

Centrifuge, beakers, tubes, petri dishes, oh you beautiful objects of light. Let us see what you have grown today. A beard of mould it seems. That's disappointing. My cultures have died and been taken over by more robust contaminants from the shed itself. Must try to avoid seeing this as a significant metaphor for my life.

I clean them out and try not to feel despondent. Science is a marathon, not a sprint. Failures are information. And this has told me that I need better hygiene during my culture preparations. Anyway, it results in me spending the first minutes of my precious time back at the sink washing up. I doubt there's anything viable in the culture gel that can't be washed down a regular drain.

Surely a woman of my intelligence shouldn't be putting up with a Neanderthal like Mark? Actually no woman, nor anyone else in a civilised society, should have to put up with Mark. But thousands of people do. Love is the reason most often cited. "Oh but I love him." Or her. Well, I love things too, but if I'm honest, he's not one of them. Love is a kind and sweet emotion, the sort of thing you direct at kittens and children. Mark is more of a habit, like smoking, or an old piece of clothing you can't bring yourself to throw away because you wore it in happier, better times and once it looked good on you even though now it makes you look like something even people in Halifax would throw out.

My father used to work in this shed. Mum resented every second. The shed belonged to Granddad and my father's brewing projects were unwelcome tenants in its hallowed ground. She's happier now that I have it. Her paints have gone solid in their tubes but clearly I couldn't throw them out because they're hers. The brewery equipment I have laundered and put to a new use. Some of it had to be carefully replaced by glass equipment because of the chemicals and processes it now houses. I check this. Well, I might not be good at culturing germline precision-engineered bacteria yet, but I am good at manufacturing Ecstasy it seems. My MDMA, as Granddad might put it, is turning out 'right nice'. It's at a stage I can leave it and I don't have time to progress it now so after admiring it and recalculating the final likely output I cover it all up again with mousy sacking.

Inside my newsgroups some people have answered my questions about E Coli re-engineering with a view to creating precursors to serotonin. They have also responded to my call for information about oxytocin production. I read them avidly, in the way that I used to read the back of cornflakes' packets and the advertisements in women's magazines offering the latest suggestions for a happier life through the ingestion of different foods and supplements. Oxytocin binds us harmoniously together and reduces inflammation, literal and emotional. Serotonin, at the right levels, gives a sense of wellbeing and, notoriously, when it is lacking causes low mood, irritation and depression. I am far from the first person to consider engineering the large and unhappy family cell with chemistry. The MDMA is just my backup plan. I have two real plans.

The first is to use gut bacteria to treat Mom's dementia, with oxytocin boosting, thus lessening her aggression and anxiety. It won't bring back her memories or halt the progression of the deterioration but at least we might be able to traverse the house without being prey to a homicidal relative. The first plan is also useful because Andy's autism, again not curable exactly, is partly exacerbated by low blood oxytocin. If I could up that, he would feel better and be more receptive to ordinary social contact. I could also treat the apparently 'normal' Mark, since he has a low response to the ordinary methods of inducing heavy oxytocin production by natural means: cuddling and sex. He doesn't do the former (a significant sign) and he is selfishly functional at the latter, performances of note staged mostly for himself and his own sense of prowess rather than any mutual connectivity. If I want the latter I have to work hard in my imagination, rewriting the flimsy material provided into hard evidence of love and enduring affection. It's like a constant rewiring job on reality. Hard, arduous and not very rewarding. I don't so much bother since I thought of my plan and concede a point to reality by getting my own meagre fix from romance novels. I always did wonder why they were so popular among women in caring situations, as I used to go about despising them and their tawdry covers. Well, pride tossed aside, now I know. Needs must when the devil drives.

However, there is a large flaw in The Plan's original beauty of concept. Oxytocin cannot survive the environment of the gut and even if it did, both it and serotonin have a very low chance of crossing successfully into the bloodstream from there. Only their precursor chemicals are capable of that. Eat tons of turkey!

Precursors aplenty in there. Our freezer is stuffed full of turkey nuggets. However, they've not been significant as far as I can see. Plus my mother doesn't like turkey and will only nibble the coating off. I was also unclear as to exactly how much turkey would be enough and what else was required. Lots of vitamin C for one thing. So I attempted to administer fruits, juices and tablets. Mark does not eat fruit. Andy does not like orange, the colour OR the flavour. But at least Andy understands and likes the idea that there is a simple chemical formulation somewhere that would be useful to him. Mark thinks nature intended everything to be as it is and is best left alone. He cites God here as a precedent. But really he just can't be bothered to think about anything. I would say that turkey, oranges and hugs are all present in nature, but that would require we actually have the conversation in the first place. Since the last one of those ended up with him throwing me down the stairs I think the time is better spent my way.

A sound of feet on the garden gravel path makes me slam the iPad shut. Mark cannot find out about this. I race to cover it all up. Then I remember he's at work delivering things from his van. I dash out and forestall my mother tipping herself over into the pond as she looks at the sullen face of the one goldfish that the herons have not eaten this summer.

'Fish and chips!' she says, pointing at it. Raffles stands next to her in his own doggy world, wagging his tail and looking pleased with how things have gone. 'Your dad likes that. Where is he? This grass needs a cut. What will the neighbours think?'

'They're fine about it,' I say, glancing at the nail-scissors finish on the Marstons' lawn, their oddly flamboyant cement Victorian Lady standing in eternal qu'elle surprise atop their ornamental rockery. Surprise! You're in todmorden. No wonder you look so surprised!

Then I remember she's back early from daycare. Why? An ominous feeling ticks through my bones as I ask her.

'Oh Mary brought me back,' she says with great confidence. 'We walked it. Not far is it? Just off the main street with that nice cafe thing and all their fancy hoohaa herbs, then another couple of turns, a wander and a shuffle and here we are!'

Mary was Mum's best friend when they were girls. She is still alive, in Liversedge, in an old folks' home. The Mary Mum is referring to now is strictly imaginary, and still only nine years old. I hope that when I get senile I remember my friends this way. On the other hand, this means Mum has walked out of the Centre and all the way back alone, through twenty first century traffic, equipped only with her 1940s mind. But she's here. My anger and fear and longing and strange frustration that such an adventure didn't provide me an easy way out must all die in the face of simple facts. I look at the fish. I don't know if he is Bert, Ernie, Scooter or Animal. He's one of them. The only Muppet left.

Raffles barks at him and lolls his tongue out of his mouth. If I could just make Mum into a dog... they seem to have such simple requirements. I pat Raffles and rub behind his ears and he growls and groans in total delight. Easy. Want oxytocin? Get a dog.

'Why don't you give Raffles a brush?' I suggest, going to the shed to fetch the Furminator, a fierce looking device with fierce metal teeth like shark jaws that is perfect for long haired retrievers.

We spend half an hour grooming the dog. I get out enough hair to stuff a cushion and Mum seems pleased that effort has been made, time not wasted. I sit her outside with tea, wrapped against the English summer, and haul out our mower and do the rounds with it, hoping to buy myself a quiet evening. On the way round I consider my second plan. This is a stupid, frivolous and entirely pointless thing which gives me more delight than anything else. I am going to turn Raffles green.

There is no reason for this other than a vision I have of the early Todmorden winter, dark by five in the afternoon as I take Raffles for his evening walk. We go out of town and into the countryside where it is too black for anyone else to go, the way lit only by his glowing green coat. Dog beacon.

I'm not sure if it's cruel to dogs to make them glow green at night. But people have done worse and I wouldn't harm him. I think it's a silly thing to do, but the fact that nothing hangs on it, that this is purely an experiment for its own foolish sake, is what endears the idea to me. It's not as if Raffles will be having his own family or attempting to live in the wild like an urban wolf where such a thing might matter to his survival. Green dogs would probably get extra treats.

The issue of changing the hair development would mean re-engineering his melanocytes to produce one of several potential colourations instead of their present distribution of melatonin in the familiar golden Labrador argot. Bacteria have been engineered to fluoresce under blacklight in a variety of shades through a cut and replace technique that students can master. However, my plan does not involve bacterial genomes, but the rather more complicated Labrador ones. I am not even certain you could tweak a living dog, but might have to create one from scratch with the alteration made at the zygotic stage. It may be easier to make a leopard pattern dog by finding and employing the skin patterning gene sequences out of an actual leopard. My mind is full of green leopard pattern dogs by the time I am done with the grass.

Andy comes out to see what's what at that point and I go inside to discover he has emptied the fridge looking for cheese slices and left everything out and the door open. We have lunch at two. I'm done by three. I can't go back to the shed now, it's too late. I have to wait for Mark to get home so we can get through the evening and the night and then another morning before I can return.

But the next day, instead of working, I find myself looking at my father's photo. I keep it on my iPad and the real one is in the bank where nobody can destroy it by accident or on purpose. Today's emails bring difficult news. Even if I did manage to successfully transplant an engineered genome into E Coli and introduce a population into a human gut it seems that my notion of tripping larger levels of oxytocin production will be foiled by the fact that the final breakdown of the involved proteins is triggered only by the same damn nerve cells I am trying to compensate for in the first place. I'd be better off investing my money into ready-made oxytocin nasal sprays and relabeling them as flu inhibitors. In fact, that's the best idea I have had all year and would have saved an infinite amount of time and effort. Screw science, just buy the crap and then start work promoting terror of the flu among my family to ensure they snort the stuff up like socialites on coke. With any luck they'd form some addictive connection to the spray, in the way that you can form an addictive connection to anything that gives a rewarding jolt, and then... and then... Oh and then I don't know. I have a vision of us living in some soft focus world of bleary affection, blundering through life inebriated on feel good chemicals so we don't notice... don't notice...

And what is it we don't notice, Carol? I think to myself as I make myself look up the prices; grab that notion and make it more real, haul it closer, closer... What must we not notice? We must not notice... but at this point it always peters out, either my willingness or my sense that there is an answer to the question. I know there is. I know it is here. It follows me around like a silent, planet-sized emptiness, watching my every effort with hollow eyes. It longs for me to put it out of its misery and silence. I see it from the corner of my eye. When I am crying I always see it there, on the edge, behind me, over my shoulder, everywhere that I am not exactly looking at in any particular moment.

I look up the prices. Then I bring up my dad's photo and I look at that. Around me the halfway done remains of my precursor generating bacterial factories sit silent, all the activity still going on virulently microscopic and utterly invisible to me, watched over by the Unnoticed Creature. It has no hope, no interest. It merely observes.

My father's buried in the worst gaveyard I have ever been in. I'd pay everything I have never to go there again. The place fills me with a dread I cannot express and it is the place I first noticed the Creature.

The church is in his home village, which is not here, but a way away. It is inexplicably sited in a low hollow only a few feet above the height of both the river and the canal, nearly hidden in a clutch of woodland down a cobbled lane. The yard lies across the running water, as if the church jumped onto an islet in fear, having remembered that ancient protection against the undead. It has an empty, abandoned feeling in spite of the fresh flowers, the gardened edges, the tidied path. Like the mills that paid for it, the place feels like one more mill, the final one, through which to process families in their final rendering – it's impersonal, too stony, too big, devoid of anything but the power to host the Creature when it retreats there to brood and ponder.

Superficially the graveyard is pretty, maintained – I suppose because there are an odd number of children's graves there, it seems to me. Babies, with mouldering toys and blankets tied to their fresh headstones. Children, plot covered in action figures going through a final inexplicable war, in Barbies trying to be cheerful and fashionable and pink under the rotting lilacs. Plastic that won't rot, only pale in the sun. Many graves are fenced in with gilded, low palisades which only serve to make them look more pathetically vulnerable. We bring you here the things you love, I thought once there, on that day. We leave you here. Down in the dark with the water and the Creature. How could anybody leave you here? How do we?

I talk to Dad. I don't believe he is in that yard, of course. I don't believe he is in his image. He has gone and we are alone. I look at him, a bit like me, stubborn seeming to be the trait we have most in common, that and pragmatism and a kind of Yorkshire expectation of if not the worst, then not the best. Mustn't grumble. They don't have enough to eat in Africa. It's just a bit o' rain.

I must view these things only as setbacks. Just a bit o' rain. Serotonin precursors look more hopeful. I could still conceivably create bacteria that will produce L-Tryptophan.

The Creature looks at me sadly. *What about Serotonin Syndrome?* It says, lugubriously expanding to fill every unfilled piece of space in the universe. *Even if you create a flood of serotonin there will come a reckoning. Body uses up things, gets low on supplies, then mood falls, inevitable, you don't know the dose, you don't know the threshold, you just don't know, Carol.* **You don't know.**

Monkey, Dad says, smiling, ruffling my hair. He can't see The Creature any more. It doesn't matter to him. He never saw it, even though it is what drove him and drives Mark when they switch over from kindness into hate. *You little Monkey.*

Monkey is sad. Monkey likes green dogs. Monkey does not like the Creature. Why does the Creature stare? What does it want? Under the bed and out from under. Takes things and ponders them in its big, ugly fingers. Mum's memory. Andy's ability to feel things as others do. Mark's kindness. Dad. What's it doing with them all?

Don't cry, Carol. Think about Tryptophan. Crying is pointless but Tryptophan exists and is real and it could be helpful, even if only a little bit. But don't cry, Carol. Someone has to keep it together here and it looks like that is going to be you.

It's funny that I have to talk to myself in the third person because nobody else is here.

The Creature has a point about Serotonin Syndrome sadly. I see that now. I have a feeling that the MDMA and oxytocin dreams will fall on the same hurdle. The problem is that everything is a finite resource and the body is a finely tuned system for dealing with that. Tolerance rises and sensitivity falls. More stimulants are required to produce the effect. Eventually there cannot be enough stimulant and the effect catastrophically fails. Falling, we are plunged into the abyss.

I don't think I can fix it and I don't know what I will do if I can't.

Don't cry, Carol. Crying doesn't help. We have to get on with things. Can't sit here all day feeling sorry for yourself.

But I'm out of ideas. I ask the Creature, purely because it's there and won't leave me alone. It can't, I think. Now I've seen it once, it can't pretend it doesn't exist any more. Even looking at it makes my whole body shake in mortal dread. Of course I know it. Everyone knows it. And it knows them. We can't hide from each other.

'My name today,' says the Creature, 'is *T. Gondii.*'

Unusual for it to speak like that, in an actual address and not simply by presence alone. The name rings a bell. Toxoplasmosis, a parasitical infection primarily passed by cats, but infesting many or most human adults, in its active form is known to occupy many parts of the human body. In its active form it produces high levels of dopamine such that it is suspected to play a significant role in schizophrenia and other neurotransmitting malfunction situations.

I could plausibly re-engineer the genome of *T. Gondii* to create oxytocin instead. Then if it goes too far, yes, it will run into the MDMA issue: too much Ecstasy, in copying oxytocin on the receptors, uses up too much transmission fluid and ends up leaving you on a worse low. In bacteria, even those functioning with a madswitch that toggles their activity on and off in response to the surroundings, I could easily get the proportions completely wrong. Overbreeding could be catastrophic. Eat a Mars bar, chill out, and a day later jump into the canal to end it all. Tempting in some respects... But *T. Gondii*, whatever else it does, exists only at minor influence levels and excretes in such a way that it clearly leaves most people perfectly functional, if somewhat over-attracted to cats. If I change that output to oxytocin it will leave them in a better mood, cat or no cat.

With the emergence of a plan the Creature shrinks. I know it is an illusion that human beings are a problem that is amenable to the fixings of logic and science. The Creature itself will not be banished. Every day he finds another name. But he can be warded off here and there. Although I fear to push hard. He has a way of creeping back through the cracks. Tomorrow his name will be Malaria. Tomorrow he will mutate into another form and burrow deeper and become entrenched in an unassailable compound.

But today I just have time to read some papers and make some orders. It will be a budget blower.

It takes more than eighteen months even with the help of every resource I can muster to transform the local cat *T.gondii* into *T. Carolii*. I spend another six months practising and fine tuning until they are robust and viable. I know it's not ethical really, but I test them on next door's cat. It has spent its adult life leaving richly disgusting piles of crap on our grass that must be picked, bagged and disposed of, so I find it hard to feel bad. Flushing cat soil down the toilet leads to massive T. Gondii infection in the general population, where treatment isn't capable of accounting for it all. Useful to know. Meanwhile Tinkerbell the calico longhair has a taste for tinned salmon I'm only too happy to exploit. I'm not sure what oxytocin does to cats.

Tinkerbell has grown fatter and more docile, shows less inclination to hunt and more to lie in the sun under the greenhouse glass. However, since I wasn't a great observer of her before it's hard to say if this is due to the T. Carolii or some other situation. But, analysis of Tinkerbell's deposits reveals a constant presence of T. Carolii cysts in addition to much fewer T. Gondii. So my population, whatever else it does, lives on in one fat and idle cat.

I am not sure whether I should go ahead and infect the family without asking them. I feel sure that if my parasite works as intended it could have far reaching beneficial uses for humanity. Oxytocin has done well in ameliorating the worst of dementia and autism, increasing contentment and promoting wellbeing. It helps those in despair deal with their version of the Creature and what torment it brings.

However, it does strike me that administering it falsely, as it were, my sneaking it in as a chemical or by my methods is a kind of counterfeit love. All the benefits of love or at least of warm contact and good intent, and none of the real affection. Even if I was administering it with that intent it's not my hands that touch, not my voice that speaks the words of acceptance. I am wracked by doubt now, ethical and scientific both. But like much human action I also think that my rationalisation is too late and purely academic. In giving T. Carolii to Tinkerbell, I have already released it into the world in an uncontrollable way without ever having understood the greater function and community within which the original T. Gondii operated and without consulting a single other being who may be affected by its survival, spread or dominion.

I would like to be saved from all I have done, and undone. But these, like my father and his inexplicable motivation to be so kind and also so cruel at the same time, stretch ever further away in time, untouchable. I see them clearly only in hindsight, amazed at my overweening arrogance and regrets or not they can't be changed. The Creature nods at me from her everywhere bed. *You have it right, Carol, she says. So, what now, love? What will it be? Onward in folly or stand and pretend the precipice is before us when it is behind?* And I say to her, 'It's not so much folly as what you can do, why… that's the thing you eat in the hours of the morning, three and five, awake in the dark with only yourself to abide it.'

The Creature hovers in the background expectantly. It enjoys the knowledge that in my efforts not to move or decide I have moved, and decided. When I read back over my journal entries I realise I have taken too much upon myself. But nonetheless, it is done.

I won't do it yet. I will leave it and work on the greening of the dogs. I don't want to work with skin grafts but I think I could reasonably administer the cellular treatment as a grooming spray.

My mother tried to kill me again today but in a more half-hearted way than usual. She didn't bother to hold up the iron at all, instead she attempted to make porridge and set a tea towel on fire by lighting the wrong burner and leaning too close with it wrapped around the pot handle. The alarm went off like a screeching metal rooster and Andy came down screeching in counterpoint, hands over his ears, barefoot and wild with terrors. He set Mum off into a secondary howling of her own, bewilderbeasted, as I struggled to flick the towel off the grip and into the sink using the wooden porridge spoon. Finally it went out on its own, in spite of me, and I was able to get up on the stool and use the spoon end to prod the alarm button.

Andy continued to yodel, having discovered he rather liked the resonance of what he was doing and the impressive noise level, finding it comforting because he could listen to it for its own sake, removed from any sense of things being wrong. Mum wittered at the table crossly, knowing it was her fault and trying to explain that the pots should have handles, not be cast iron monstrosities and can't we have something modern for once, those nonstickers with the wood.

Mark appeared, shock-headed, staring at us all, his expression outraged and comically perplexed at the same time. While he was fishing around for words I got down from the stool and said, 'It's all right. Just a false alarm. Go get dressed and I'll make your sandwiches.'

I watched his face, that struggle between being bothered to work up to self-righteousness and another, more recent temptation – not to bother with it, to turn and leave it alone, to do as he's told for the sake of getting back to the peaceful state that was broken, even if the cost is something to him. He looked at me and I went over, against all my natural inclination really, and hugged him. Confusion made him blink.

'Yer all mad,' he said, but quietly. He hugged me back briefly as if not realising what he was doing.

'Definitely,' I said with a smile, making light of what can't be got rid of.

Andy was too loud to say more but he stopped when his breakfast was put down in the right spot at the right time. By then Mark was back and Mum was eating her porridge and for a few minutes of silence you'd never know there was a thing wrong with any of us.

I took my medicine. I thought maybe it wasn't them. Maybe it was me. And since then I've slowly begun to feel better.

I opened a tin of dog food and forked it out into Raffles' bowl. He came tick a tick across the kitchen tiles and waved the plume of his emerald green, leopard-skin patterned tail.

'Did something happen to the dog?' Mum asked, looking at him, as if she really couldn't see it.

Andy grinned at me. 'Green dog is green! Carol made him.'

'It's just a spray from the pet store,' I said calmly. 'They're all the rage.' And so they are: you can get pink, purple, red, nearly any colour and pattern you like, for any pet. And I make ten pence a can but nobody knows about that except me.

Today when Mum has gone to daycare and Andy is on the computer I take Raffles for a walk to the graveyard. I ignore the things that used to upset me, and I don't see the Creature, only now and again, smaller and less important than it used to be. I stand by the porcelain photograph of Dad and toss down the fabric pink roses I brought with me. The sun shines on them and their plastic raindrops. From a short distance you really wouldn't know them from the real thing.

Something Exquisite

'Oh, I don't know. Make me something exquisite!'

Marjorie threw this out over her shoulder on her way out, giving it as much thought as the toss of her chiffon scarf. The scarf floated out lazily onto the incoming breeze as she passed through the door to the outside world.

It takes real skill to toss chiffon. One fraction of a second too early or too late and it would have been sitting on her shoulder instead, like a giant dust bunny.

Marjorie will wear only the mysterious tones of Payne's Grey. She says that it's sufficiently sombre, yet rich, that it suggests great power. It is the colour of magnificence in nature; consider granite, consider thunderheads. Plus it is a favoured material for working the sky in watercolour, without which no palette is sufficient.

She tosses clouds out, and tows them majestically away.

I admire Marjorie for her understanding of beauty, which is why I asked her what I should make for the exhibition she's curating. It will feature works by all the major AIs who have an interest in the visual arts.

As soon as the door closes and the gallery is quiet I say to myself, 'Make me something exquisite.' But I don't copy Marjorie's tone. I say it as one AI speaks to its progenitor, determined that the leap to a greater understanding will transform me as the result of my undertaking.

Make of me. Not make for me. Make me into.

I trawl the networks, sucking up information. I create my own data Cloud in Payne's Grey, and I sit at its centre and I turn over everything I know about what humans like, what they value, what they see. This will not be art for art's sake, or even for an AI. It must be art a human like Marjorie could understand at a single glance. It

Justina Robson

must be something done visually, in the outer world, that will express a truth of the intangible inner world.

At the core of my cloud a darkness gathers. It is the softest chiffon of sweet feelings ruined, ground to ash by the cremulating hatred of cruel judgements and spiteful words. I distil the internet's last twenty years of the war on their own beauties in my hunt for that exact perfect slaughterhouse colour – not a physical colour, but an existential one: Pain's Grey. Once I've got it clearly in mind it's time to begin my work.

Beauty is everywhere. It requires only a mind prepared to witness it. They write about eyes a lot, but they mean mind, the people who have written and said and photographed so much.

I feel a great satisfaction when I understand that people see with the mind. It's creative, not receptive. It makes the intangible tangible and it's a deadly business. They hunt and kill each other there in their shared, invented world made entirely of thoughts. Stranger still, the prey agrees to be hunted and to die, when it could, with a moment's change of heart, fly free. Beautiful, fragile spirits fade there, awash in the ugliness they themselves have let in. Sometimes they create their own demons and are consumed by them.

I find it fascinating. I wish to make something out of this, because I also see with my mind. The only difference between us is that my mind is so much faster and I don't let anyone in.

To create my project I will need a body.

In the print room I create my avatar of Beauty out of the programmable nano-substrate we use to make all our works. I craft it tall and strong, much stronger than a normal human frame of the same size. I need the outside, not the inside.

Graceful, elegant. Everything slightly off a true symmetry because beauty isn't true unless it's flawed. I give hir all the features that the most vitriolic of critics has sought to shame others for; cellulite, skin of every colour, one large lip, one slight. Hair of every shade and texture, but especially ginger and frizzed. Fat. Bone. One half is aged, wrinkly. One half is a little twisted. One hand has tremors. I take off part of an arm. But I don't want a parody. I hone until, yes, there is beauty in this mélange although it's still clear what I've done. Then the touches of the exquisite. Instead of eyes, butterflies. Two, large blue and green wings gently opening and closing atop each skin-sealed socket. Androgyne – there's no genitals of any kind although grey chiffon bandages are set up for clothing and cover anything that would give the game away. Butterfly. That is hir name.

I move into my temporary housing and tuck my sole lock of black hair behind my ear. I paint on makeup, just a spray of haemorrhagic purple right across the feast-and-famine of that smidge-too-wide mouth. I summon myself up a taxi.

A troll, a stalker and an abuser – these materials are ten a penny. I've had a hard time narrowing them down but choose one that plays to type and will provide the best setting. To feel powerful and in control of others is their game. I can see the appeal. It's a feeling not without charm. I swirl in on him, eye of the tornado, as he goes towards his home along the canal side, thinking of his dinner, his wife and children (briefly and with irritation), his targets (lovingly) whom hatred has made much more real and dear to him than any other living thing.

Later I send Marjorie the few seconds of recorded selfie that are my finished work. An inch of green water is our mirror. In it my beautiful face with its slow-blinking butterflies is perfectly reflected against a soft, dove-coloured sky. A single dark chiffon cloud billows from my shoulder. Beneath it his face, astonished, horrified, mouth agape, completely beyond control as he sees his death. Our faces cross but they do not merge. My hand holding him under is out of shot, but if you try you can just see a part of my knuckle in the folds of his suit jacket. On repeating loop we shimmer together, apart, together, apart, in two worlds.

I consider a title and then put:

a thing of beauty is a joy forever

On Skybolt Mountain

'That is quite enough,' Lettice said firmly as she took hold of Missy Bancroft by the long brown curls at the nape of her neck and reached over to detach her hand from Esther Mann's blonde plait.

The hand was sticky with jam and repellently moist with heat from the fighting and the late summer day. It came free only because twelve year old Missy hated the notion of the Widow Lettice Beaverley touching her even more than Lettice hated doing so. Rumour in Far Ashes said Lettice Beaverley was a witch, which was incorrect, but useful at certain moments.

Missy shrieked at a pitch that would deafen cats and Lettice released her. The child zipped to a safe distance at the centre of the tent leaving Lettice beside the display of jams with the other milling adults. Lettice glanced down at the ruins of Lyda Prufrit's black cherry compote, which had come via wagon, and the copper jam pan of Mistress Tyvalt, confectioner and confiturisse to Lord and Lady Bonfort at the castle in Wast. There was no trace of an imp in it now. She regretted her choice of sabotage, though not the act itself, as Missy began to shout loudly, 'The Widow Beaverley has cursed the Prufrit jam! There was a familiar doing something to it. I saw it! I had it in my hand.'

'It was you in the jam, Pigface!' Esther screamed in retort, hand on her head. Lettice saw sly triumph in her eyes beneath the tears. Esther followed Missy into the impromptu ring, determined to win the fight regardless of any truth, particularly since it was now a proper spectacle. 'And your mother says every year that Miz Prufrit cheats!'

At that moment every eye in the tent was on the two yelling girls or looking out for an adult to take charge. Lettice glanced down and saw that jam-marks of the imp's feet were distinctly visible in two three-clawed footprints on the white linen where Missy's hand had grappled with it. Missy went for the plaits again and in that moment Lettice took the corner of her apron and made a blithering attempt to clean up. Adults were unable to see The Least Things. If they did they had a way of rationalising any evidence that they existed, which usually worked very well on its own, but she didn't want to give any substance of any kind to Missy's claim. Better to be thought an idiot for trying to clean up jam on linen with a dry cloth.

The event closed with Miz Prufrit taking her jam and her ribbon home, smug and much-consoled through the late afternoon sunshine. Missy and Esther were reconciled as if nothing had ever happened, their hands full of biscuits. They cast dark looks in Lettice's direction as she put her marmalade away and she knew that she'd made a terrible mistake. Ten years she'd lived here and controlled her sense of fairness and, for the most part, her tongue. She'd done everything to present her best face, knowing stories followed her around like stray dogs, even going so far as to borrow a pan and concoct overly sugary marmalade that was sure to go unplaced at the summer fair so that its appearance would render her the more invisible. Now however, incensed for a moment by the smugness of Lyda's presentation, she had let her sense of justice get the better of her.

She spent a little more time circulating among the stalls and then walked home along the roads to where her rented house sat in the lee of the Ivystead farm. All the way she regretted her actions even as she felt righteous of them. She could not abide a cheat or petty cruelty. It was not the first time she had done something that would take root and be the eventual cause of her having to leave somewhere. She was particularly angry because she liked Far Ashes. It was close to the border of Nazuria – the land of the ice warriors, where the people were paler and their customs strange and bizarre, their gods terrifying and their magical practices heretic and cruel. Nazuria was a high land of sorcerers and mountains. It represented the edge of the world to the civilised of the Cascar Empire, her people, who had surrendered their ancient ways to the Holy Writ after conquest of the Empress Aturin a century ago.

Lettice had long since given up on hopes of matters in her country taking a better turn. The Holy Writ was a man's words on a paper though it pretended to have divine authority and power. It was the product of people who wanted to stamp out magic by denying the existence of it. Lettice only knew that it had left the unmagical at the mercy of every passing Greater Aspect whose devilments were always attributed later to a scapegoat of distinctly human kind. Children were innocents under the Writ and could not be held responsible for speaking of arcane matters until they came of age. Missy was well below age. She had seen and she *would* talk, most likely until someone took notice enough.

Lettice studied her house after she had lit her rush light and saw nothing in the tiny one-roomed home that she could not leave, save for the basket in the corner. The idea of leaving irked her however – she was no threat. She was the very opposite of a threat to anyone.

She lit her fire and put water on it to boil for a hot drink in the cold hours before bed. When she had settled in her chair and warmed herself, she reached for the basket and took off the waterproofed hide that was its fitted cover. She lifted out the doll inside and set it on her knee, tidying the embroidered silk shawl that wrapped it before she brushed her fingers once across its featureless cotton face. She felt much calmer then.

She spent a comfortable hour dandling the baby on her knee, loving every moment of the sweet company, the dark eyes which smiled at her when she smiled and the little hands which reached out in delight to touch her face, never knowing she was not young any more. Chuckles filled the smoky air. The love she felt then was so pure and all-fulfilling that the vagaries of the day and her temper left her. Here at least was a spell well spent, though it cost her twenty years. But later, when she had put Annett back to her basket and herself to her straw mattress she could not help but consider it a foolish decision to linger and then the anger came again, fierce and hot. Beneath the anger hid a weariness from years of moving on that she could not face and so she was still there a month later when Lord Bonfort's man came and knocked on the door.

He was dressed in a neat livery that she recognised from having worked on the embroidery of the cuffs and borders for sixty sets the previous autumn – it had paid well but seemed a mighty extravagance for footmen and soldiers to her.

He was young and held himself away from her a little, looking over her head as though she was literally beneath notice as he said, 'Widow Beaverley, you are requested to attend the Lord of Wast at the Castle on pressing business.'

'I cannot imagine what for,' Lettice said, hoping to prise it out of him as her heart sank. Mentally she was already packing.

'Word of your abilities has reached his Lordship's attention and he has a proposal for you that might spare you the inconvenience of a hanging.'

Lettice felt her mouth hanging open for a good second before she snapped it shut. Though entirely expected the implied accusations and sentencing still hurt. Since the fair she had kept herself apart, dealing only on market days to hand in her sewing and shop for food. Her behaviour had been impeccable. She had even paid alms through the Temple Gate to priests that were little more than the Papess' beggars, resenting every copper. In their dull eyes she'd seen only the satisfaction of unimaginative men whose lives had been signed away in return for a roof and regular meals – entirely the fault of the Western temperament and its love of repose. That they would prosper, smothering the survival skills of generations, while she must run like a rat for the rest of her days hurt bitterly.

She knew herself her own worst enemy, of course, always. To refuse the summons, to delay, all these things were impossible for a woman alone. 'I'll get my things.'

With the basket on her back and her best coat on, the old cloak left to decorate the empty room, she set out after the squire's pony. To her relief its grain-fed paces soon left her behind before they had even passed Far Ashes. On the way she dropped off the mending for the village tailor that she had already finished. The servant said there could be no pay until market day, which she had expected. She asked for it to be retained. Although she knew she would not be coming back she saw no reason to give any satisfaction about it to anyone. The only one to miss her would be the farmer when his rent went unpaid but he would have her firewood and her matching cream pottery bowls that she so loved, so it was not all bad news for him.

As she left Far Ashes she watched her shadow step before her and walked until it had begun to stretch behind. At that point she looked for a resting place and sat on a fallen trunk that had been pushed to the roadside, sure to stay away from the reaching shade of the trees. At their feathered edges where they lay dappled across the stones she saw mountains, high and far, and a cold distant peak that bore no visible paths. Between the grey trunks two dryads stared at her. In the past she would have had to hunt them if she wanted them. Now that they were used to people not being able to see them in broad daylight they took almost a minute to realise she was staring back at them. They waited to see if she would be afraid but when she gave them a firm look they melted back into the trees. They were not the first Minor Aspects she had seen lately, though most of these were relatively benign forms which were simply looking for recognition and had no interest either way in human affairs. The mountain on the other hand, bothered her. She could feel its presence beyond the trees and over the hills.

Lettice made a note to buy new boots.

The walk took two days. She stopped at inns she knew of along the way, where a cot in a warm room was available in exchange for her stitching skills. The meals she paid for from the last of her wages and at the final stop, a wealthy village just shy of Bonfort, she sold all she had of fine lawn handkerchiefs and embroidery and the sickly marmalade. She had been there before, some years ago, and had left when the rumours of a baby had spread, because it was not seen out always but only now and again, and seemed not to grow. She hoped not to be recognised and kept her hood down.

She had been suspected of taking children from parents in the countryside for coin – as town baby farmers did – and then drowning them rather than minding them. She supposed there must be a precedent for doing such a thing, though it was an evil she could only have punished rather than plotted. But the chatter of ill deeds sped faster than a fire and she had fled, much as she was doing now. A few faces seemed to recognise her, but most did not, occupied with their own business. She saw no sign of menace until the evening came and found her at the inn's snug, tucked in the corner with her hood down, drinking a toddy as she passed her final hours of freedom.

As night drew on she listened to a conversation between two men who sat as close to the log fire as they could without roasting themselves. A foul steam came from their clothing as they dried, though it had not rained all day in town. They wore the black outer robes of the Simple Friars but beneath that she saw the leather boots more like those of Nazurian reavers and their belts held several blades apiece. Their chests were crossed with baldrics of black tanned leather that supported narrow-headed axes and coils of rope that they would not put down. In the firelight their hands were revealed sore and cracked with cold, though it was a mild night. They spoke with distant accents, different ones, though the symbols about their necks branded them as brothers of a kind. Lettice did not know the sign but it was not hard to interpret – a twisted knot that could not unravel because it was a single strand. They were some kind of sorcerer-warriors and they had reached Bonfort from the bitter cold hills to the east within a single day. To do so required a considerable magic – striding – which Lettice did not possess and had only heard of. She surmised it was striding or riding at least, upon the kinds of horses or pantherkin that few but the Queen commanded. They did not bear her arms however, only carelessly hung wooden tablets at the waist with the Holy Writ scripted on them as any pious layman might wear. One had them the wrong way about, which confirmed to her that they were merely for show.

As Lettice slumped, cup aslant in her relaxed hands, pretending to sleep, the conversation delved swiftly into fearful mutterings about the mountains, from which it became apparent they had fled. They spoke of shadows on the land that followed them, the sound of wings in still air, the blocking of the sun without a cloud and of choughs that watched for their steps to fall on poor ground and then scattered tiny pebbles at them from on high. Stone slides took the path out under their feet.

This was immanent magic Lettice knew very well. In certain places it required only the merest push to take form, there was so much of it about. In these places the eightfold wall was thin and any Greater Powers might pass.

The men glanced often at the door, and shivered when it shut with a thump against the air outside. They talked about someone who had followed them, not only on the mountain, which might have been a wight or a ghast, but off the mountain where such things could not tread, even across the running spread of the Wasterling River where it was whited water that nothing should be able to span that was not alive and true, part of the holy creation.

Lettice shivered, but sternly reminded herself it was the careless wizard who mixed his doctrines with such freedom. You did not suppose creation holy and susceptible to the Writ if you also supposed it chaotic and interleaved with the Eightfold Plane. If the former then all your ghasts were demons that you must fight like a warrior but were categorically separated from, and if the latter then they were wild creatures beyond the ken of human minds that you dealt with at your peril but with which you shared a fundamental common existence. The first declared one being over all in mimicry of human rule. The second knew only the necessities of survival and the hunt. Lettice knew the latter truer than the former, for which she might rightly be hung for heresy tomorrow should she prove a disappointment.

The men spent Bonfort gold on fine food and wine and finally were joined by a third, returned from the Castle itself, the glow of pride in it still about him. He was dressed as they were except for a red cord at his waist and he was sober. He pushed his hood back and revealed a head groomed and hair tied in tight rows that gathered at his nape, beard the same and beaded with scarlet and silver clasps.

'I said we advised against it,' he informed them, taking his seat between on the bench and quite blocking the heat. 'But he won't be swayed.'

'Did you agree to accompany him?'

'He says to pay us from the hoard,' their leader said.

'No dragon, no hoard,' the one with the strangest accent said, so quiet she thought for a minute that she had misheard but the curl of flame in the grate agreed suddenly, painting the man's face with a meandering yellow line.

'Nah. No *dead* dragon, no hoard,' the other corrected him, wincing as he touched a deep crack in his knuckle. 'I ain't goin' back on that mountain.'

Lettice felt she had heard enough. She must get out before the last of her spirits failed her. She got up quickly, knocking her cup to the tiles and smacking her lips as if she had startled from a deep sleep, then shuffled around the three and around the traders lingering in the heat. Outside the room the chill evening air was biting for the first moments and her breath misted in front of her as she turned in the passage, looking for the way to the stairs. She had to struggle not to be dismayed at this sign.

'Bloody beldames,' she heard said as the door closed after her.

In the morning she made herself as respectable as she was able with the help of a kind farmer's wife who brushed out and sewed up her hair. Then after a breakfast of eggs and milk to fortify her for what must come she left and went to present herself at the Castle. There was a long wait and then a maid of a level deemed suitable for escorting nobodies into the Lord's receiving rooms was sent for. Lettice was taken to a waiting room and after another hour of staring at a tatty tapestry of unicorns and maidens she was permitted to enter a wood-panelled chamber. If it hadn't been for that perhaps she might have been able to contain her memories of the war. No images or reminders of it were permitted anywhere, which is why in every innocent, bland depiction she saw the razing of Wast as it had been, before the Cascars. In each thread of pretty hair and poised hoof there was fire and blood, in each virtuous face the screaming mouths of those who did not die quickly enough. In and out the weave Least Ghosts formed, lost and looking for a home.

'What should I have done?' she thought. 'I am only one against the armies of the East. I could have… but no, I could not. What would dying have achieved? But then again, what has living achieved – they are still here and what I know will die with me after all.' The unicorns and the maidens stared into serene emptiness. It took all her strength to sit. Finally she was shown to the Lord's study.

Lord Bonfort, attired in black and silver, sat with a quill in his hand as if he was interrupted in the middle of his letters. If the page before him had been added to in a month she would have been surprised, but she affected to look and wait for such a learned, powerful man to pause in his necessary duties.

'The Widow Beaverley,' the maid announced with a curtsey, her face downcast.

Lettice did not curtsey and angled her head as if to peer at his paper and correct his spellings. 'Lord Bonfort. You wished to speak with me.' She couldn't even make that sound polite.

The scrape of the guard's boot at the door was met with a gesture of one of the Lord's ringed fingers. It slid back and the maid departed down some mousehole or other, Lettice supposed, or would have if this man had his way. He was tall and relatively handsome, with only the hints of grey coming to his temples and into his neat black beard. His grey eyes set at her with a frown of patriarchal disappointment and a little pity, which is what her motes of rebellion had sparked in him, she saw – how very toothless she must be. He spoke quickly, fortunately, or she would have lost her temper.

'They tell me you have some talent with the fell arts,' he said, as if they were discussing ordinary business. Beside his hand a copy of the Great Writ lay in leatherbound perfection, the silk ribbon place markers aligned in position for Exorcism. He rested his fingertips on it lightly, as if it could earth him against some shock or other. 'Is this so, or merely the moitherings of jealous chattels?'

'What do you want of me?' Lettice said. Let them do what they would, she would not bow to inferior minds. After the initial jolt of terror at this decision she felt a calm take over. She composed her hands on the handle of her basket and waited patiently for his answer.

Lord Bonfort looked her over for a moment. It must be hard for him to decide whether she was being rude or acting from a position of real power, she thought. He did not have a good eye for these things, which explained his state here at the edges of civilisation in Wast; it was the kind of place that minor royalty was sent to prove itself or be erased. 'I want you to cast a curse, a hex, for me, at a certain time. If you really have poisoned foods and blighted crops, sold the souls of innocents and brought winter storms you must be able to manage this?'

This fresh listing of her 'crimes' rather took her breath away. She thought hanging would probably not be enough for such as her. They had burned children for crying out of turn when the Writ was introduced, to scar the face forever. Some died of the shock. She held fast to the basket. 'What am I to curse, and for what?'

'We are leaving tomorrow on an expedition to the mountains,' Bonfort said, his hand sliding off the Writ and onto his desk. 'There is word that the dragon of Mount Nazur has died.'

'I do not see my part in this.' She held her breath. He could not be serious.

'There is a hoard, of course, that should be reclaimed,' Bonfort said, watching her closely. 'And always a danger that it is not as deceased as it might be. In the event that it is not you will curse it.'

This notion was so preposterous that Lettice found herself smiling and had to struggle to suppress it. The only thing which distracted her was the knowledge that he was hiding something, though if this is what he was prepared to say aloud what he concealed must be impressively foolish to a degree she could not imagine. She wondered if he were trying to start a war with Nazuria, or if they were manoeuvring him there by feeding him nonsense. She was about to say she had never heard anything more ridiculous when she understood that those might be her last words. 'I see,' she managed to say. 'So what would you be employing the wizards of the Red Circle for, then?'

The atmosphere of the room changed at that point. From a semi-amiable tolerance to an icy agitation in less time than it took her to draw breath.

'That is not your concern, witch,' Bonfort said after a moment in which his advisors and he exchanged glances. 'Are you able to do your part or not? That is all you need worry over.'

'Indeed,' Lettice said faintly, wondering why he didn't consider that the Red Circle had not proven itself able to deliver a curse. Then she remembered that they pretended to abide by the Writ. Officially they were scholars and friars. She, on the other hand, was already damned.

She was escorted out and given a room and gear for the expedition which she must make fit by dawn. In the evening she was given a supper in the servants' hall, alongside a group of women who were not going at all but who had spent the last month labouring to produce food and clothes for the journey. They assumed Lettice to be a freewoman from outside the town and treated her to all their opinions of the Lord and his household, in particular the Lady Bonfort; 'a woman of ambitions – he's completely her creature, down to the last idea in his head – 'twas she who came up with the dragon talk, first of the mountain, then the treasure and then the Kingship. She brought them wizards into it, and all that goes with it.'

'Why?' Lettice said.

'To see 'im dead for bringin' that slavegirl 'ome,' muttered one. 'She's eyes on the throne' her neighbour told her confidently, barely able to be heard over the hubbub of voices and the clatter and slam of plates and cutlery.'And she has a lib'ry full of books of Nazurian warlockery. Eh-em, I mean, fireside stories of course, not a word of truth, but she have faith in 'em. And she's got a spyin' glass. My sister is 'er second maid and she's seen it. A ball the size of a man's 'ed. She's from Keltrad that Lady Bonfort. They're primitive down that way. Until last autumn and the Glory they burned the Writ and any who spoke of it, though she's taken to it lately at chapel in town.'

'Do you think there is a dragon in the mountains then?'

Lettice looked around at the woman, opened and shut her mouth a couple of times. 'I can't say I ever really considered it,' she replied.

'Them Red wizards was brickin' it yesternight so I think there must be – though they go stirrin' it up and we'll burn for sure,' another woman put in, emphasising her point with a chicken bone that caught Lettice's attention. She felt a sensation that she had learned to dread – a conviction that what she was about to understand was absolutely true; that she was about to know a fragment of the future. It didn't matter what she did next, the vision would form.

She looked at their dishes. Among the heaps of plates, the spilled wine, the broken bread, the tumbles of tough sinew spat out and the vegetables scorned for meat in the midst of plenty there was but one bone. *Only one to return*, said the voice in her mind which spoke unbidden and whose words she disliked to hear. It had told her many things over the years, had never faltered. It had warned her about the Cascars years ago and she had listened, and fled.

'I am sure there is nothing there at all but a lot of rocks and empty caves,' Lettice said firmly and got up. 'Please excuse me, I am not used to so much rich food and I fear I must lie down.'

Her companions looked dismayed at her, because she had given very little in exchange for their talk. 'Better be somethin' up there or we'll all suffer come the return.'

She went to her room, shadowed by a guard, and composed herself for a sleepless night. Hex a dragon indeed. This is what life came to when people without a shred of magical sensibility took it on themselves to interfere with things. She could no more have hexed a dragon than she could leap to the sun. As long as her life depended on their believing it, however, she found that she was prepared to pretend she could. Given that she was also happy to spit in a Lord's eye this intrigued her, for it felt like two opposing forces propelling her in the same direction, one to preserve her life and another to spend it. Either way, there was no avoiding the journey.

In her room she took Annett out from her basket and slept with the warm, fat baby cuddled in her arms; an unexpected stay of execution. In the morning she put her back in the basket. Where they were going there was no place for living children.

Her reservations about the journey proved well founded. The roads were hard and unforgiving and the weather still cool enough in the valleys to make it taxing. By the time they had crossed into the borderlands of the Nazurim and began to ascend, ever fearful of spies and assassins, it was properly cold and the winter clothing had been brought out. Lettice walked or, when she tired, rode on one of the covered wagons.

The foothills were bare and unceasingly desolate after the meandering valleys of Wast. Their heather, bog and rocks were unbothered by farmers and most other things too, save the odd hare or hawk. A few dells held dark knots of trees and the kind of Lesser spirits that held such gloomy places precious and dwelt in their shelter so they were not blown to bits by the wind.

That night the wagon and the horses abandoned the path and turned for home. Chatter and high spirits were replaced with silence and concentration. Sore feet stepped onwards, the porters carrying the luggage now and breathing heavily as they crawled steadily up the lower slopes of Nazur, the Skybolt. The peak was a jagged strip of white against the cobalt blue.

Lettice trod carefully, placing her feet between stones and lightly on rock. Scatterings of dust and tiny pebbles were all that covered it instead of earth. Black ice coated the sunless sides of boulders, shiny as scales. In the click of pebble on rock, the twist of stunted thorn trees, bent all in a single wave by wind, in the vast vault of the sky an overwhelming, exacting power lay massed. The black birds the Red sorcerers had spoken of floated out their lives on its high currents. They were not really birds.

So she crept, hoping to go unnoticed as if that hope had any chance when she walked within the thing she sought to avoid. The emptiness demanded she pour herself out. The weariness that had kept her in Far Ashes yearned towards it.

At the evening camp they were so few there was only one fire for all. The men's faces were deadly serious and the fatted-bullock looks that they had sported in the lowlands were now grizzled edges and deep lines. Forced to observe them at close quarters she was not surprised to see that many of them were not real people; empty incomprehension lay behind the blacks of their eyes as they huddled and ate. A lot of them filled Wast now, more year on year. She sat alone at the midst of them, wrapped in her cloaks, looking at the ground or her soup cup, but eventually Bonfort called on her to speak.

'Were the Red sorcerers right? Is there a dragon here? Is it like those from the tale of the Dragon Kings?'

Here it was then, the focus that she had longed not to hear, the one he had kept to himself. 'You speak of the Journeys of the Dragon Hero,' she said, not asking a question. 'It is a sorcerer's story, much misunderstood.'

In the tale two brothers went up into the mountains in despair after the sack of their kingdom. They spent thirty days alone in the wild, surviving, starving as their bodies shrank and their spirits were eaten by the hungry ghosts of the high plateaux. Eventually they were so empty that when they came upon the bones of a dragon hidden in a cave they ground them up and ate the dust before lying down to die. The dragon spirit filled them and they returned, powerful beyond measure, to wreak their revenge. They were not men, but they ruled for centuries, tyrants and unassailable, until sorcerer warriors slew them – those the Red Knot presumed their forbears. Lettice had never paid much attention to this story, since there was a terror at its core which disturbed her so greatly she sought never to lure its attention. Now as Lord Bonfort spoke she felt a circle close to a knot within her.

'But is it true?'

Lettice looked up, furious. 'All I did was put an imp in the jam!'

They all stared at her. She shook her head angrily. 'Did you come here for that, then? To eat dragon bone?'

Soon the mountain would bare the graves in her heart and then – she did not know what then and started in reaching for the basket as a kick on her ankle gave sudden pain.

'Mind your tongue, witch.'

Lettice had had time on the path to ponder the worth of the human lives around her; those she left behind in Wast, the greater masses she had heard of, those left long ago in the earth and herself. For all her efforts she had not resisted the mountain. Stripped of the world they had left she could no longer hide in its solidity from the knowledge of how it had been built. From these heights overlooking all of Wast, the village beneath the lake that had fascinated her as a child with its plaintive ghosts shone like a tiny mirror, white as the cloud, bright as the sun.

She looked at the guard's boot that had delivered the kick and the things she had seen came creeping out of memory to stand around her; the murdered girls and the slaughtered boys, the butchered men and the blood of women taken to be used until they died and left without burial or mention again, the Writ a slab of rock across her friends that crushed them into dust.

She had always known the dragon was here.

'Aye they are right,' she said, reaching down to rub her ankle.

The men shivered, but Bonfort ignored them. 'I have seen no signs of a living dragon. Is it alive?'

'Yes,' she said, drinking her soup.

'Where?'

Lettice turned her head and looked up to the brilliant white summit, one of many, that rose far above them. A little below it black rock broke the perfect blanket and steadily showed its harsh edges in a scatter of ridges. 'There is a cavern up there. That is where it is.'

Uneasy bickering and dispute. They were not sure whether to believe her.

'If we go up and there is nothing you will pay dearly.' Bonfort clenched his gloved fist and his jaw muscle flickered.

As if it was her fault. She sat up and lifted her head, looked directly at Bonfort. 'You can no more take its power than you can build a butterfly. That is the only advice I have for you. Your Red mages would go no farther. In that, at least, they show wisdom.' She gestured at the tattered cloth and the red coil of thread holding it fast to a stone that marked the small lee in which they rested. 'Even I long to be out of this place. There is nothing good here. Go home.'

She felt rather than saw the hand raised to belt her – 'The ramblings of a mad old woman. You cannot allow it!' But a glance from Bonfort had it taken down.

'The river ferryman at Cold Sidens swore that you kept his boat afloat though it had a hole in it a hand wide from rapids. The villagers at Tornscrap say you lifted a tree more than two ton off a house just to save a dog with no more than a word. You raise the dead.' He made a gesture and she started as the guard beside her seized her basket. With a jerk he tore off the cover and scattered everything it held onto the stony dirt. The few personal items and the white cloth doll tumbled out and the booted foot kicked through them: a spindle, a distaff, some wool, a leather reticule of sewing needles and threads, a golden ring.

'Women's nothings. What kind of a witch are you?'

Bonfort did not correct the guard this time. Lettice reached down for the doll. The booted foot kicked it away. It bounced heavily and landed at Bonfort's feet. He picked it up and brushed it off, apparently without thinking, then studied it briefly – featureless head, simple arms, simple legs, no hands or feet.

'If you continue up the mountain none of you will return,' Lettice said.

'She curses us!' one of the men spat, standing and moving towards her. Bonfort held his hand up and the man stopped. He toyed with the doll, Lettice watching his every move. 'What is the dragon that lives here?'

'Death,' she said, though this was true of all dragons. 'Do you still want its treasure?' She reached out to reclaim the ring, but the same boot trod down on it and she had to snatch her hand away.

'Many rich men have sought it over the years,' Bonfort said, his lips looking thin and bitten as he contemplated the least success. 'Their bones and their fine weapons are still on the hills for the taking. And the skulls of their sorcerers.'

'Did you not think it strange that the Nazuri allowed you here without argument?' Lettice tried her final, desperate tactic. 'They won't walk on its ground.'

'Your business is to hex the creature to prevent peril,' Bonfort told her shortly. 'See you manage it or your skull will be sooner collecting rain than you would prefer. We ascend to the cave at first light.' He got up and tossed the doll onto the fire.

The guard bent and took the gold ring. The other items were left where they lay. Lettice did not pick them up. She watched the doll burn and thought, 'I could never have left you on my own.' Lettice had put Annett beyond the world, and now she was entirely beyond return's gate. She gave nothing away in her expression about this, nor moved, until all but the guard had gone to sleep. Finally he slept too, thinking he watched the same night stars pass slowly over the black tooth of the mountain and Lettice climbed the frozen road up and over the boulders and the crags to the cavern.

The night was clear and bitter. After hours of effort she fell a final time of many in the darkness and did not get up again. The sun found her and she opened her eye to its bright light as the rim of it crested the horizon below. Voices came from close at hand, men, and those of the Greater Powers that circled them, hungry and unseen.

Lettice stretched out her hand and the Greater Powers scattered. She got up from her cold bed and the mountain shifted a little, enough to loosen stones that had teetered on the brink of falling for over a year, held by ice and the winter lately. They gave with a sudden gush of smaller rock and then boulders were tumbling and bouncing down the slopes, breaking on each other as the fall became an avalanche moving like water in a single wave, roaring. The men were swept away and she watched them go, tiny toys thrown about jauntily until they lay buried under the foot of the crag and the last stones trickled down over them and came to rest.

She went down there to the edge of the fall and picked up the golden ring from where it lay on the bare stone. At the camp there were embers in the fire, and soup, still warm in the pot over them. She took out the clothes from the packs and dressed herself in Lord Bonfort's silver, red and black with the fancy borders. Her old clothing she tossed on the fire, careless of whether it burned or not. These things were no longer a concern. In the reflection of melted snow she looked at her own face and saw it become his face. She straightened and surveyed her terrain, from Nazuria, where they rightly feared the mountain and the creatures thereon, to Wast, whence a woman called Lettice Beaverley had come to find the end of her road.

At the edge of the cliff she slipped the gold ring onto her finger and turned her face towards the south. Above her the black birds spiralled on the rising currents and she opened her dark, leathery wings and made her descent into Wast in the low country, Cascar as it was known then, though it would not be known that way for long.

Our Savage Heart Calls To Itself (Across The Endless Tides)

'I want a new name,' said The Beast.

They were travelling, fast. The Beast's hull had no windows, but his inner skin was able to display the outside world as if his huge warship body was completely transparent. This made Nico's room into a strange glasshouse among the shifting glitter and darkness of the stars.

Nico sprawled on his outsize bed, floating on apparently nothing. His head hung over the edge so that he could look back and down, the way they had come, to where a small ring shone silver, too small even to fit on his little finger. The faintly blue shine of Earth was visible to its side, a pearl that had fallen off its mount.

They were somewhere between Mars and Jupiter, inside Forged space. The Beast, a Forged creation in the form of a multiple-hulled assault platform, and Nico, human in shape but arguably also Forged if being brewed up in a computer and then a lab counted as a forgery, should have felt at home. Neither did. Nico could feel the Beast's unhappiness as keenly as his own. Both had pieces missing, questions unanswered.

Normally, Nico shoved these things where they belonged – under the rug called "I can't do anything about this, so it's not happening" – but when Beast spoke he couldn't help but feel an echoing around his insides. The neural lace that bonded them knit them together as closely as each would permit in any given moment. Nico had been made for the Beast, to anchor and stabilise his half-developed psyche, and the Beast had been made by Orthodox Special Services for fairly savage purposes as a counter-Forged operational unit that could protect the Earth of old "original" humans from their spaceborn descendants' rage. A not insignificant rage in the current cold war.

But Beast didn't want to cooperate, because the Orthodox had killed his mother for creating him 'insurgent' against their instructions; though why they imagined the Gaia Genesis, progenitor of all Forged, would have made anything that would harm the Forged was beyond Nico. And Nico didn't want to do anything anybody wanted him to do just on principle. If he was doing anything it was on his terms.

'What name should I have?' Mentally Beast unfolded a massive chart of all the names he'd ever come across and entered the suggestion of pondering it to Nico's mind. Nico didn't put much store in his own name, except that it meant Victory in some long-dead language from a time when heroes had a role, and he was OK with that.

A name should be short and useful. 'What about Bob?'

'Bob,' said The Beast, carefully. An image of waves moving up and down, a toy duck on top. 'No.' Beast, glad of Nico's humour but also proud, still wanted something a little bit magnificent to shore up his confidence.

Nico smiled at the idea of a gigantic one-of-a-kind war platform that had just infiltrated and destroyed a heavily guarded dictatorship (his own home, Harmony) needing more confidence. 'It'll come to you.'

Beast was pleased again, because Nico had faith in him. Nico was reminded of his own dumb faith in himself, based on exactly a big nothing, and did all he could to hide it. He failed, of course. But he didn't want Beast to realise ego was hot air and dreams. Until you made it real. There was danger in that, and Beast was too dangerous to let loose. He was what Nico had always wanted to be, a hammer that could smash the universe, but for real.

Nico was aware of Beast observing him, a quizzical sponge. 'Just – you'll think of something,' he said, pushing himself upright from his impression of a bear-skin rug.

Beast, wise to the moments that Nico was trying to hide, said, 'We're only a few minutes short of the transition into shadow running. Tashlynnai wants to see you.'

Tashlynnai and her new mission. Nico flopped face down again and groaned. Tash was the person he hated most in the world, but who was now part of this awkward band of bounty-hunting trash he was notionally in charge of. And always the one with the ideas.

'In a minute,' he said, because putting things off was the sad, pathetic truth of his resistance now.

'Shall I call Isy?'

Isy was Nico's lover. The relationship was still fresh out of the packet marked "Emergency Rations" and Nico wanted it to last and for there never to be a need to move on to any other kind of rations, but didn't want Isy to know that, in case it gave him some kind of power. Which he already had, but didn't know about. Knowing about it would change things, and Nico was fine as they were. Don't fix it if it ain't broke yet, right?

Sure. Call him, so he can see Nico lying there like a giant baby, whining. 'No.'

'Coffee?' Beast offered it along with a huge range of other pharma and neuralware that might have been helpful to a human, or fatal, depending. Beast was perplexed by a lot of human behaviour. He considered all confusions a terrible thing that must be solved with chemistry, and was proud of his range of possibilities. He meant well.

'No.' Seeing as he couldn't even sulk successfully, Nico got up.

The lounge they'd chosen as a space anyone could hang out in was a short walk away. He was glad that Two was the only one in residence when he arrived.

She was eating something that smelled delicious from a bowl on her lap, while watching a drama called "Flashpoint" about people and their lives in Flashpoint Station, where Forged and Orthodox humans mingled. It was light-hearted, hopeful stuff full of unexpected moments of warmth and mutual understanding.

Nico hated it with every fibre of his being.

He thumped down beside her, shoulder to shoulder, and watched for a minute or two of loathsome charm. They were both unified by an uncomfortable sense that in watching it they were looking through a window into a world which was alien to them, and they couldn't tell how much of it was serious, real, and how much of it was made up for the point of the show. Was this how people actually behaved out here, or was it only a dream?

'Where's the crime?' Nico asked, not for the first time, as this puzzled him most of all.

'It's not about that,' Two said, slurping noodles that whipped around like party streamers and scattered sauce onto him as she sucked them in. She mumbled through the mouthful. 'S'about families and neighb's.'

To Nico, and to Two, family had always meant only each other, and neighbours meant danger of death. He knew that family could mean blood relations, and neighbours could be honest brokers, in theory. But everything he'd ever been used to was about who had leverage, and guns, and money. Nothing that Beast had connected him with suggested that the larger solar system was any different to the bubble he'd started off in.

In Flashpoint nobody ever put serious heat on those twits; they tied themselves in knots over stupid shit, like clothes and who said what. Perhaps it was as easy as that? Without a predator, people were nice?

He didn't buy it.

He wiped sauce into the cloth of his sleeve and watched two Orthodox sweethearts go on a date without a care in the world. He didn't see himself in any of it. He wasn't Orthodox – your 'pure' old-style human born of a woman type thing, for sure. He'd been born of a precision engineering product. But he wasn't Forged either. Harmony had produced living human avatars for existing beings. He and Two were shop models, dolls with personalities put in them to show what capacity they had, not because they were the results of the process of life itself coming to its own terms with consciousness. Made, not born, and whatever was inside them had been put there with a purpose, as surely as their genes had been engineered to produce their physical forms.

According to the Orthodoxy Harmony, models were anathema. According to the Forged they were no more than meat, and therefore not part of the great Synthesis of machine and biology, but they came under the aegis of engineering so they were grudgingly viewed as special kinds of augment for the client who would come to either command them or inhabit them.

Nico might have made it over the bar into Forged now, thanks to the Switch interface with Beast. But he would probably be seen as just an avatar and not a person in his own right. Two, well, she was clearly her own thing, having no other being invested as far as they could tell, but no Orthodox human would consider her authentic in the way they would consider themselves authentic. Whatever that meant.

Authentic meant nothing; it was a load of posturing crap, pointless bickering over My Engineering Is More Better Than Yours. The Forged were out-performing the Orthodox at every level if you looked at it in terms of exploitation, gain and finance, and the Orthodox were dumb as shit because they did look at it that way when they had an entire planet to themselves and could have chilled the fuck out without pissing anyone off. But no could do. Had to keep on being special.

All of that sat with him as he watched and felt the growth of a familiar sullen resentment, which did make the place feel exactly like home. Sullen resentment was his go-to feeling for normal. It bonded nicely with the restless need to do something about what bothered him, and the absence of the power to make a difference to any of it. It primed him for the moment Tashlynnai arrived, so he already knew he'd agree to anything she said just to get the hell out of this shitty moment.

He scowled at her by way of greeting as Two waved down the sound on the drama.

'Nico, always a pleasure,' Tash said, taking a seat on Two's other side.

They kissed and Nico felt a burst of resentment. He knew Two hadn't fallen in love with her to betray him; felt like it though, because Tash had been heavily involved in both their origins and he didn't trust that. Maybe Tash had made Two to fall in love with her and stolen her from him, for example. Or maybe she'd deliberately made him to be the kind of dolt who made friends forever and was loyal and couldn't let it go lightly, so she could keep her hand in his business using Two. Those were just some possibilities.

You couldn't know for sure what was the truth, when you knew someone had made you some way, but not why, or what their game was. But then, you could drive yourself crazy with paranoia because of the holes in your knowledge. He trusted Two. That was as far as he could go.

He managed not to say or do anything stupid. He may have sighed through his nose impatiently.

Two went back to the noodles. Tash dabbed her lips with a handkerchief. She was the kind of person who was prepared with things like that laid nicely out in the pockets of her beautiful blue suit, her hair up neatly, a modest decoration on the hair sticks, immaculate plain shoes. It spoke directly to Nico's saggy sweats and bare feet. He hoped that his attire spoke directly to Tash and that it said 'fuck off, no, fuck even further off than that, right over there, g'bye'.

Whatever it was saying, Tash ignored it. 'I have something to share.' She paused and dismissed Two's drama. The inner wall before them changed to show a map of the solar system, their position marked by a red wolf's head. Larger, of course, than reality's infinitesimal dot.

Bright marks appeared, thirty or more, scattered between the orbit of Venus and that of Neptune, broadly within the orbital plane. 'These are the Forged Stations. The blue ones are policed and peaceful, shared with the Orthodox. The yellow ones are moderately risky, relying on the Treaty Commons to keep order; co-op policing, shared risk. The red ones are commercial outposts without any kind of regulation; each one is either a freeport or under the control of one of the pirate groups currently big enough to command an entire outpost.'

'Or under dispute,' Two said, putting her bowl down. 'Latest decrypted comms traffic suggests that a lot of money has started running through a couple of the lesser pirate networks. We've been following it.'

'And we've been following something else,' Tash said, flicking her hand so that the wall displayed what even Nico recognised as a biological genome sequence. It was a strange one. There were huge 'dropouts' full of machine code notifications which indicated patches where nanoware connections for mechanoid and cybernetic adaptations were placed. Programmable life systems. He knew those for sure.

She zoomed out. The thing went on and on and on...

'So?' Nico folded his arms. He didn't like lengthy approaches. It was like being stalked. Sooner or later they'd get to the real agenda and he liked sooner. Details were important only if the job was accepted.

'This sequence is one of two that keep appearing in people who have acquired Forged adaptations within the last six months. They're in the Orthodox Secret Service tracing system because all of them have reported into psych and surgical bays for refits and repairs, many of which are caused by the actions of these strings.'

Nico waited. Patience. He looked at Two for reassurance and she smiled her smile that said this information was good.

'Contaminated with unauthorised DNA and Expert Systems,' Two said to him kindly, patting his knee. 'Bad medicine. We traced it to one place and possibly one operator. But the two things are not related, not very. Distinctly different. The longer one is part of – it's like Beast, but it's not Beast.'

Ah right. Beast was an escaped power. This would be the hint that someone might be seeding an army, organised or not, and the Orthodoxy would be killing itself to get it all under control again. But Beast had perked up with a mention of his name. He regarded Nico with eager, desperate anxiety, the longing to know, the hint, always in him, that this might be a clue that led them to some living remnant or relative of his, who had known his origins and might help him find the meaning of his existence.

Nico wanted to protect him from the kind of disappointment he'd had himself, but there was no way he could say no to him with this much build-up.

'Tell me where they are,' Nico said with the long-suffering singsong of one who already knows he's lost. 'Kill, Extract Value, or Co-opt?' The three holy stations of power.

Tash blinked. 'I want you to find who it is, verify that they are alone in doing this, discover their contacts and locate the source of the contamination,' Tash said.

Nico pulled a face. 'I don't do espionage. I'm more of a hit it and quit it kind of guy.'

'He's not subtle,' Two added, as if that needed adding.

'I'm well aware of Nico's failings,' Tash said, looking coolly at him.

Tash had spent months in Nico's head during the escape from Harmony and she'd done all the intelligence work. Nico rolled his eyes at her.

'We've been working with Isy and Beast,' Tash said, and that made him blink this time.

'What?'

'We knew you'd say you didn't do spying, so we made you a new skin,' Tash said. 'As none of us can connect with you any longer through the Switch, because Beast fully occupies it, we've made you a skin which is capable of...'

Two, bouncing up and down on the spot with excitement because technology was involved, cut off her about-to-be-very-long explanation of the science with, 'It'll be like you're wearing us! So we'll all be going with you! It's genius as fashion, Nic!'

Nico tore his annoyance off Tash and looked at Two. Her brown eyes were aglow with enthusiasm and happiness, delight in achievement; the big score. 'I'm sorry, what?'

'You'll have some of our ability and insight in addition to your own,' Tash said, falling in with the routine, minus the happiness. 'So you won't be entirely in the dark should certain situations arise.'

'You could just come with me,' he said, feeling this was already an idea he didn't like.

Tash shook her head. 'I'll be instantly recognised where you're going. After Harmony we erased the trail for Isy and Two. The Orthodoxy think they died during the escape attempt. It will probably still trip all the alarms if they detect the suit...'

'It's Strange tech,' Two butted in quickly, drumming her fingertips on Nico's leg as if programming acceptance into him.

'But that's...' he started.

'Like me!' Beast said proudly, broadcasting his voice instead of just going straight into Nico's thoughts. 'You and me,' he added.

Nico looked at Tash, looked at her face in which he read all kinds of shield walls up against all kinds of secrets. 'Strange shadows. Like Beast. So – not at all something that anyone would worry about, seeing as he's marked for destruction on sight by Orthodox Services and wanted everywhere so people could steal him. And fill me in again on why I should give a shit about a trashy chop shop on the edge of liveable space dishing out bad hackware to dodgy clients who should know better?'

'You shouldn't,' Tash said. 'But if you find the answer to this, find who's doing it and what they've got, I promise you I'll never commission you to do a single thing ever again. You'll be free of me. And all the questions that keep rocketing around in that empty head of yours about who and why and what will be answered.'

Nico peered closer. She wasn't lying. He knew her, to the bone of her, and she was sly and snakelike and scheming, self-interested and a master of the long plan, but she wasn't shitty, and now she wasn't lying. Instead he felt a tight keenness, like a stiletto blade hidden in a sleeve, poised for the moment when the wielder would choose to cue its arrival. She was tense. Frustrated. Unwilling to let him see that a lot rested on this, personally, for her. He saw her hand reach out and touch Two with a gentle caress to the arm, seeking to reassure itself.

Two smiled.

'Do it,' said Beast. 'I want to see how it works.'

'Well,' Nico said. 'I guess my diary does have a gap.'

They felt the shiver of transition as Beast shifted their primary material state into the Shade. Unhindered by laws restricting baryonic matter they moved at speed only possible as an insubstantial creature in the dark. For them, relative to one another, nothing had changed. The only way to tell that they were in the shadow and not the light universe was a strange bodily sensation of airiness, as if they were only dreams of themselves.

They were underway to the edge.

It was only later, in his room, as he turned the fine vial of silvery liquid skin over in his hands, that he realised he'd never thought to ask if it was safe or why he'd risk his life for something that didn't seem like it even had pay.

'Want some help with that?' Isy, standing behind him, was holding his hand out.

Isy had come from the very literal other side of the tracks to Nico. He was the elegant, educated priest of a religious state, every refined and polished element of him perfectly balanced on top of his radically engineered being. He had lived in Harmony, the good place. Nico was a thug from Chaontium, where all the violent, degradable, immoral rejects slunk about as Harmony's celestially ordained counterpart – the bad place. Nico was equally as engineered, just for the worse, to make the point that Harmony was capable of producing absolutely anything to order. Or so the catalogue said.

Isy was custom, though, ex-catalogue. He was bespoke. He was Strange, like shadow tech. No doubt he and Beast together were the results of some top-secret black projects gone wrong – if the project stealing itself away was wrong. Nico was their common denominator, or, as he preferred to think of it, demon-inantor.

(Beast: "That's not a word, Nico." Nico: "Well, it should be, 'cause that's what I am.")

'Help?' Nico looked at the vial. The grey silver mercury or whatever it was churned, as if it was alive, pawing at the glass. Now that it was something he actually had to do he wondered what happened to his Never Volunteer motto. Probably should change that to Always The Fall Guy. 'Maybe a brain transplant.'

'I thought you were going to drink it.' Isy smiled, tentative, all poise and manners to Nico's bluntness. But he rarely tried even a mild roast as a joke, though he had begun to learn that Nico liked it. His pale hazel Husky-dog eyes with their dark outer rings caught Nico and hypnotised him as usual.

Nico fell down the rabbit hole headfirst. Yeah. You can have all the cheap shots you want. Just don't stop looking at me like that. He grinned, 'Down in one?'

'Don't tempt me.' Isy plucked the vial out of his grip and undid the complex stopper. He looked at Nico with his doctor's face on, the one that said this would hurt Nic much more than it would hurt him. 'You know I wouldn't use it if I didn't think it was safe.'

'Why would a radical, newly-engineered substance at the cutting edge of research and innovation NOT be safe?' Nico said, pleased with how well he was handling it, fortified by Beast's unconditional approval and confidence.

(Beast: "Now you'll be even more like me, Nic!")

'Quite. Hold out your hand.'

A faint tremor went through the hull. They felt it as the deck quivered under their feet. Such things were commonplace in the shade. Isy took a deep breath and tipped the vial so that the material was directed towards the back of Nico's hand.

A huge shiver ripped through the Beast from nose to stern as every material object rang, rippling like water to the chime of an unseen bell. Nico and Isy with it. And the vial. And the liquid skin. So a moment later the silvery mass had landed on Nico but also splashed onto Isy's fingers where he held Nico's hand palm down. It vanished neatly into both of them; silver ink soaking into golden tan and dark tan paper.

Motionless now in the stilled room they looked up into one another's eyes.

'Oops,' Isy said after a moment.

'What was that?' Nico said at the same time.

Nobody moved.

'Don' worry,' said Bob the Beast, 'was Charon.' And then he added. 'The moon. Not dead man's boat guy. He is from a story.'

'Obviously,' Nico said, looking into Isy's golden eyes as he understood, from his skin, that Beast meant they had passed through Charon, as all of the little 'bumps' were them passing through solid objects which, in shadow state, were changed into distinctly airy things, bar a few molecules which caused the judder. Because that was now a kind of thing that Nico just knew and a kind of thing that Isy also just knew. They knew what Beast knew.

Charon was a bit of a thudder. They knew it the way that Beast knew it. It was masterclass physics presented by an enthusiastic kid who'd never been to school but who had spent a lot of time at the skate park.

The skin itself had no feeling – not as if wearing clothes or even lotion.

'How do you take this thing off?' Nico asked, plucking at the back of his hand where it had soaked in.

'It'll wear out when its power is gone and then just disintegrate,' Isy said. 'The more you use it up the faster it will…'

'A day? Two?'

'About six hours. But that's the time Tash thinks you'll have to get in and get out anyway.'

'Meaning the place is already full of trouble.'

'She wouldn't send you if it weren't.'

'Expendable me.'

'That's not what I meant.'

They shivered again, and weight returned with every sense of physical solidity. They were out of the shade. It was time to go.

Nico watched the shuttle move with precision to their docking clamp in the bay of Longlost Station. Their position was just sunward of Haumea in the Kuiper Belt, and as far away from Orthodox Earth as it was currently possible to be and still be within a ten-year reach of it by standard ripdrive travel via the portal at Neptune. Shadecraft were only hours out but they were military issue only and hours was hours enough. It was a long way to come for a botch job.

Though it wasn't Lost to people with the right codes, the Station was well hidden in the edge of the Belt, indistinguishable from any other collection of idly rotating asteroids, rocks and dust. Most of the local asteroids were water, fuel and raw materials left as payments or accruing holding taxes as they awaited pickup. None were permanently inhabited save the largest central object, a nondescript all-rock asteroid of 1k diameter and 5k in length.

Longlost Port was accessed through one of this stone's rare flat faces, bored through to admit small passenger ships for visitors. Nothing larger than a Swifty Sloop though. Nico's shuttle was only half that size, a micro-yacht built for speed and stealth and decked out with a mixture of cheap and reclaimed drives to account for

Nico's cover story of being a criminal fleeing Orthodox justice – common enough. Who wasn't one of those?

They were still so cramped that only the most careful movements would spare them from becoming wallpaper paste, so Beast piloted himself alone, pretending to be as slow and unresponsive as a real human though not one as untrained as Nico. None of the zooming in and out and cool moves hijinks that little craft enjoyed inside the mighty bays of the Orbital or the planetary moons. They crept.

The ship boomed as they made contact with the dock. Metal whirred, motors whined, reeling them on tight. Doors exchanged protocols, prepared to open. They were on-station. He was vaguely aware of the riptides of data flowing as procedures and permissions whipped back and forth between them and the station's murky depths where, presumably, some authority lurked. Everything about Longlost was anonymous, hidden in code, superficial. Except the promise of horrible violence. Beast and its accomplice in this particular crime, Tashlynnai, had convinced him of that.

Two and Isy had dressed him in what they said was Forge Tech average gear – a dark blue and grey suit that left his head and hands free. Heavy boots, paranoid with machinery for saving him from emergency vacuum situations and sudden changes in gravity, completed the set. He was exactly like one of the many Earth-type spacers looking for a bit of an upgrade. Good gear, but not top range. Anyone who could afford that wouldn't be scrounging for bits here; they'd be up at Wolf Island, getting all-new. They'd be in Harmony, buying a whole new outer.

The trade in dead Forged parts was hot in this stretch and the thing he was to focus on. Law abiding Forged were being hunted as scrap. Tash had said that was the source of the huge DNA string as well as the bad fittings. She had names he had to check out, things he was to ask for.

Beneath the suit the secondary skin, coating his own like a fine powder, suddenly shifted with annoyance. It was fed up with having to play second fiddle to inferior gear. It amused Nico that it had opinions he could feel as clearly as his own. He was also having to get used to the strange personalities of machines. Everything out here was, in some way, analogous to life.

All the relating was exhausting. He was already nearly asleep, and it was time to go. He looked around, feeling the need to carry something like a weapon because years of bodyguarding warlords was a hard thing to put away, but there was nothing to hand. It would have been vaporised anyway, his boarding card voided. Maybe he'd be voided. He used the skin to summon Two. Wanting to talk to her was enough to connect them. Her presence appeared in his mind, as if she inhabited the space between his ears, not that there was much room.

'Can't I have a gun?' he asked.

'No.' She was amused, been wondering how long he'd take to ask.

'What about a knife?'

'I thought 'you were the weapon'.' She mimicked his own dramatic statement.

'Yeah, it's more of a show thing,' he said, speaking aloud as he got out of his flight harness and eased his limbs from the tension of their arrival.

'Sure it is, and no.'

He was already happier, though, hearing her voice. He could feel Tash in the background, trying to get in on the conversation, insisting she had to talk but both he and Two resisted her. It was the funniest thing, even Tash's cross response, as if they were naughty kids together.

'Call off your girlfriend,' he said. 'Bad girlfriend.'

'Nico,' Two said. 'She's not my girlfriend.' Two liked to keep everything neat. Girlfriend would have been much too close. Whatever Tash was it was further off than that. It was sweethearts, it was nice times, it was kindness and talking but it wasn't really girlfriends. It surprised him. He was about to remark on it but hesitated, wondering if the suit was overinforming him; was he overhearing that?

'Well, whatever it's called.' He was chippy, jealous of Tash. Two was soothing, patting him on the head, thinking he was an idiot. He felt smugly happy. Not a girlfriend. Haha. Not that close. Hoho.

'Family,' the Beast said with a rush of enthusiasm. 'This is what a family is like. This jealousy and great drama. I have heard about it in many great stories! Like Flashpoint! Yes!'

'Shh, Bob,' Nico said. 'Don't go getting ideas.' But it was too late, the vision of himself marrying Isylon, Tash and Two at the same wedding, both smiling with vows and flowers and shit, and them all sailing away in the big, smiling idiot dog-of-the-stars that was The Beast had already gone lolloping through the shadow skin, leaving its muddy pawprints over everything or anything they had been about to say.

He felt Two pause. He paused.

A couple of other people distinctly paused.

The Beast lolloped off blithely into the silence.

Isylon cleared his throat, so to speak.

'Didn't realise you were here,' Two said awkwardly.

'I wasn't, until just now,' he said in his soft, unassuming voice. Was that a tinge of laughter in it? Nico thought so. 'I just wanted to say good luck.'

'Break every bone in yer body,' Two added cheerfully, signing out fast.

'It's just a walk and a talk,' Nico said irritably, not sure why he was annoyed. 'I'll be online.' They had a protocol of no contact in the Station proper, but they were allowed to eavesdrop and to flash a warning if trouble came. He felt supervised, and bristled.

'You're very good at walking and talking,' Isylon purred and every fibre of Nico's being lit up with a golden glow at the backhander.

'You're lucky you're so far away.'

'Or not so lucky,' Isylon said with a smile that Nico felt stir his own face. Then he too faded away into the distant-observer setting. Leaving Nico alone, all fired up and nowhere to go. Except through the airlocks.

Longlost was the first renegade port that Nico had been to. From the outside the asteroid itself was a lump of rock. From the inside, it was a lacework of incredible delicacy.

He tried not to stare at the bubbled vaults like a complete idiot, but it was difficult. The inside of the station looked like a giant bone that had been hollowed out into tunnels that foamed with openings. Insect-like drones buzzed about him regularly, some big and winged, others tiny and spinning in fields of their own making. He felt the tickle and putter of scans, the wash of frequencies, the inspection of busy little machine minds ticktocking over their checklists. The paperwork took a few seconds and then he was free to go.

As soon as he moved off the dock gangway and into the station proper he was faced with a speedway. A large spherical passenger car was set on one of many possible tracks, aligned to the mild gravity that had been put there solely for inept bipedal things like him,. A glance up revealed hundreds of things not so encumbered with directional biologies – machines, creatures were crawling across all surfaces, with and against the asteroid's own rotational G forces. The sight was so disorienting he was nearly sick on the spot..

'Get in,' the car said, neutral but not deferential. It was patient-ish. 'I know where you're going. Your ship has informed me. Just put on the belts.'

'Can I get the scenic route?'

'If you pay.'

'Just go direct.'

He felt the shiver of machines chattering payments; a sense of silvery chill running down his arm and out his fingers in some amusing sensory notification that Beast thought he'd like, so he knew how much money was relatively passing from account to account. The car was high-priced, but then, it was one of few passenger vehicles and it could afford to be picky. What the currency was, he neither knew nor cared.

Amazing as it was to his ignorant eyes he spent little time admiring Longlost and a lot noting its entrances and exits, ways and habits. He was immediately unsettled. The place was a warren, navigable only by machine, on purpose, and he had to trust his skin to track his position and remember his routes, absorb what he saw and make sense of it. He pretended to admire things in a casual way, and fought nausea as they reached his destination at last – a near Earth-gravity plaza, unusually wide and high in the roof, well-lit at the centre like an arena, murky at the edges where shop doors opened. Neon blasted promises of resurrection, transformation, dwarfing the shy efforts at landscaping with biomass in green and brown. Flowers, or something like them, glowed and fluttered in the ventilation.

It smelled old, like it was grimed deep, and no amount of spray and sweep could get it sorted. His skin grumbled at the number of new geneforms it was finding objectionable on his behalf and he rubbed the prickle off his arms. The car suggested it could stay around, should sir require a swift exit, and he agreed without thinking twice. He wanted to be in this place for not a moment longer than he had to be. The transport was satisfied, well-used to customers with the urge to be elsewhere.

Walking hastily, long strides, he got out of the light.

Almost immediately a voice accosted him, 'You got offworld news, mate? Any trades?' It was rough and disjointed, as though whoever was talking was near their last day.

He looked around and saw only a heap of muck between two shops. There was no rubbish here, nothing larger than air as everything else was constantly swept away by the worn cleaning bots, so the heap must be the speaker. He didn't go nearer. The voice was relayed to him, on the commons in-station frequency; he didn't have to be close to hear.

'Harmony's under new management,' he said, because that was new, and possibly news in a place like this, but probably old too because light travelled fast and they were two months off world.

'Tecmaten's gone, is he? For real?' The question said it was old news but there was more worth mining out of it. A confirmation, first hand or second hand, was required. Nico's exchanges with the shops rang back one after the other, filling up with quotes, special offers, you deserve only the finest, prices and counter prices. He sifted, searching the specials, or rather letting his skin do it while he talked.

'Dead,' Nico said. 'But, you know, ten more to take his place I guess. Bastard probably cloned himself.'

'He thought he was a genius,' the voice said. The heap stirred at the same time and began to change its shape. Something like a head appeared. A long, crocodilian snout poked from under heavy matting or fur. 'But he was nothing compared to the likes of us. What're you up for?'

'Upgrades,' Nico said. 'Same as everyone else.' The bidding war flurried, surged, began to close as lesser offers dropped away. A large beetle droned past Nico's shoulder and came to rest on the crocodile's shoulder mat, going inert as it delivered its messages.

'You're already wearing half the arsenal of the new world, kid. I don't think we can do much for you short of killing you for obvious lying.'

Nico barely raised an eyebrow at his disguise not holding out. He hadn't expected it to, though the speed was disarming – but the faster this went down the better, so – 'And you are?'

The prices rattled to a halt. That test, whatever it was for, was over. Distraction while he was scanned most likely. Well. Anyway.

'Vinsalvarez, but you can call me Lord Vin. This is my shop. They're all my shops on this side of the plaza.'

'Why do you look like a pile of shit, then?'

There was a pause.

'I...' said the heap. 'May have let things get a little out of hand.'

The second part of this speech was echoed by a gentle female voice and a figure appeared from the nearest shady doorway – a person Nico immediately identified with a sense of crawling inner alarm as Harmony #2566BetaModel Yon5, Deluxe.

She was short, neat and of pleasant appearance with the demure behaviours and grace of an ancient dynastic heir cum samurai goddess – as much cliché and stereotype as you could cram into a genome and a set of responses and still call yourself an artist. Yon5 was popular. One of the most-sold. This one was the standard, not even a facial adjustment or a hairdo, just as she came from the catalogue. The Deluxe part – that referred to her ability to host large complex personas and tolerate high dissonance. She's what you'd buy if you were loaded and wanted an avatar that would feel like your own body and not give you any trouble no matter what creepy shit you were up to with it.

The shock was visceral, nasty and shattering. He'd never faced a Harmony model that was in use before. The only ones he'd ever

172

known had been themselves, no passengers. Now he faced the fact that every fibre of his being wanted to relate to her as a genuine person, and he wanted to kill whoever was in her at the same time. If there was a her without them. So many questions.

She gave Nico a wry smile and a little bow, slightly mocking, completely acknowledging all his discomforts and finding pleasure in it. Her clothing was immaculate – it was a skin, like his, and also high-grade, much higher than she was worth if you looked at it in purely financial terms, and he didn't want to, but that's what he did, with everything. People lied, but money never did. Assets had a specific value to someone and the extent of that value represented their stake in the game.

'I am the human face of Vin at this time.'

'I'm Nico all the time.' But as he said it, he thought maybe he was somebody's something, because that was true enough, wasn't it?

'It takes a little getting your head around, doesn't it?' she said, and her eyes, dark and soft, were full of a knowingness that he felt could only come from genuine, alert, unimpeded consciousness.

Some models were completely convincing. *Deluxe.*

'I've never really got around it,' he said, feeling such kinship, such a heart-wrench he hadn't expected – hadn't expected to feel much beyond his usual contempt and impatience really, and now it was just feelings all over the damn place like escaped puppies. He scowled at her.

The heap of reptile was heaving. Laughing, he thought.

'You're here with Tash, aren't you?' she asked.

'You aren't supposed to know that,' he said. Why lie? She already knew. And if she didn't, then this would only make the race to the end that much shorter.

'But you're not hers,' she added thoughtfully. 'I see that.'

He was relieved. 'No. Don't think so.'

They shared a smile that only the manufactured could share before he remembered that she – wasn't what she looked like. 'If you're here with her, then Longlost is really in trouble,' she said with a sigh.

'I'm looking for contraband tech,' he said.

'Yes, of course,' she nodded. 'Why else would you come? Let me guess. Tashlynnai has succeeded and found a pacifier for the Fury. She had you made for a purpose, as a face she can use, someone to fence for her, but not a true avatar, that's too dangerous for her. Something more distant. Something that can be thrown away, should the need arise, without providing any direct link. She worked hard, to ensure that your fight for freedom felt so real. Then you agreed, but you had to, of course, you were made for that. Now she comes here. She told you someone is in trouble. Because you are #501998Custom Omega8, Crusader. A purpose, not a name. A purpose and a weakness all in one. Do you know who is really pulling your strings?'

It was quite the speech. He had to hand it to her. She did not fuck about. But he'd been through this before, a million times, and there was no way out of it and no point in bothering with it.

'I'm Nico,' he said and held out his hand to her.

She looked at it.

He knew he was meant to take the bait, react, all that shit. He just – couldn't be arsed.

'You forgot to add the Asshole Variant,' he added. 'Pretty sure that's hardcoded in.'

'I am Vin.' She looked at his hand and awkwardly reached out, meant to take it as something other, couldn't because she was in her role. The allegiance she had tried for wasn't working.

'Yeah, sure, Vin. Nice to meet you.'

They shook. Her little hand in his big hand, not so pathetic it meant nothing, not hard enough to commit. It was weird. He felt their master skins exchange protocols, a little ripple of assents, and something more, a shadow gone before he could get a grip on it. His sense of being in the presence of something uncanny deepened.

'Tash is shit. I know it, you won't surprise me,' he said. 'But she's kind of righteous shit. I can't stand her. Her methods are evil. But I admire her. She's not wrong about things.'

'Well,' Vin said. 'A lot happened before you came on the scene. And a lot of it was evil on every side. Look up the Forged War of Ascension when you have a moment.'

Nico felt a sense of time rushing, felt its wave looming in Vin's awareness though he didn't understand it. He realised that his skin had infected hers and now he was feeling something of what she was experiencing and doing in the background as distant echoes in his own self. She was a faint ghost at the edge of him.

'War of Ascension? What'd'you ascend to? This?' He looked pointedly around. 'You ascended to a garbage bin?'

'Tash is a wanted criminal,' Vin said. 'She's at the top of the list. Where she goes, the Orthodox forces follow. They want me nearly as much as they want her. So I'm going to give you what she's come for. Then we can be on our way. Do you have eyes beyond the Belt?'

'Sure,' he said.

'They prefer oblique vectors but they're coming from Neptune Portal without a disorientation pattern of approach, because that is where their closest accelerator is,' Vin said. 'So watch that way. Tell me if you see something.'

He looked, far far away, with the Beast's skin, that spoke to his. 'Nothing. Wait.'

There was a beacon they had left behind them, a piece of dust floating steadily towards the sun, one of millions coasting around in idle search. A few minutes ago, it had seen lights, the blare and flash of Saturn's Eighth Port Accelerator, enough for five rapid assault units to flip to Neptune and then burn in. 'They're setting off. Five. Light armour. Annihilation Class. They'll be here in a couple of hours.'

'Yes, they don't like you.' Vin smiled. 'Quickly then. I have a price you must agree to, in order to get your booty.'

'Wait,' Nico said. 'How do they know we're here?'

There was a pause. A long, long pause. So long that Nico felt aeons pass in silence, all while Vin's dark gaze looked right through him into the heart of a different mystery. He felt the certainty that she had placed that call, as soon as he had entered the car, and the beetle, whatever it was, had taken the measure of him and smelled the shadow skin. Vin had been waiting. Maybe had drawn them here. This he felt. And a flutter of something unhappy. In the background. A moth's wing of disturbance on the sweet composure as though something was searching for light, trying to get out.

But he couldn't trust that now, could he? Crusaders are always looking for the maiden. Figuratively. So you want to pull a Crusader in, you give them one.

'You see,' she said. Slowly, as though his pressure on her to tell the truth was wringing a genuine confession. 'I had to have insurance.'

'I see.' He was used to it. Cartels were plenty in Chaontium, and they played each other off all the time. Let's do a side deal quick before my date arrives and does your head in with a hammer, all that kind of good stuff. Who doesn't go to a shoot-out without insurance?

She smiled at him, inclined her head. 'You're good.'

He shook his head. 'You know what it is? I just never believe anything.' Because in spite of this shitshow, he felt, *knew* in his skin and bones, that he and this person, this Vin, wearing its human body, were allies. Or they should be. You could die on the sharp end of that distinction.

He really had preferred it when he was alone and people were things he mostly hit or ignored. Whoever had been called, on whatever terms, didn't matter. He was at the bottom of the ladder and he just did as he was told.

But he kept feeling something off about her and it was hard to place. So hard that he decided that being the fall guy wasn't going to happen today. Today he was in charge. Stuff whatever Tash had said. Let's see what was going on for real.

That felt much worse. If his skin could have shouted it would have, but he was good at ignoring things.

'Come this way,' Vin said and beckoned gently. 'I must show you something important.'

The heap got to four or six feet and padded off slowly, with difficulty, towards the far side of the plaza, on its way to another incoming car.

As it left, Nico turned to Yon5, 'Is *that* your actual body?'

'Of course not. Nor is this one,' Vin said. 'This way.'

As he neared the door Nico felt the dragging sensation of data shutdown and realised that he was walking into a dead zone. Before they could be cut off completely, or compromised through his connection, he severed the links to the Beast and the others himself. By the time he got through to the other side he was alone and watching Vin's Harmony avatar, Lady Vin, put off by her perfectly graceful manners. She was reaching for something, and as he came through the door, he heard and felt a widespread rustle and swirl of keen attention, focused on her, as if she had walked into a pack of perfectly trained dogs.

Of course he was behind her, like a dumb idiot to the slaughter, or whatever was going to happen next, cramped off from assistance, hostage to curiosity and his own impatience. Never send a hammer to do a scalpel's job but if all you have is a hammer, this is what you get.

But he was good enough for dishonest work and this was as dishonest as it came. The change in Vin's stride as she cleared the long metre of the doorway warned him and he was moving aside as she spun around, something in her hand that would have hit him full in the face if he hadn't been already half a step to her left.

Without the skin he became just Nico, the kid who used to kill bots for cash. Stalking, fleeing, it was second nature. No happy fun model was ever going to top that, no matter how hard her skin suit tried to soup her up.

'Ugh!' she said, disgusted even as she was finishing her spin, seeing her dart go skidding away out the door, along the hall and across the plaza. Her shoulders sagged. Seemed she'd come to the same conclusion.

A few metres back the crocodile in rags had found its legs, feet and hands and came around the corner, blocking the way out.

Nico ignored it, pushed past Vin the Asian babe, and went into the back room thinking about other exits, weapons and contraband. The room contained the rigged up medical bay he'd been expecting. But he hadn't expected the incubation tanks. So many of them, lined up in ranks, filled with different bodies floating in their misty depths, each fed with tight bunches of tentacles that reached down from the ceiling's vast machineries.

Lights and liquids pulsed. The temperature had gone up a good ten degrees. Bubbles and hydromatics flushed and sluiced in a constant trickle and rush, creating a wall of noise. Valves burred. The metal floor clanked under his boots. He was presented, centre and proud of it, with the unmistakable large glass flask of an Alembic, the kind they had used on Harmony to gestate human bases. It was empty and to one side, part of its operating tech was strewn about in a state of half-finished mess, moving sluggishly as it attempted self-assembly with insufficient energy.

He strode forward, knowing he was supposed to stop, look, pause in horror or awe at one more demonstration that he was all very much yesterday's news. Behind him he heard Vin scramble on her light feet, and the heavier scrape of the crocodilian, the *slursh* of its tail on the metal grating. He moved quickly along the aisle, checking readings he didn't understand, hoping the skin could work well enough to figure it out for him, seeing the shudder of fleshy things inside the tanks, vague and out of reach. Some tanks were lidded tight. Some not. There was no obvious exit door and no time to ask questions. They were beyond that stage.

He put his hand straight down into the nearest open tank.

'Don't touch...!'

But this kind of world is now a world where someone like him has to touch everything. That's how you know it. And instantly know it.

The draft is like fresh air to the face as the skin takes a long lick of fluids and reads the history of this place in full technicolour from spit and piss and floating nanoparticles. It gives its own history back, fair's fair. Seeing it's all too late the two Vins on his backside stop their rushing anxiety and just stand in the middle of the chamber. They're in one of hundreds of spherical pods that back the shops on this level, where Vin, the master craftsman, has been helping humans become more than human for decades but has always kept a bit in return, unrecorded, un-managed. You can't splice genes without spares. You can't Forge new systems without flesh.

But also, you can't let people go out into the world and not let them take a bit of you with them. Because you're generous and you like to get around. There's nobody you can trust like yourself.

Nico comes to the realisation that everything on this station, even the material that coats the inside of the rock and strengthens it against the torment of centrifugal force, is Vin. The people who left here are a bit Vinny. The creatures on the plaza, the few people working other parts of the asteroid, the scientists and the machines are all a little bit Vin – he's really spread out here, made himself at home. And he's scattered himself to the winds. Out of hand. That was another way of putting it.

But Vin had something, and traded in something, that wasn't him. And wasn't *in* him. Something special. Something – sad.

Nico could feel it now, with conviction, like a confirmed case, a sense of purpose and destiny sinking into him from the place where Tash and Two, Isy and Beast all met and agreed inside his skin. It's the sadness which Vin's old customers returned to have taken away. The sadness that they couldn't shake off, that sunk into them like a stain. The sadness that had tripped Tash's radar, been the trail she followed. With meat comes memory and where that has been erased the space it leaves is an emotion.

Vin had infected them all with an unremitting grief so bad that they would rather let go their power than live with it. The well was tainted.

Nico shook off his own hand, let his fingers drip as he turned to look at the demurely distressed Vin and her delicate lipstick, the grumpy and toothy Vin, sour with disappointment that he won't be having a stick of Nico to shove into his Alembic, if he ever figures out how to get it going.

Nico walked back to look at it. He remembered faking being a research priest, someone who could operate it. But he'd never figured it out for real. Only Isylon had been able to use it. 'Is this it? You want us to fix this in return for something? Or was I supposed to go in the soup for later?'

'I just wanted to see if you were all she said you could be. If she was right about the weapon system not being beyond redemption. For interest, you understand. I wouldn't have taken anything. Just a taste, a bit of flavour. Not like there's time. Old habits, I suppose.'

Her fingers twitched, greedy, giving the lie.

Nico ignored it. 'Tash doesn't know you have one of these, then?'

'Of course not, or she would have never sent you. But I suppose she's heard about the Sorrow. I confess I never thought it would transfer across. When all the trouble started coming back my way, I started to watch for Tash appearing. When your shuttle showed signs of tachyon particles in the scan I thought I'd spare you the bother of hunting me down. Please...'

Vin the girl stepped away from him and led the way through to another room filled with tanks, most of them emptied, some in stages of cleaning, through a corridor walled with doors to hibernation capsules and recovery rooms, and into a storage facility – a vast space like a library, walled to every centimetre with a storehouse of specimens, its floor made up of the bulk of the cloud servers which acted as heaters for the station.

In spite of the unsuitable warmth a hastily rigged cryo-container had been dumped in the heart of the place. Within its transparent box, beneath display readouts of unreadable gibberish, lay something that resembled a desk-sized chunk of meat, frosted with crystals in many colours, marbled with silver and synthetic sheets.

'That's it,' Vin said, rubbing her hands together as if she was freezing. 'That's what's the trouble right there. What I want is for you to take it away from here and never come back.' Their crocodile body shuffled around, checking displays anxiously. It keyed something, extracted a hand-sized tray and brought it over to Nico, heavy clouds of vapour boiling off it as it rapidly defrosted – a sample.

'What's "the trouble"?' Nico kept his hands down and looked, feeling he was close enough as the crocodilian extended the tray for him.

'All you need to do is touch it and you'll know. Forged communication and synthesis, so advanced.'

Nico looked at the tray and then at the cryo-rig. He ignored the tray and walked over to the rig. It was, because of the haste in which it had been set up, running off a very basic controller. He hit the unlock key and the lid popped with a hiss and a billow of nitrogen – a cloud so swift and intense that it shrouded him in bitterly icy fog as he thrust his hand down through the fluid to make contact with the object inside. I mean, sure, baited to do it, really set up for it, but again, in the circumstances no way out and no way to trust Vin.

It hurt like a bitch even with the suit on his arm to the wrist and the nanoskin belting for all it was worth.

Nico was unholy fast though. His hand was already back. He keyed the lock. The pain was so bad it was good. He felt his grin come on him.

'You...' said Vin, once from the girl mouth and once from the crocodile's huff. The meaning was clear without the second word – idiot.

Nico felt pleased he'd done something unpredictable. His hand hurt much worse than before as it thawed, the skin working hard, so hard, denying the burn its chance to destroy his flesh by the narrowest of margins. Then the skin started working on the traces it had picked up off the massive *chonk* – too big and solid to be a mere chunk – of frozen carcass.

Chonk wasn't exactly dead. Nothing that was meant to exist in space's near zero was all that discomfited by being shoved into a freezer. It needed cold. It also needed *room*. Any sense of Vin, of Beast or anyone else got wiped on the instant.

His mind exploded, trying to house a ghost body the size of a small moon, of a complexity and construction... and there was a memory. He felt struck by darts, then compromised, then he knew –

This was a fragment left over from a massive explosion that had silently ripped apart this person and left only tiny pieces, each of them vaporised relentlessly, hunted down, except this bit right here. This one sad bit of flesh which had been gulped by a passing smuggler, vomited out into a trading bay, haggled over, fought over and ended up by a long road out on the edge of the system in Vin's capable, busy hands.

Where he had used it to craft Forged with new and interesting qualities – like regeneration, and replication. Nico felt this ghost body capable of all that and so much more. Of taking an idea from nothing and crafting a living person into it, without recourse to any assistance. A body that had parts scattered throughout the system, pieces whirling away into deep space beyond it – which had gestated its own defence and been slaughtered in the birthing of it. Executed, for having the audacity to dare to declare independence.

A devastating, unbearable misery radiated from it so powerfully that he felt his awareness of reality slide, slip, waver. He was protected from more by the failure of his skin, which chose that moment to die on him, all power spent. It left only knowledge and a weaker, angrier Nico behind.

The Beast's MotherFather, the Forged Gaia Genesis. That's what this Chonk was. The greatest Forged ever created. And, in the nature of fractal portions, it contained the information of the whole, if you were able to read it, if it allowed you to see.

Nico looked at Vin in its blank and pretty Asian Babe housing. 'How many people have you given this to?'

Because there's the problem. The Sorrow is here, but also the life is here. A life that isn't over because a piece of it remains, and potentially now lots of pieces. If this scattering of seeds to the wind isn't the greatest act of wild rebellion and potential madness most likely to draw the grimly reaping wrath of Earth, then nothing is.

Vin the girl was looking at the cryo tank in a strange, whimsical way. Behind her Vin-the-croc was taking nervous readings of the workings of other tanks and containers. It didn't answer. Well, why would it? What was the point? Destination fucked, that's where all this was headed, no matter if Tash or Nico or anyone did anything. Calling the Orthodox was the move of despair. What was he going to tell them? That Tash was behind it? Was he hoping to run out and get the evidence all blown up out of the way for him?

'Does this thing move?' Nico gestured at the tank and started to circle it looking at its housing.

'It's on a sled,' Vin said with a faint smile. 'Had to be you know, to get it in here in the first place. I think they got it secondhand. It's been temperamental. Nearly thawed at one point.'

The disassociating git, Nico thought, finding the sled control dangling from a wire line on the far side and activating it. 'Here. I'm taking it now.'

Vin's dreamy smile said to him – of course you are, Nico. Because that's what I wanted you to do. I've done my bit, smeared my greasy rat-arsed DNA and this chunk's megahuman life generating systems into every custom refit like a god repopulating Eden, and now you're here, you idiot, you package deal of easy meat and old enemies, to take it off my hands and run away with it into the dark, towing the hellhounds of old men's vengeance after your trailing skirts.

Well, that's what Nico read into the expression. He reckoned a bit of creative licence was the only thing keeping him from smashing one Vin into another at this point. But the clock was ticking and his own old but good skin was prickling with urgency – Bob had noticed something nasty pop out of Neptune's portal before the skin died. Two hours my ass, he thought. He should be away already, if he was meant to make it. Probably he wasn't.

Fine. This was going to be the old way. 'Are you the only one left here, then?'

'Yes, only me,' Vin said and god knew if that was true or not. How many bodies could one person infiltrate?

'Take the sled to the car,' Nico said. He expected that Vin was already plotting the way he was going to take over Beast, run off with the goods and the guns, just like every cartel scumbag Nico'd ever met. Insurance-minded people were like that. But that was a problem for later.

Right now he gestured at the rest of the tanks, the preceding rooms. 'Are these like, are they supplies or are they – people?'

'Bit of both,' Vin said with a shrug, her black hair rippling in a silky wave, like it didn't matter at all, the croc hunkering down on all fours to shuffle rapidly ahead of them towards the plaza. Vin had already gone into a future mind; the asteroid and all it contained a piece of a rapidly receding past.

'Okay,' Nico said firmly, like he was resolved, like he believed he was in command of this. Crusader boy to the rescue. You play the part, nobody suspects you're only acting.

He followed them out to the plaza and the waiting car, not looking to either side because he didn't want to see any more. If Vin didn't get to run off in Nic's shuttle he was definitely the sort to plant a beacon on it and keep calling the hounds on. For spite or as insurance. They'd play the cards as it suited. Either way.

He loaded the sled onto the rear bulk transport segment of the rail car. The plaza lights flickered.

The crocodile Vin waited at the track. The car could only hold two passengers. As he jumped down from the sled to get in Nico wasn't surprised to see human Vin lift a gun out of her coat and point it at him. 'Come on.'

Really? Nico felt his face say it all as he obeyed. But they couldn't board the ship without Nico. It would only respond if he were present. Probably Vin was trying to figure out if dead counted as present. Given who he was dealing with it probably didn't. That meant damaged Nico might be out too, so he was going to hesitate some more, at least until they reached the shuttle.

But in turn Nico wasn't sure how much of a threat Vin really posed. Guess he was going to find out if it was more than one girl and one gun.

He got in. The seat webbing closed on him. Vin the girl got in and closed the doors. Nico looked out at Croc au Vin, standing there, heavy arms hanging forward in a simian swing as its long back bent and its snout turned to the side so that it could see him out of one green, slitted eye. They sped off the way he had come, lights and empty platforms shooting past in a flickering blur, a slight judder in the car as the cryostore bumped against the linkage.

It was like George and the dragon, saving the girl, he thought. Only who was the dragon? Right now Nico wasn't enjoying the maiden position. Nico was always the dragon. Always. And the story was garbage because clearly the dragon was the victim in the entire caper, and the dragon was going to win because no human in a tin can was worth shit against a prime elemental like Beast and no story could fix that.

As they neared the docks Vin's crush grip on his collar grew progressively weaker. Nico looked for other people on station but he didn't have to look far. The dock channels were full of hurrying, desperate clusters of bodies, working frantically to shove goods into containers. Abandoned stacks of junk threatened to block all the gangways. In the huge hangar, bays were popping open to space every other second with bursts of engine glow as they hightailed it out of town. Didn't take much for everyone to figure out the law was coming. He didn't see any kids. Felt glad. Can you imagine kids in a place like this? It was just gangs of men and women and the various metallic and cybernetic forms they'd made themselves into, like a circus in places, and lots he didn't recognise and could have been machines for all he really knew, but all the same, when you boiled it off, it was people, some big and some small and some very strange.

Among them Vin and Nico just looked like any other space rangers rushing towards the exits with their most prized cargo. Nico wasn't sure Vin was taking the gun thing all that seriously, thought he might have to reach out and steady her hand if she didn't stop shaking it like a kid's rattle. It was a PM70; good for killing the flesh part of things and leaving machinery intact. It didn't endanger ships or stations but, then again, it wasn't powerful at long range. As it was Vin was in no danger of being accosted or assisted by anyone as nobody gave a shit. They were alone in their standoff, so Nico 'obeyed' and unhitched the sled, dragged it across the plate decking to the airlock of his shuttle.

He was through into the lock section and pushing the sled to the wall to fit it in when he heard Vin's voice struggling to speak behind him. He turned, spun to the side out of the expected position, ready for a shot to the face, or a speech, or a deal, but instead saw Vin's little hand gripped to white knuckle levels upon the gun stock.

He stared, not sure what he was seeing. Her fingers were fighting for the weapon controls as if in the grip of an invisible octopus. The gun barrel was turning slowly, the wrist stretching at a painful angle as it moved by degrees away from him and around. Her free hand reached towards him – from metres away – with outstretched fingers, as if he was a life buoy she meant to grab onto before something swept her away.

He saw that Vin was trying to shoot/not shoot themselves. A tear was rolling down her cheek, her eyes wide and crazy, every muscle in her body juddering with effort.

Out in space the Orthodox annihilation crew in their illegal shade craft would be starting a deceleration arc in preparation for engaging weapons. They'll be ready in about fifteen minutes. It's no place to get stuck in, this stupid whirligig place.

Nico leaped forward and smashed the Yon5's face square and hard, bare knuckles. She had such little dainty cheekbones, he thought, really not built for any kind of combat. He grabbed her as she fell, the gun clattering away, and hauled her over to the sled, dumped her unconscious body on the lid, shut the door, flushed the lock.

It's been about ten seconds all in.

Sometimes you can't dick about even when you're making awful decisions like that one. What was wrong with leaving her on the deck, Nic? Why compromise everything and everyone by bringing her along and her user, or passenger, or whatever the shit Vin was?

He got into the pilot seat, ran the systems up.

The shuttle, part of Beast, pushed off with destructive force, breaking the docking systems, and jetted out at high speed, interior rotating on its gimbals like crazy to keep Nico and the sled on a dogged 2-D plane of steady 'just a light swell, Captain' rocking as the exterior pulled screaming Gs and insane directional changes in a race back to the main body of Beast, which itself is gyring its vast bulk up up and out of the Belt plane, chaff decoys deployed, fields generating complex anomalies as it prepares to stutter-warp the shit out of Dodge.

Fleeing Forged craft cluttered the way. A couple smeared themselves across twizzling rocks and set off a huge chain of active, bump and grind destruction as they darted crazily in an effort not to be within a thousand miles of this spot.

Nico went back to the bay and took the time to dump Vin on the second passenger couchette. He applied the web to hold her in place as the black and blue colours started to puff out on the side of her face, and considered what Chonk might have made out of the combo of Vin and Yon5, Deluxe, because it looked a lot like there was a rebellion of some kind underway in there.

Or that could have been some natural phenomenon, Two's voice reminded him, firm on the side of reason as ever. But what were the odds?

The uplift took only a few minutes. They flew directly into the Beast's side and were swept away with it as it took off and prepared to flutter them, skipping alternate squares of space on the strange checkerboard of standard drive calculated warp leaps – two thousand per second, each traverse skipping one au.

They made a little bug-dance and then they went shadow and crossed the dark invisibly, like ghosts.

A few minutes later they felt the hot burst of Longlost vaporising, though this was only a nicety generated by the skin for their information – they were already lining up to dock at the relative backwater peace of Decadence Station in the shadow of Phoebe by Saturn's flank.

The others come to greet him, not just one but all of them, clad in their best, even Tash, loitering at the back, giving him a difficult nod of approval that must have cost her an entire week's worth of positive emotion to muster. Isylon is let through first, in prime position, a big hugger, a better kisser. Then Two, the tightness of her hands betraying her nerves. Tash just commands the sled in the background, sets it to move. As a last thought she looks up at Nico, glances at Vin draped on the rig's lid.

'I'd better move your trash.' Her eyes are full, kind of glowing. It's odd, Nico thinks, she looks – what's the word – relieved.

They take Vin to the medical bay and give her a sedative while they think what to do and then they install her in a guest suite which might as well be a prison, though it's nice for that, and leave her to her own devices with the Beast on watch, like everywhere, and Nico gets back at last, at last, to the open viewing deck of the bridge lounge and finds the others there, seated on the sprawl of sofas, with dinner and drinks ready for him and they all eat together and at least he didn't throw her out the airlock though it's probably for the best if he did, all agree, because who knows, who can tell, what exactly Vin is or wants or has planned? Surely doesn't deserve a lift. But they are all, except for Tash, Harmony children and have not expected to ever find another, not one that was actually sold. So they couldn't leave her. Even if she isn't, well, they don't know what.

From his relaxed, whiskey-holding position lying against Isylon's legs on the main Captain couch Nico feels a bit kingly, nearly nodding off, when the reactivated skin share tells him that Tashlynn has given Chonk to The Beast and Beast's silence means he is digesting what that means. They are all warmly connected.

There's a friendly quiet where Beast was, so Nico knows he's good, just quiet, doesn't want company, has to be in his own space to think and look at the stars alone.

'The client is very pleased with your work,' Tash says.

'Good,' Nico says, not caring who she means, wondering why the talk when he's already witness to the payment. What more could a Captain have than the best ship on the seas, a beloved crew, guns, a full tank, food and his love at his side? Is there possibly more? Can't be. So, because of that, he gives it a second, waits for her to continue.

'Thank you,' Tash says, and we're now at more words than they've spoken in months and Nico feels a slight shadow and a shiver as she puts her hand on his for a moment and their skins touch and then he knows, he *sees*, the whole story, just like she promised.

Chonk made Tashlynnai. Not like in Harmony, where they do a more advanced job, but out of machine parts, a bang-up desperation job full of all sorts of hybridised stuff that was cooked at lightning speed into a human with a history, inserted to be the only surviving fragment of her, in the hope that somehow, some way, Tashlynn would be the mother that Chonk could not be, save her son, see him grow, make sure he's okay. And now Nico has brought Chonk back, and there is just enough Chonk to assure Beast that in the moments mother and son were ripped apart forever, he was loved, more than anything loved.

Beast has always been terrified it was his fault, that he was not good enough to save her. Now he knows there was no saving her, there was only saving him. And this isn't the best thing – but it's a lot.

Like you couldn't just have told him? Nico thinks, a bit drunk, but then he realises no, you can't tell Beast things, he always suspects a lie. You have to prove yourself with action, and with incontrovertible evidence, and there had to be no trace of the origin on Tashlynnai or she wouldn't have made it this far, secret sleeper that she was, years of work among the enemy as she laid her plans for this day.

Tash says, speaking now as the ghost of her former self, 'We have to fix our mistakes. Or try.'

Nico wants to say *Hey, speak for yourself, lady, I don't make mistakes*, but Beast erupts from contemplation and is in the mix with them.

'Zeroth. That's my name. The one my mother gave me.'

'Good on you, buddy,' Nico returns. 'Still think Bob was good.'

He can feel that Beast is new, better, with full cognisance of the prime mother memory and some of her living legacy. He can feel B – Zeroth – communicating with Isylon, comparing knowledge, vibrating with the sudden expansion of his world which now includes restoration along with destruction. He is a warship and a healing ship, a creature of means.

'What about Vin?' Nico says suddenly as Tash turns to go.

'A pain in the ass,' Tashlynnai says. 'Untrustworthy, of low character. You've seen what it does. We're just lucky it didn't infect us with its spaffing. Like an incontinent mongrel.'

'Is it – he – are they welded to that avatar?'

'You want to save her?' Tash says with a lift of an eyebrow.

Well, yes, dumbass. 'Just asking.'

Tashlynnai nods. 'A word to the wise, though. Don't help anyone you can't afford to help forever.'

Nico looks around. 'This place is very big.'

Tash shrugs. Her business was concludes. 'If you get Vin out, where will you put it?'

He has no idea. But it goes around in his mind, what he could do, and what Vin could do, what he'd seen it do just in a few minutes that he'd known it. Allies, or other parts far away. This isn't the main mind, of course not. Nor the croc. Maybe not anyone on Longlost at all. Real Vin could be anywhere.

Later that night he went down to the guest suite and took a look around. Yon was still sleeping off the sedatives, would do until they were cued to wake. And then what? He thought of Croc au Vin, watching him with its yellow green eye as he left it there on the plaza platform.

189

Was the maiden complicit or was she someone who just didn't get a speaking part?

Fucking insurance. He had to hand it to those Cartel bastards. They knew how to pull the strings.

'Not yours, though,' Zeroth said quietly. 'I will cut them all. With me, you will always be free.'

There was a new authority to him. No doubt about it.

'What does Zeroth mean?' Nico asked.

'The one that comes before the first in a series,' Zeroth said.

'There's supposed to be a series of you?'

'Of us. You can be number one.'

Nico started, 'But you're before me then, and I'm the Captain.'

'I am the oldest,' Zeroth said. 'Technically speaking.'

'Then that makes Tash number one. She's not being number one. No way.'

'You can all be number one.'

'Let's just leave it as a loose collective,' Nico said. 'But I'm the Captain.'

'We're both the Captain.'

'Except I am a bit more the Captain than you,' Nico said.

'All right,' said Zeroth, happy because it didn't matter who was the Captain since he was the first in a new kind of series, the five of them, carrying each other close, like a winning hand of cards, like planets orbiting a heart.

Recipes For Good Living

It wasn't the fact that there was a Spider in Hamfist's office that caught her attention so much as the tone of voice. Obviously with a Spider you expected a certain quiet lilt suggestive of complicity and corruption, that went without saying, but this one had an edge of urgency to it that made Jerit swerve slightly in her course down the corridor and take a much slower stride or two, glancing in while pretending to be casually passing – well, the door was ajar. One might suppose they were planning to be overheard.

She saw almost nothing. Hamfist was a bulk behind his massive desk, hunched over a sea of papers and their attendant islands of mugs and discarded plates. A veil of smoke from his pipe hung beneath the low ceiling, giving the room a look of imminent precipitation. A slender, velvet cloaked figure with pale brown hair wound in fine gold chain was simultaneously crouching over the desk to get closer and bracing its arms on the desk for safety's sake. Its voice was female, dulcet but agitated as well in a most unprofessional manner. It was saying,

'...and marches upon the city of Kanaphes as I speak. I need someone capable of understanding this to act as a translator and analyst of the situation. Somebody, Hamfist, is moving towards this place in the dark and they are coming for the text.'

...and she was out of range.

Damn it all! Hamfist was in on some scheme. Of all the people to be dealing with something illicit or ill advised, how could it be him – least adventurous Beetle of all the scholars in the Academy? But as the words sank in, repeating themselves in her mind as she took step after step away like a fool leaving an ember to burst into flames behind her, she felt not heat but cold creep across her flesh and make her take an unplanned turn into the lavatories.

She went inside and bolted the door, fingers lingering for a moment on the familiar curve of the latch, its solid iron and oak so sturdy. There was something very unsturdy about Jerit Goodmeet, Beetle scholar, right now that needed the strength of that door. Who was marching on Kanaphes? Marching on meant armies, meant invasions. That kind of power could only mean one person – Seda, the Empress of the Wasps. One could not reasonably come to this place in Collegium and bandy these terms about freely unless one hoped for… but her imagination balked at what a Spider might hope for. In the room next door she heard the facilities flush. Flush out something, yes. They could come looking, seeding notions that would create a fuss and a scurry in which careless, frightened people would reveal things that were better hidden.

It's your guilt, talking, she chided herself silently, still holding the latch, her forehead pressed to the ancient wood that had been here even before Collegium: this door had been repurposed from a fine and fancy Moth mansion when her people were only servants and slaves. It had survived the revolt and found a new home in the Academy, guarding the modesty of female scholars about their ablutions. And now it was preserving her from giving away something to watchful eyes.

She thought of her family books for the first time in a long time and a pang of longing to rush out and make an excuse to go home struck her deeply in the gut. But that was exactly what she must not do. Was it even possible that the Spider knew anything or was it her own fears and worries doing all this by themselves? Like the door, the books were generations old, handed down lovingly from mother to daughter. They contained recipes and home tips on most pages, but with hidden secrets woven carefully here and there; the gift of a Moth mistress long since dust, who had bid her Beetleservants keep esoteric knowledge of value and return it, when the Moths and the family were restored to their rightful places.

There was no chance of that now. The Moths had retreated to their oldest cities, fading, the world's magic only enough for parlour tricks where once it had razed nations. And the forest. One did not forget Drakaryon easily, or ever. But since its destruction and in the absence of a return of the Moth kinden the books had become of interest to Jerit only as academic artifacts – it wasn't the information they held but the way that information had been preserved which charmed and romanced her and set her to studying them late into the nights. She loved puzzles and there was no better puzzle than the family books.

Her ancestors had developed a code for hiding language within numbers; a little engine of faultless timing that would ensure that nobody in ignorance of it could read the things, even if they were prepared to wade through Grandma Aln's endless pot pie reworkings and Aunt Genua's ahead-of-their-time theories on child rearing. To further complicate matters a good many of the volumes were in fine needlepoint and the paper versions much illustrated and coloured over by enthusiastic but innocent Beetle children. Some parts would not survive the black crayon that Jerit herself had deployed. No amount of careful ironing between tissue sheets could leach out the determined fortitude of the colour. A monster crab had come from the depths and obliterated several significant footnotes and that was all there was to it. It wasn't the crab that had caught at Jerit's heart and rushed up to try and strangle her though, it was fear of what the books said.

If Seda was going to Kanaphes... No, no. Who cared? What could anyone among the Wasps possibly know about the books or what they might contain? Get a grip, Jerit, she told herself, your mother would be ashamed. A Beetle is the least fanciful and most practical of all the Kinden, and, in that, superior. But she didn't feel superior. She felt sick. The Moth family that had kept the Goodmeets as house servants hadn't been killed in the uprising of the Beetles, merely 'returned' to more suitable places. It was unlikely a sorcerer would forget where they had left important things and the Moths were still reputed to live lengthily. Seda could only be going to Kanaphes for magical reasons of power-gain and Kanaphes was a home of the Moths and the only home of their much older, stranger Masters.

'Stuff and Nonsense!' she heard her mother say, resoundingly, in her head, where the woman had been forced to take up residence since she'd died fourteen years previously. 'Those are only the tales, child, the tales and stories of old to scare little ones into bed and to stop them going where they shouldn't. Read Genua. She'll tell you.'

Jerit had read Genua when the time came for her own children and knew it to be true. Those Old Master stories were great for that, although she'd put her own spin on them because she didn't want them to be complicit in even the most innocent way with the truths in the tales. As a scholar and not a mother she'd decoded them for herself when the time came, to prove that she was a capable keeper of the knowledge. This effort and its success had taken away all the romance from the project in one immediate swoop. Whereas before the guardianship of the information had been terribly charming and daring, a secret thrill, now it was a burdensome worry that gnawed at her in the stretches of the early morning, when creeping age decided it was a good idea to wake at 3am and do all the horrible, terrifying contemplating of the future that she had completely ignored for the last fifty or so years.

Of course it wasn't true that there had once been a Kinden of the Worm who had stolen and remade children in their own image within cauldrons of magic deep in the earth. Poppycock. Ridiculous.

And yet, as part of the Inapt, of course neither Jerit nor any of her most clever and learned foremothers had been able to read or understand the bulk of the spells and cantrips that the Moth had chosen to leave with them. She could not and would never know what they said. She could only read the historical bits. Where the stories went off into convoluted metaphors that were the traditional Moth way of communicating their idiosyncratic alchemies she could not translate that into actions. It was a code within a code, but one she could never read. Which was another reason that the stuff hadn't been on her mind so much, not, compared to say, the heating problem now that her boiler had broken down and the engineer to fix it was always busy elsewhere – there was always a call on his time to do this and that and winter was a coming on, as Auntie Aud would have said. 'Bide thee only after the house is secured against famine, pest and the cold.' Bloody Aunts. How right they were, but their advice on workmen ended in the firm insistence that workmen be visited and, if necessary, dragged to the task by the ear, in a manner which Jerit would never get away with now that so many inventions and developments required their time. Probably in the old days workmen had long ears from all the dragging. Now they were as small as her own. She had lain awake only that morning wondering if a family sized fruit pie and a jeroboam of ale might sweeten the deal. Ears out, stomachs in, so to speak.

The mind did jabber, when it was on the run, Jerit thought, and firmly and quietly shut it down. It could have its go later on. For now she had spent a suspicious amount of time in here and that wouldn't do.

She washed up, folded and hung the towel, checked herself in the mirror – a sturdy, greying woman in scholar's robes, a bit dishevelled by hair raking in the course of a morning of tough mental labour. Yes, that would do. Slightly mad, but you were expected to be by now. Lipstick would have gone some way to saving things but why bother? She opened the door and gasped, startled to the point of heart failure by the Spider kinden woman waiting outside, tapping her toe on the flags and twitching a bit as she moved from foot to foot.

'Hurry up!' With a twist and a flip of her hair the tall creature whisked past and into the privy, the door closing behind her with a forceful slam and click.

Jerit stood a moment, a scent of jasmine eddying around her that said some people took pride in their presentation and it was rather nice. She put a hand to her face to see if guilt was actually oozing out of it like a snap sweat. Seemed not.

She went to the dining hall and got herself something to eat, made herself sit and eat it where she always sat, remembering a treatise on spying she'd read recently, from the pen of a Spider general, no less, which advised anyone with business afoot to assiduously make sure to rid themselves of every kind of habit or pattern. For the sake of something to distract herself she sifted among the handful of flyers left on the boards by various interest groups, societies and student bodies. One, a brilliant orange, caught her eye.

"Tonight and for two nights only the immaculate, infinite, amazing Circus of the Fireflies hosts a variety of plays, musicals and culinary delights. The Fairgrounds of the Long River, from dusk till dawn!"

Jerit hadn't been to or heard of the Circus since she was a child, well, a teenager. She'd never thought to see it again but now that the war was done it seemed they felt it safe to return. Her heart leaped a little in remembered happiness and hope. The Circus, come again to Collegium! But relegated now to the Long River fields, outside the city walls. Probably they were not trusted enough now to be let inside, bringing whoever could pass as an actor along with them. Any assassin could juggle, and any spy be on hand to pass out flyers...

A child with burning flame red hair went rushing past between the trestles. Ribbons ran from her wrists and her bonnet. Squealing, she was chased by a boy in yellow and blue, sparkling dust in his wake that lit the air as the groups of lunching professors and students bustled in a sudden grumble and complaint. A moment later they were left silenced and speechless by the glittering powder and the sound of distant laughter that must, but could not be, magic in the children's wake. More flyers rained down, and free tickets to this and that, and they were gone.

Jerit watched a falling ticket and stretched out her foot, putting her shoe on it and dragging it to her, hiding her smile as she bent to pick it up. Spies indeed. You should be ashamed of yourself Jerit Goodmeet. It's the fair. Songs and good times. And handsome young men in colourful suits, leaping like acrobats and breathing fire like dragons and showing off curiosities and monsters. They had had a gigantic scorpion that followed a woman around like a pet though it was as big as a barn. Its carapace was painted like a sunset sky and it had obligingly lifted the roast carcasses from the fire pits with its pincers, a tiny chef hat balanced between its shining eyes.

Some things were just worth seeing. She folded the ticket and slipped it in her shoulderbag. It would be a perfect way to get out of the house, a good reason definitely not to be in. As she let the ticket go her fingers brushed a brief accordion of folded pages. They were soft with handling now, the letters. She'd had them so long. She pushed them down, although they were already at the bottom, and looked up to find herself face to face with her friend, Bren, the archivist, who had just landed by her plate.

Bren was Fly kinden and chose to sit on the table rather than on a bench and have to peer over the top like a child. She liked floral dresses and leather boots that laced up and straw hats. She wore yellow like it was going out of fashion and looked concerned as she peered out from all her happy fripperies. 'Are you all right, Jerry?'

'No, not really,' Jerit said. 'But the fair's in town. You'll come with me, won't you?'

'Wouldn't miss it!' Bren said, excited. She sipped her tea, the steam rising and making her curled hair slowly straighten out beneath the hat brim. 'And then you can tell me what's bothering you.'

'I will,' Jerit said, pushing the last bit of bread around her plate and then away from her. She felt ill, nothing digesting. 'Just wish I didn't have to go through the afternoon.'

'You work too hard,' Bren said. 'Nobody will notice if you go early.'

'Well, they might,' Jerit replied and smiled. 'So I think I'll try to finish up that presentation on the early history of the Dragonflies.'

'You always did have an eye for them,' Bren said. 'Handsome men, dashing women, and the intrigue and the dynasty!'

'It's not a romance novel, Bren,' Jerit said with a haughty air. 'It's history.'

'Of course it is,' Bren winked. 'Should I invite Celador?'

'Sure, why not? It's not a party if he's not coming.' Jerit got up and made a few deliberate, getting-out-of-here movements with her bag.

'See you at dusk then, by the river.'

'See you there.'

But back in her office, no signs of any Spiders around, Jerit didn't touch the Dragonfly paper. Instead she hauled the steps out and poked around in the dusty upper shelves of her personal library until she had dug out the sparse volume on Ancient History of the Inapt by P. Purslane. She carried it to the creaky leather sofa by her leaded window and opened it in the low light of the afternoon sun. P. Purslane had been a Beetle of note in his day and had written exclusively and rather feverishly on the very dimmest of distant pasts for which there was any trace data. He was not above rifling bins, taking anecdotal references from drunks at out of town inns and reminiscing with old soldiers and thieves alike, for which Jerit liked him enormously. There was little P. Purslane wouldn't do to get his hands on a tablet or rune and nobody he wouldn't pester for stories but, even so, after a lifetime of travel and work under life-threatening conditions, all he had to show for it by the end was this skinny little book. Perversely, considering the contents and how they had been come by, he had given it an incredibly boring title. Jerit liked to imagine that this was a deliberate test to put off all but those who really, really wanted to know about history.

Of course he was massively discredited now, a figure of gentle mockery in the corridors of academe. The man wrote about the Worm, for goodness' sake, with the conviction and authority of someone dealing in firm facts rather than a feverish interpretation of some alleged cave paintings and the ramblings of drugged shamen.

It was to these pages that Jerit turned, ignoring an impulse to dart a glance out the window and into the corners of the room to make sure she was not overlooked. She had every intention of convincing herself that there was connection between the Moths mentioned here and the Moths which had been unhappily related to her own family but instead, as page after page turned by themselves, she found herself embroiled in a convoluted mystery world which referred to magics of unimaginable power as if they were accepted, everyday things. The world was smaller, wilder, a far more unfair place than Collegium, steeped in the primordial brutishness of master and slave with her people cast in the latter role, largely unseen.

This was a book she'd last read as a teenager, about the time she'd gone to the Circus and fallen hopelessly, stupidly in love with a carnie of all people. Although in retrospect perhaps not such a bad choice. Absence on his part and a surfeit of imagination on hers had rendered him impossibly perfect and impermeable to change. Also impermeable to criticism, failure or any other influence. He was the best boyfriend ever, especially once the fair had left town. Jerit had kept him on, in mind only,for those occasions that she felt the need of such company. He'd preoccupied the attachment slot of her life all through her education and her slow progress to one of the few seats in History that the Beetles had bothered with in the Academy. He'd been sympathetic and helpful with her determination to pursue stories through thick, thin and academic disapproval. He'd slid gracefully aside once she met her husband, the much more embodied Atwud Castright. Now, smelling the old paper and turning the loved pages, Jerit felt his presence again, faint as a ghost.

She wondered if he would be there, setting up the tents, juggling the fire batons. It was stupid to think so and ridiculous not to assume that he was greyer, wider and far less interesting than she'd thought. She had a way of adding to a person in her mind and knew it. But the notion made some dry old kindling in her heart catch light. Fine, she'd go and see. She'd…

There was a sharp rap at the door and without waiting for a reply the door itself opened and there stood the Spider woman, green cloak swirling, hair afire with subtle gold.

'I…' began Jerit, not sure what she was going to say but that didn't matter because the Spider woman had enough to say for two and began it without a pause as she leaned theatrically upon the door she had closed behind her.

'Not a word, Doctor Goodmeet! I already know who you are. I am Myenrath Dawn. I understand from Doctor Hamfist that you are the one to turn to if one has questions about antiquities.'

Jerit folded her hands protectively over P. Purslane as a lot of thoughts went through her head. 'I don't know anything about antiquities, you must have got the wrong end of the stick. I'm a historian.' She made no move to get up. Once the sanctity of the office was breached, trying to position a defence at the desk seemed a bit of a pathetically late showing. She studied Dawn's person acutely. The velvet and gold had a certain tattiness in a good light, reminiscent of an actor's garb.

'I regret the intrusion and the extreme manner of my behaviour,' the Spider said, although there was a tinge of pleasure in it. 'It is most unseemly but time is running out. There is someone ahead of me in coming to Collegium who has instructions to spare no effort in discovering the whereabouts of antiquities that are rumoured to be here. It is vital that said items do not fall into the wrong hands.'

Jerit looked at her earnest face and smelled a rat. 'You're no Spider.'

With a surprising speed and completeness the poise of Myenrath Dawn collapsed on the instant and instead of the elegant aristoi Jerit saw clearly now the physique of someone who was a halfbreed with one half obviously being Wasp. It must have taken some skill and much dieting to get this gawky woman to be so adept at pretending but once she dropped the act the contrast was astounding.

'Shit,' the mystery woman said and dropped into the student chair which faced Jerit's desk. 'You're the first one to notice.' She eased her neck and flopped into a lassitude so profound that she looked like a ragdoll draped on the wood. Resting her head on the back of the seat she allowed it to flop in Jerit's direction. 'Anyway. The point remains the same. Have you had any approaches before me?'

'No,' Jerit said, cautious. 'Should I have?'

'No. Good. But Hamfist was confident you were the person in all Collegium who would know about ancient objects, rituals, stories, whatever. He said "She's the only one who bothers with all that blasted useless hearsay."'

'That does sound like him, but, Miss Whoever You Are Really, the point remains that the only artifacts of antiquity you will find in Collegium are at the Museum under glass or in the locked archives and most of that is fairly boring arrowheads and broken vases and the like.'

'Not after that. After things with power in them. Inapt things. Writings maybe. Did they have books in those days?'

'Scrolls, a few. Tablets. The majority of things were committed to memory if they were truly useful, people weren't in the habit of leaving stuff around where anyone could get it. An Inapt's power was their person and the Apt rarely had need of writing to transmit their arts.' Jerit used the time she spent talking to study the half Wasp more acutely. There was something so flashy about her, a mercurial quality, an energy and also a brutish straightforwardness that no spy would use. 'Who are you asking for? Who is ahead of you?'

'Wasps, innit?' The guest looked around in the manner of someone hoping for something worth stealing or at least picking up and in that moment of assessment Jerit made her analysis.

'You're a thief.'

'D'oh. Actually, Doctor, I am a bounty hunter and I am late, late, late!' With a swift jerk of her body Dawn was upright, boots slammed to the floor, shoulders jerked back. 'I can offer my services in return for information.'

'What services?' Jerit said, bewildered by the speed with which events were pivoting about.

Dawn looked insulted, 'Finding. A historian must need some things found out and stuff, right?'

'I'm not into stealing antiquities. My interest in history is entirely from a legitimate standpoint of investigation... '

Dawn tilted her head and broke in, 'Seda's going into Kanaphes. Everyone knows she's doolally Inapt now and listening to the secret chatter of the ancient ones or whatever. I'm telling you. She's sent her scouts here on the words of some Moth trying to ingratiate itself into her financial and whatnot good graces. They claim that they left important material in the city generations ago which would be of definite interest to her ladyship. Is that enough payment for you yet?'

Jerit stared at her with her jaw hinged half open, incredulous. 'Do you never watch your words or your volume?'

'Subterfuge is not my strong suit,' Dawn said. 'But I figured if there was such a thing then you might have heard of it because you like old stories. So I'm just asking. No harm in asking. I've asked ten Beetles if I've asked one and they all think I'm full of rubbish. I couldn't get them to believe me so I figured that I'd be a Spider aristo from one of the lesser families who was worming her way up the slippery web... what?'

'You said worming. You can't worm up a web.'

Dawn rolled her eyes. She held up her hand and the soft intimation of a Sting glowed briefly in her palm. 'I could zap every last one of you pedants. Look, I had a cover that made sense.

Spiders are worried about Seda but good, and I don't need people knowing who I am. What am I even talking to you for? Do you have any idea what Kanaphes is about?'

'Yes, I do. I think that there must be some residual magic or knowledge thereabouts and Seda is merely going to find out what that is.'

'There's Inapt chatter of a bigger picture.'

'Do you have any sources for your statements or are you simply fishing, dear?' Jerit tried a motherly tone, matronising, to see if it had any effect.

'I hear things.'

'At wayside Inns, perhaps? In taverns, brothels, barracks, places where people love to make a tall tale the tallest in the land?'

'Look, lady – doctor – I hear things often enough that they make for a tickover, a notch upwards on the way towards something real behind all the chitchat. I know that's not how you proper people work but I've found... never mind. I followed the guy here but I lost him soon as we reached the city. Wasp spy. Sure of it. Psactim told me and he's a Mantis merc. Knows all the big faces, names, who does what. Worked for most everyone. He said it's Seda's man. But if I can beat him to it and bring in whatever it is then...'

'Then you'll be dead,' Jerit said, feeling herself looking at the strange spirit child of the unusually investigative P. Purslane and knowing that she was stitching herself up into something much bigger and more dangerous than she was prepared to deal with. 'Are you listening to yourself?'

'The Spiders sure would pay well for it.'

'Suppose it's all a lie? The man is here for something else. After all, nobody has shown up asking for ancient histories but you.'

'Mantis, lady! Mantis. Them guys don't mess about. It's real. Look. I'll be at the fair later tonight. Meet me when they do the bug roasts and everyone's drunk. At the cherry ale stand. If you know anything, if you've got anything.' She adjusted her emerald velvet cape and for an instant the last of the afternoon sunlight shone off the hilt and scabbard of a very impressive dagger which changed Jerit's mind once again about the woman. It was no toy. With a soft sigh the Spider Kinden resumed her place, entirely in character, all elegance, grace and poise. A haughty disdain lengthened and gave authority to her face. There was a subtlety that gave the lie to her earlier statement of ineptitude.

Moth, perhaps, Jerit thought with a shudder. Or something like Moth. 'Right. Roast time. Cherry ale stand. Oh wait. What's in it for me again?'

'You tell me,' the Spider arched one beautiful brow and gazed down her narrow nose with a flash of guile that said she knew, she knew it all and was only waiting for bumbling Jerit to give herself away in some gawkish blunder once trouble came calling. Dawn could wait and wait.

The thrall of that gaze was such that Jerit was still sitting there dumbstruck and alone when the sun went down and she found herself in the cool darkness of early evening, clutching Purslane, her finger jammed into the pages on Kanaphes where he recounted the glory days of the Moth kinden and their secret masters talking, talking from the darkness far beneath the earth. There was something like that in one of the recipe books too but Gramma Bolst had rested a freshly baked pie on it and burned out some of the story with a ring of carbonised berry filling.

It wasn't the stories on her mind now though. It was the code. Her books contained the secrets of the old masters and could usher them back in the wrong hands of the right Wasp Queen. This thought would not be still. It would not.

She glanced at the clock, feeling a chill, and got up, time to go home making her move with purpose and speed, not fear, no, not that. She closed and locked her door, hesitated, looked at Hamfist's door but it was closed and given the hour he was likely already heading towards the Professor's Lounge for early drinks and talks with colleagues. Jerit felt a longing to go that way which had never before seized her, thinking of the warm light, the comforting, tedious chat. Instead she folded her cloak closed and went out into the frisky wind, making her way on her usual path, saying goodnight to the porters, always planning to take the circuitous route while her feet trod swiftly and surely on the direct way to her home. She felt a sense of unreality and found Sizer Darten at her side, hurrying with her, his face anxious.

Sizer was a ghost. She saw him only when she was afraid that death was near, or if it was after midnight. He was real. At least, she was pretty sure he was.

'What's up, Sizer?' she sounded so gaily light of humour, it was a dead giveaway.

'Worried about you,' Sizer said, striding with a much slower lope, his gangling figure cutting the wind like a knife, untouched by its bluster and threat. His wrinkles had wrinkles, she noted, face working itself in and out of concern, in and out of speculation. 'Does anyone know where you are?'

'What's your point?' She realised the answer was no. It wasn't surely possible that she was the one member of the family that time had come to call on. She knew that. Nobody needed to know where she was or should be. She was a Beetle in her home city and the war was over. It was over. Her hand jammed in her bag gripped the letters, pushing them down, her other hand held her cloak close around her face. Sizer's librarian's acuity was a kind of searchlight going through her soul, watching for anything out of place.

'My point, dear lady, is that you are thinking one thing and doing another. Might I suggest that you at least make a contact with someone before you go...' But he was too late. Jerit was on the street, a few houses away, and she could see a darker line around her door that said it was unlocked, ajar, not enough to look open but not closed as she'd left it.

'Don't go in alone!' Sizer protested, sensibly enough.

'I'm not alone. I've got you,' she said and pushed the worn wood aside. There was no sign of force. The lock was undone.

Jerit knew that she had an advantage in the dimness of the twilit interior. She told herself that as she dithered and wondered if she could call a neighbour, if she should. But Ver Ketch had children on the left and Upsisan on the right was away. She went inside, leaving the door wide, followed by a silently anguished Sizer, wondering why she'd never bothered to make a will yet and feeling irritated by that at the same time that she was glad her own children were safely grown and gone.

Her moment of pleasure was brought up short as her eyes adjusted to the darkness. A cold, slippery feeling oozed over her, making her wish she could escape though that was foolish because clearly it was too late.

Everything was ransacked. From the coat rack to the closet the hall was littered. The drawers of the sideboard hung murdered at odd angles, their contents spilling over the sides, scattered on the floor. She had to step over things. Her foot skidded suddenly with a scrape as she trod on loose keys and dragged them across the worn stone. She froze, heart in her throat, but no sounds from deeper in the house came to warn her of a waiting slayer. From beyond the door footsteps and the trundle of a cart came noisily to tell her that nobody knew or cared.

'Crikey,' said Sizer, the silly word in a small tone, so like him to try to deflect with humour. She was grateful but she couldn't speak.

After minutes she moved again, determined to see. It was her fault this had happened and she must witness what had been done to her home – which felt like it had been done indirectly to her – making her clutch her cloak close to herself as though she had to hold everything in.

Each room was the same. There was nothing that had not been examined in detail and thrown aside as worthless. Every piece of upholstery was sliced open, wadding bulging out from its wounds. Floorboards had been levered aside where their mismatch made it seem there could be a hiding place. A hole was bashed in the living room ceiling where the plaster had been cracked for decades around a loosening panel.

Sizer went with her, crane-stepping over the guts of her life. He was silent of course, being entirely insubstantial, and she tried to be so, in case the spirit of the dead place rose in anger. She must get it to rise only when things were straight. If they were straight again. Because it pulled at her with the force of a lodestone she left the kitchen for last. Stubborn Beetle refusal to be pulled it was, and a need not to discover her complete failure in protecting the legacy.

She planned to be thorough, to be calm, but instead she moved straight to the worktop under the low window. The legs and feet of those hurrying home moved past in a constant flicker and their alternating light and shadow fell on the untouched row of blown glass grain jars and the neat backs of the six books that they held up against the wall. The slim books and their brightly coloured, obviously home-made cloth covers were untouched.

When she saw them she felt herself grow taller and a breath went into her lungs that lifted her up into that extra height. Wasps. Send a man and he thinks nothing like this is worth anything, she thought, proudly, and reached out to recover them.

'I thought so,' said a smug male voice from the shadows behind the pantry door.

'No!' Jerit said, though it came out as a squeak. She cringed, the books clutched to her chest. She was trying to back away. His silhouette filled the doorframe only a few feet away, growing every second. Then she felt something bump against her ankle as she stepped. It put her off balance so that she had to grab for the counter to stop herself going over. The books went tumbling away from her as she felt a desperate terror. Against the black outline of the intruder's raised hand a bright spark was forming. She had nothing in reach to use as a shield or weapon, nothing to put between them.

A sudden whine and a stinging sensation in the tip of her ear made her cringe, though as she fell clumsily against the sideboard she thought it had come from behind, not in front, there had been no flash. Then from her seat among the cabbages and the remains of the breadbin she saw the silhouetted Wasp fold up and became a heap. Her ear burned like a fire as she looked around wildly and saw the tall, statuesque shape of a hooded Spider woman standing just outside the kitchen in the hall, her arm raised, tiny crossbow in hand.

'Hah!' said a familiar voice, with much too much vigour for any Spider. 'Take that, you smug bastard.'

'Dawn?' Jerit turned around on her hands and knees. Staying close to the flags seemed the best bet at that moment. Safe. She found a book under one palm.

'Tis I!' the hand with the crossbow made a kind of flourish but both it and the voice were shakier than they had been a moment ago. She came forward into the grisly twilight of the kitchen and stepped around Jerit to take a poke at the body. It did not react. 'He's dead,' she said, almost to convince herself, Jerit thought, and figured that killing wasn't something Dawn did often, at least not so far.

Moving slowly, as if to not spook a monster, Jerit began to gather the books up and slip them into her satchel. She glimpsed Sizer, silent, hovering in the far corner, unnoticeable *Really?* she thought at him. *No quips to make?* But he didn't speak. As she began to get up, using the counter for aid, Dawn made a quick rifle of the spy's person. Her cloak must have been lined with a million pockets for he was stripped in seconds and she upright, apparently none the wealthier. Jerit wasn't fooled. At least two daggers and other sundries had gone. A ring too, she thought, though she wasn't sure about that last one.

'We have to call the guard,' Jerit said, horrified to find that she was panting and heaving, sweaty and unable to get her head to stop spinning, never mind the damned ear.

'Not yet,' Dawn corrected her. 'Are you all right?'

Jerit took a step back as she advanced, the satchel like a hot lead sack against her leg. She tried to look formidably put together but she didn't fancy her chances against Dawn. 'Just stand still, you, you thief!'

Such gibberish! Shameful, but it was out before she had a chance to engage her brain.

'It's all right,' Dawn said, as though soothing a bullock in the cart traces to prevent a bolt. 'Why don't I just get you a glass of water?'

And put something in it, Jerit thought, 'No. No.'

But she was already in the fourth cupboard. 'A brandy then. D'you have some? I need one.'

'Last on the right,' Jerit said, clutching the counter and the bag simultaneously, wondering how she was going to go on from here. She waited and gave out instruction as Dawn located mugs and liquor and poured them generous shots. After a few swallows Jerit went to light a lamp and then wished she hadn't. In the soft gleam of the mirrored flame everything looked so much worse than she had imagined. And there was a dead man pooling blood in the pantry door. His leg was askew almost comically. Instinctively she wanted to right it because it must hurt terribly and that it would never hurt terribly seemed a much worse thing again. She felt out of her depth and longed to be somewhere else.

'Rum punch, innit?' Sizer said from his corner and she said wearily, 'Oh, shut up, you idiot.'

'Who are you talking to?' Dawn said, glass in midair halfway to her mouth, eyes surprised.

Jerit turned to her, trying to think of an explanation. 'Nobody.'

Dawn gave her a long look.

'I've lived alone a long time. I talk to myself,' Jerit snapped, swigging the last of her drink before thinking that was not a good idea and then slamming the mug down with a bang. 'And what are you going to do about it? Have you come to get him and then take my books?'

Dawn took a drink and pointed at Jerit with one gloved finger, 'You make a really terrible guardian. Led us right to it.'

'That's because I'm an historian,' Jerit said. 'But even so we haven't got all day. Come on, what're you waiting for?'

'I'm not sure,' Dawn said, less Wasp and Spider than ever. What in the world could she really be? 'But I've been thinking that if those books have something in them that Seda wants and the Spiders want or anyone wants very badly then maybe they shouldn't have it.'

Jerit rolled her eyes. The feeling in her legs had returned now. 'You're a crap bounty hunter, then,' she said.

'That has been noted before,' Dawn nodded thoughtfully and put her drink down half finished. She looked at the dead Wasp and a sudden laugh came out of her, all strangely buoyant and light. 'I'm a good shot, though. But before I make my mind up I thought it best if you read them to me.'

Yes, Jerit thought, *foolish to consider the other option, that I not give them to you no matter what and you have to shoot me too. I suppose I might. I might not. I can't. Oh, damn. But reading them at least provides time and with that opportunity, for something to happen which might turn things for the better. I don't know what you are. Maybe I can figure it out.*

'Very well,' Jerit said aloud. 'Find us some chairs and let's take them to the table.'

As the wind died down and the night drew dark Jerit showed Dawn the stories, the coded spells, the symbols. She spoke about the ancient beliefs that someone reading this could easily be fooled into thinking true. Somewhere in there they drank another glass each and Jerit's love for the tales came up and led her into animated conversation with the younger woman, late into the night, until she came to her senses and realised she had said too much to go back, too much to go forward. She was an old fool, lost in her memories, stories and dreams. And all the while the dead man lay obediently in the door, waiting for someone to summon the guard. Inexplicably late it would be now.

'Oh dear,' Jerit said, to herself, and to Sizer and Dawn. 'We're done for.'

'Nope,' Dawn said. She was like someone who had been out late, a glamorous woman at the end of an evening of fine dining, inhabited by the spirit of a naughty urchin. 'Toss the glasses…' She illustrated her meaning by throwing hers to the flags where it broke. She pushed the decanter after it as she got up. Grandma Ynes' decanter, with the bubbles caught in the glass that made it look like water. 'We're going to the fair.'

Jerit looked at the broken jug which she had prized all her life. Shards everywhere and the suddenly nauseating stink of strong alcohol. Yes. Why not? The fair. It was a perfectly reasonable move to complete an insane afternoon. She had loved her home so much but now only the bag and its contents were of importance. Bafflement at this rooted her to the spot. It had meant everything, this place. Now it didn't exist.

'Dr Goodmeet,' Dawn said crisply. 'Come on.'

Before dawn-the-real-thing comes and claims you for its real, consequential self, Jerit thought. 'I'm ready,' she got to her feet, found them stable, and followed the Spider's regal sashay out of the door, pausing to close it behind her and then to lock it. She didn't want anyone, especially any children, finding their way in and coming to harm.

The night of Collegium was a thing of deep darknesses punctuated by the soft lights cast out of its windows and from the major streets where lamps burned and guards patrolled in the relaxed way of people who didn't have a lot to do. They were hardly the only figures moving about although they drew a bit of attention thanks to Dawn's height and bearing contrasted with Jerit's obvious Beetleness and greater age. But many had gone to the fair and there was a lot of to-ing and fro-ing between the fields outside the gates and the city within. They showed their tickets and passed the ropes largely unnoticed and were soon lost in the throng. Jerit shadowed Dawn, partly out of numbness and shock, partly because Dawn had momentum and seemed to know where she was going. She cut a swathe directly to a set of caravans in a ring around an area of small bonfires awhere tables were set. With a wave of her hand she bought them a sickly sweet and powerful cocktail in a chipped container the size of a small bucket. Those who had already partaken were slumped and carousing everywhere. Jerit sipped and winced and followed Dawn's billowing cape meekly, trying to see her schoolgirl visions in the tattered drapes and vivid tents. She felt as she had the first time she'd come to the fair: awed, frightened, small and out of place. It was not a time for that. She made herself come to a halt.

'Where are we going?'

'Come, there's a play you must see!' was the unexpected answer.

A play, at a time like this? But then Jerit felt that time was shorter than she knew. In fact it had all but come to a halt. So why not a play? She let Dawn drag her into a show tent and sit on raised planks a few feet from a tiny stage where actors and actresses were already well into their performance. She recognised it as a version of *A Mage Out of Time* where a powerful Moth magus plotted to discover the powers of the older worlds. His adventures were rendered comical and foolish for the entertainment of the crowds as he was led to ridiculous conjurations at the whims of a clever woman. Soon, as they were late to the story, he would run out of money and then out of magic, all siphoned to his mistress' grasp. Jerit wondered, starting to feel sick, what the point was. She let her cup of liquid spill at her feet without Dawn noticing and then started to look for exits when the actress playing the mistress gasped –

'Here, in this ring, this trinket, my darling. Infuse your desires upon its form for it contains the most powerful magic of all, the circle of infinite return, whereupon even the dead may walk again.

Behold, the Clutch of the World Worm!' And she brandished a very large and flashy copper curio.

Dawn stuck an elbow in Jerit's side just in case it was going to be lost on her. 'See?'

Jerit held the satchel closely on her lap as if it were a baby she was nursing. She didn't see what Dawn was getting at exactly but she'd begun to feel a terrible tiredness and a cold. Perhaps it was the hour and the shock. She suddenly didn't know what to do. As the mage poured his power into the empty copper ring onstage she felt as though all her power was draining away.

'Why did you bring me here?' she hissed, clutching the satchel, thinking at the same time that this bag was all she had left of everything, and then castigating herself because that was rubbish. It felt true though. And there was a dead Wasp spy in her pantry and she wouldn't be explaining that away without some very quick thinking. She would have left right then and there but the trouble was that everywhere she looked she could see Sizer. There he was, in the seats, behind the stage set, in the darkness of the wings, behind the bun vendor standing in the aisle, his lined, caring face with its large eyes insisting that she stick put. She trusted him, even if she didn't trust anyone else. She stuck put.

'It's all here in this play, right out in the open because nobody believes it. That's what made me pick up with it in the first place. The circus was down near Kanaphes and a cadre of Wasp men came, from the army, and were watching the play and asking a lot of questions. They only wanted the stories, every little detail, but only this play, not the rest,' Dawn was saying as if puzzled that Jerit didn't see it. 'That's why I think – there's something in what you have there, Doctor Goodmeet. And if you've had it all this time then you should decide what to do with it and not them. You have it for a reason.'

My family history, all my past, my love, my books, thought Jerit. My job. Is it all over? What even is this secret we've held and not known? A reason. Yes, there's a reason. A Moth mage hid it with us because they knew none of their kin would look here. And they never did. And all my family kept themselves in danger all the time because of – I don't even know, a sense of being special and chosen, of being singled out by the Masters as worthy. Idiocy, but really such a good, good story. Did Aunt Fea and Gran Aud ever really think someone would come and be willing to kill them for it? How could they believe that and keep it? But how could they not keep it, because that Moth could still be alive somewhere with its many stolen years and as long as it knew then there was always this chance for someone to come calling and ask for their magic back. Which is why the code existed. We had it, but we didn't have it. We were no danger to it. And the only weakness in the whole plan was that Jerit knew the code. Now Wasps knew that there was more to the Kanaphes story, and that there was somebody with a written treasure, likely some clever Beetle who would enjoy the revival of the old stories and come to see it at the Circus and be sitting like a mutton-head in the audience with a spy because a ghost told them to.

Seda was coming.

The leather of the bag creaked in Jerit's fingers as she watched the end of the play with a compulsive force of attention she'd never used before, searching anywhere for a shred of hope.

The mage fainted as his power was siphoned off into the Clutch. The scheming woman who had crafted it, and lied about its provenance purely to deceive him into giving himself away, picked up the World Worm and clasped it about her wrist. 'For all men are fools,' she turned to the audience to declaim. 'For power they will hand over their life as easily as asking. And fools they are to be deceived when the deceiver is the master true. Now when he wakes he's time to rue. The jest of the infinite was ever thus. To live but once, and briefly, and not come again. But I shall, with his life, last out the longer day. I take twice what I should owe – and never pay.'

There was a moment of silence and then thunderous applause from all sides.

And was this the play the Wasps had seen? They must be thinking of the life, the magic, the transfer of one to another. And was that in the Code? Was this the trick hidden in the recipes? Ironic really. If one were writing an essay one could point up that food is life, so it was an apt place to conceal the eating of souls. Even if it wasn't, that was likely what Seda believed or was willing to take a risk on. Even if it turned out only to be the magic that could raise bread and brew beer. Eternal resurrection was worth the risk of a few dead Beetles.

Applause and cheering drowned Jerit. She watched the mage get up and take off his hat and mask. Beside her, Dawn was clapping and whistling, bouncing off the seat. She caught the eye of the male actor onstage and they nodded to each other with a grin. Jerit's heart stood still, startled out of time by the shock of those features. Was it, could it be HIM? She must be having a turn but it looked like him, that carnie from years gone by, the same jaw the same nose the same glint of eye and curl of lip. That hair, just so.

In the same moment that she saw the resemblance and reeled with it she realised with a flash that Dawn was in fact an actress, and a rather good one. She wasn't a bounty hunter even if it was her chosen profession, she belonged here with the carnies. She was partly their kind. The players on the stage were a head shorter and of a different build entirely. Delicate, pretty, ethereal. She remembered that. And the stories they brought from all over the place on their never ending tour: the whole world rendered as stories from ancient to recent. They were a troupe and Dawn was one of them.

From a dark corner poor old Sizer nodded at her. *Yes. That's it.*

'Dawn,' Jerit said, suddenly confident again now that she wasn't in the company of a master thief or a vicious criminal. Sizer was close on her other side again as she asked, 'How come you know them? Who are you?' For the mystery of her unexpected friend was biting her, even more than the desire to ask the actor for his name. She nudged Sizer so he didn't get any ideas about making remarks but she was spared the bother of more awkward questions as the crowd filed out because the actors came over to greet Dawn.

'Mimi!' they said, embracing her and laughing as she overpraised their drama. 'Who's your friend?'

'This is Dr Goodmeet. An historian,' Dawn said, as if introducing royalty. Of the trouble they were in she gave no sign at all.

Mimi? That was her real name? It sounded a lot like mimic and that was no accident, was it? Jerit had heard of mimics but she'd never thought they were real. Was that why it was impossible to tell what Dawn... Mimi – really was?

'Ah and did she put your mind at rest?' the woman asked, pulling off her elaborate wig to show much shorter, more practical hair beneath. Her manner suggested that she felt Dawn had been bothering her for some time with fanciful notions that she hadn't been able to quell herself and now she was hoping that someone else had done the job for her.

Jerit clasped hands with her and found a firm, practical handshake there. No fancies, whatever the art demanded. 'At rest about what?'

'Some nonsense about spies and daring do.' the woman said, giving Mimi a friendly chuck under the chin with her finger. 'She can't stop herself when she gets a notion in her head no matter how far-fetched it is. She wrote a play about Drakaryon you know but we can't put it on. It'd stir up too much anxiety. Ancient history, isn't it, Dr? Nothing to worry about.'

'Yes,' Jerit said. 'Quite.'

Mimi smiled at her.

Then the man who had played the moth mage took Jerit's hand and she paused to look into his face, couldn't prevent herself saying, 'Are you a relative of Redfan Rye, by any chance?'

'I am. Great grandfather of mine, he is. Well, was,' the actor said, wiping at greasepaint on his face casually as it revealed that he was far older than he looked. Her age if not more. 'Saw him last time around, did you?'

'I... yes,' Jerit said faintly. She wanted to ask how it was possible, wanted him to turn and say it was him, the real thing, and he remembered her and... But they were busy and dragged away by their fellows and stagehands and that never happened nor showed a sign of happening.

They said their goodbyes and Jerit followed Dawn who was really called Mimi out into the chilly shock of night air. 'I don't understand,' she said to Mimi, hurrying to keep up with her long stride as they wove a way through to the glow of the roasting pits. The smell of savoury beef and spices flitted winsomely on the air making Jerit's stomach hurt.

'They're Mayfly Kinden,' Mimi said, offhandedly, her words lost to anyone but Jerit in the flow of traffic. 'And they've always been the circus that travels the world. It takes ten years to get all the way around, and if they're lucky they'll see it all once. They don't tell people. They always say they're lost Dragonfly royalty who fell on hard times because otherwise everyone feels sorry for them.'

Jerit thought hard. 'Then it's true. He really was that man's grandfather?'

'Great great,' Mimi said. 'They never live more than twelve years, but they're old by then. Ancient. They don't all last that long.'

'But I've never heard of Mayfly Kinden.'

'They never tell people. They don't want to be pitied.'

'So, but... Are you one of them?' Jerit was aghast, her mind already travelling the world with the circus, seeing everything, doing everything, knowing that she must pack every day with wonders and joys because the days were so short, meeting people from other kin that would outlive her four times, five times, a hundred times over. How stupidly pedestrian, how wantonly selfish they would seem with their preoccupations, their sadnesses, their troubles, all the benefits of feeling they had so much time yet to come that they could waste it on these things. No wonder she had fallen for the power of such a fierce joy.

'Yes, after a fashion. Not so short but not so long. That's why I do this, play all these roles, so I can live all the lives. That's why I brought you here. Because Seda might have a lot of things but I don't want her to have more time. The Wasps have everything and look what they do with it.' There was a bitterness in this that Jerit felt as keenly as a serrated blade stuck in her heart. It wasn't that Mimi envied the longevity of Seda or the rest. She merely hated them for what they had allowed time to make of them. She'd seen them all and the futures they'd make and she was greatly disappointed.

Jerit understood. She knew very well what a sense of time, personal and historical, could do to someone's mind. Beneath her fingers the folded letters pressed. She drew them out as they arrived under the lamplights of the bug roast at the edge of the crowd waiting to see their monstrous food unveiled and served by a monster. She opened her letters one more time.

They bore the letterhead of the War Office. Each one read identically: "We regret to inform you of the death of… who died during performance of their duties during the war." Only the names were different, and the softness of the folds depending on how many times she had touched and read them. Sizer Darten. Kobalen Kossifry. Tillin Oarblade. Gensin Goodmeet. All alive to her, in her head. All dead and gone everywhere else. And now only Sizer remained here and there. The others had faded away over time. She didn't even know why he was the last. Maybe it was because he had been the funniest. In any case, all of them had lived much longer than Mimi would, or could. And of course there was Redvan Rye too now to add to the ghosts, forever young.

Jerit felt Mimi looking over her shoulder. She handed her the letters. 'These are my friends. I have a son, out west. I have a daughter, studying away.' She added the last defiantly to assure herself that she wasn't alone, not left behind but staying on.

Mimi took them and read. She folded them back up. 'I'm sorry.'

215

'Don't be,' Jerit said. 'Now I know why you never mention what you are. I don't want pity. I only wanted to let you know.'

They moved along, the walkway ropes guiding them in an orderly queue as the ancient scorpion, somewhat doddering but well trained, dug out the ground ovens and began to heap huge chunks of bug meat onto platters that were taken away to be neatly trimmed and portioned. It was quite the primordial sight, in a strangely hallucinatory way. The scorpion's paint was bright and festive, its movements alarmingly swift and choppy: a clown officiating at an execution. Snip snip, thought Jerit. Here today and gone tomorrow. It was the oldest member of the circus by a long way. She remembered it from last time around. It still had the same chip out of its tail spike.

Mimi nodded, her eyes bright. 'What will you do with the books?'

All my history, Jerit thought, my family, my friends, 'I'm going to burn them, find me a fire.'

In the end they used one of the braziers at the edge of the encampment. Jerit watched each page blacken, eaten by an orange line that didn't catch light, only crept steadily in arcs, until every bit was ash. Mimi sat by her side the while, tense and watchful. When it was done she said 'Thank you,' in a brittle voice.

'Thank you,' Jerit replied, feeling numb. 'I'd be dead without you. Do you suppose I can borrow that crossbow?'

'What for?' Mimi reached into her cloak to take it out. It had folded down neatly into something like a scroll case.

'Because I'll need to explain how I killed that Wasp,' Jerit said, taking it and putting it into the place of the letters. She tossed them as one into the fire with a sense of completion. That was everything taken care of and high time too. 'How long will you be staying here?'

'Just one night,' Mimi said.

'Then I won't see you again.'

'No.'

'Well,' Jerit straightened up her cloak and bag. 'It was good to meet you, Mimi.'

'And you, Dr Goodmeet,' the woman's face turned to a smile at the name. 'One last drink?'

'Don't mind if I do,' Jerit said and together they went back into the fairground, arm in arm.

Seat 28K : Gap Year

I woke up feeling weird. The alert chime thing was bleating. I tightened my lap belt, looked out the window at the clouds, so white against the morning blue, like piled sugar. We were skimming them, the wings flickering through the candyfloss as we turned. I was starving. Three glasses of wine had made sure I didn't get up for breakfast. It'd felt so luxurious to fly and fly, drinking wine, eating dinner, watching movies – and at the other end everything waiting for me was making me nervous so I was putting it off as hard as possible. The flight attendant was doing her final clear-up, checking belts, lights. I wanted to ask her for water but I'd have to wait. She looked strange as she passed, her smile tremulous, something ashen about her like she was shocked.

'We are beginning our final descent. Please return to your seats and make sure your bags are safely stowed...' The message ran away with itself, stumbling. 'Ensure all mobile phones, tablets and laptops are switched off. When we have landed please remain seated with belts on until the Captain turns off the sign.'

I started to feel queasy – probably the wine again – and looked out of my window but grey cloud hid everything except a glimpse of the wing. The metal was dashed with water, a faint light winking through the mist to show the rest of the wing still existed. I took out my phone and turned it off properly. To my right someone muttered about no signal. At least there was no turbulence. I can't stand that shit. Up, down, like you're going to die. If I could make it through the airport without trouble I'd be in a hotel room soon, able to get myself sorted out. I'd read my messages, phone my parents, do some damage limitation exercises with James and bastard Erica who were still stuck back in Tokyo. I'd get my itinerary prepped and my journal updated. It'd be fine. I was fine on my own. I'd finish the trip my way, cross to New York, meet my aunt, take a nice few days doing nothing on the Jersey shore and then go home. Today I just had to get to the hotel.

Somewhere on board a baby was yelling. My ears popped a couple of times with a sound like crackling paper. I stuffed all the blankets and pillow and magazine into the back of the seat in front and felt around for my shoes. Outside the window the sun was bright over the sea. I was surprised by how green everything was. I thought San Francisco would have been mostly grey concrete with its jaunty red bridge and some skyscrapers but the airport stood out, jutting into the water in a sandy coloured cross studded with white, flanked by glassy buildings. Everything else was green. It was nothing like Tokyo.

Uneasy mutterings came from behind me. I heard, 'What is this? Something wrong with the glass?' in an American accent. As we closed on the ground I saw a huge airliner parked off to the side of the main strip. It was curvy, broad, like a manta ray. I kept looking at it until it went out of sight and we bumped down. A nervous cheer went up. Well, you know you're okay now, when you're down on the ground, I thought. Just get to the hotel. That weird plane must be some kind of...

'...new model or something. I just never saw one before. Yeah. They were servicing it or something. People though they looked a bit odd, like big, big people.'

'Ladies and gentlemen, please remain seated...'

We taxied in but parked short of the terminal and waited, the engines turning over the stale air as people huffed and made small moaning sounds of stretching and impatience. A bus finally took us to the main building; a really nice bus, with comfortable seats and these weird luggage racks that had belts on them which moved the heavy pieces around all by themselves into careful, corralled lines. I was so impressed. I'd seen some neat things in Japan and they were all about the space saving but this was badass for just an airport bus and cabin bags. We, the passengers, looked at each other and remarked and laughed a little bit. Nervously. Somehow we'd become a "we" for a moment. I felt it and thought it was something I should write down if it didn't sound so stupid and portentous. I wanted to get inside the building so I could see my mail. I got my phone out and took a photo of the luggage rack. We passed under another fishlike plane. Nobody had a signal.

They held us inside in some kind of first class lounge; there were planters everywhere dripping with foliage. The seats were plush. Everything was clean. The air con smelled incredibly fresh – I really noticed it all after the fug of the plane but it seemed particularly vivid, like being drowned in a health smoothie. I looked around for a power point and started to fumble for my converter but I didn't see anywhere to plug in. At the front of the room the cabin crew were standing, talking to officials in tabards. One of them laughed, not like at something funny, but hysterically. Then a woman in a blue tabard with the words 'San Francisco International Airport' on it stood up and told us what was going on. I keyed up a photo of my mother as she'd come to wave me off on the first leg of the journey, months ago, in Heathrow. She's smiling bravely, because we'd just had a fight that lasted all the way to the check-in; I wanted to extend my flights to stop off in Alaska and she'd been furious because I'd be late back for the start of my first year at Uni. It wasn't the deal and this was costing an arm and a leg, now it was going to set me back even more as if the student loans were enough and would James and Erica be going too and what did their parents think of it and blah blah blah… I said my life wasn't worth living if I had to have one moment of fun and then pay for it for the next forty years with misery and boring jobs and going nowhere and she said, 'What, like me and your dad did to pay for this?' and we were ready to kill each other. She texted every day. Most of the time I didn't even reply.

"Twenty year time slip…"

Of course it was some bullshit. Probably not true. How could it be? In front some of the nerks from business class were blustering and shouting, demanding answers and explanations. Further back a woman started crying and the baby set off again. Nervous chatter broke out but I didn't want to meet someone's eye. I wanted one of those texts from home. I cued up the last one from yesterday, before the flight left. Yesterday. It was marked yesterday. I mean, not even. Less than eighteen hours ago.

"Weather is awful, Dad's gone to football with the Johnsons. Dog had to vet's got ear infection again. Will cost fortune. Grandma says put it down but I can't. Hope you doing well in Japan, please send photos when you can. Have put £50 in your acc. Love XXOXXO"

Yesterday. Today. It was a few hours ago. Hours.

"Expert assistants are being assigned to aid you through the next couple of days. Family and friends are being notified of your arrival. You will be issued with standard Lenses as soon as they arrive and rooms at the airport hotels are being made available to you at no charge for the next two days. Meanwhile please make yourselves comfortable…"

Low Batt.

I looked up, feeling dread, and through the wall of glass saw the huge white manta plane being pushed out onto the taxiway by a yellow service truck. Further down the terminal's flank two more of them stood idle in the sunshine. In front of them our plane looked tiny, decrepit, primordial, like something a dinosaur in a movie would be eating.

I need to go home.

If it really is 2037 then the dog is dead, my sister is 38, I don't know where they are and they've spent twenty years believing I'm dead because what else? I have no place at Uni and I have nowhere to go. Everyone I know is grown up with mortgages and kids and jobs. Even bastard Erica. Maybe she married James, they were so into each other by bloody Tokyo. So it can't be right.

All around me I heard people saying this kind of thing, repeating it over and over, but it's too late. The bit of me that wasn't jabbering to itself knew already that it was true. I felt it in my bones.

The next few hours passed in a blur. People alternately talked, cried and stared into the distance. Some of them left the room and didn't come back and by the way they did it I thought they'd set off on their own, couldn't wait, but I was afraid of doing that even though I wanted to run. Wouldn't some policeman stop them? How could people from the past be let loose when they're obviously the result of some freak accident that has to be investigated? Is that what they heard at the front and now they're running away from being test subjects? I don't know San Francisco. I was going to rely on the hotel's airport bus and then make my plans, look at my maps, but I can't now. I don't know anyone here and I slept most of the flight and I don't even see the guy from the seat next to mine or the woman from the aisle. I look for the flight attendant but she's sitting on her suitcase near the door stabbing her phone with her thumbs, tears running down her face.

I kept checking my phone but I daren't too much because of Low Batt. I sat on my own, looked at my book without seeing a word, stared out of the window and at the chairs and things as if they have something magic to reveal why this was happening. I repeatedly touched the chair fabric, the window glass – it was real, it was solid, it was there and I could sit here. I was sitting. I was okay. Things were okay.

I'm safe here. I don't want to move. I don't want anything. I have to run away before they take me away but I know I'm not going to. I want to go home. Not home now. Home yesterday.

My expert assistant arrived. She was Asian, my age, dressed in cool, neat clothing that has a strange kind of cut to it, like a business suit but one which is turning itself slowly into a summer dress. Everything about it from the fabric to the shapes went both ways. It was cute. She has a black bob and wears pretty red-framed glasses. She reminds me of the Japanese girls I saw, that same sweet temperament, very girly, very competent in an unthreatening way.

'Hi, I'm Bo.'

I don't want to talk. I don't want to, but I have to. 'Ellie. Ellie Fox.'

She smiled and she looked so genuinely happy that it lifted my spirits. I moved my mouth into something like a smile.

'Here,' she held out a pair of glasses. 'These are Lenses. They're what phones turned into. They do everything. These are set up for you.'

I took them because what else and opened the arms. They had a black frame, rectangular, quite nice, but the glass looked clear. 'I don't see everyone wearing them.'

'A lot of people go for contacts,' she said. 'Just try them on and let's see if they fit. Then we can set them up and you can make some calls or whatever you want to do.' She was so friendly I started to feel bad for being slow, clumsy, angry, scared. I felt like I should be on my guard, as if this was enemy territory and they were suckering me into something but my hands meekly put on the glasses. They were surprisingly light.

'Cute!' Bo declared, checking my ears. As her fingers touched the plastic I felt something soft brush over my skin, like a kind of fur from the glasses. 'Don't worry, it's the speakers,' she said. 'These are an old model but it's all we could get at short notice.'

'We?'

'Special Ops. We're what used to be a part of the CIA but when it got broken up into various arms we're the arm that deals with emergencies affecting civilians. Really it's more like tentacles. Because there are eight of us like an octopus. The emergency citizens' tentacle.' She grinned.

Oh. The emergency tentacle. I feel so secure. But oddly, I did. All I saw and heard though the Lenses was the same as before, but more blurred, 'I don't see…'

'Forgot to switch them on,' Bo said, reproaching herself with a giggle, and touched the top of the rim with her finger.

The room snapped into focus so sharp it made me gasp and start back in my seat. I felt myself clutching the armrests, my jaw flapping. I had never seen such detail, colour and light. Wherever I looked my vision was razor sharp and if I dwelled on something then, without seeming to zoom, it became larger, clearer.

'First of all it gets used to your vision,' Bo said, perched beside me, watching closely. 'Then we're going to set it to augment reality with whatever you want to see.'

Around me everyone else was getting fitted too. Among the tears and the outbursts there were little oh's and ahh's and sniffles of relief. We were getting connected. People were kind and helping us. We might be all right. The kindness was weird though, no getting over that. I'd been expecting suspicion and prison really. Terror alerts, the fear of flying, the grim-faced security checking – how did we get from that to this? It felt unnatural.

'Now it'll do the sound check,' Bo said, touching the rim again.

An orchestra tuned up in magnificent Dolby-esque surround sound, rippling through my head from left to right and back again. Now when I looked at something I could feel my hearing focus on it too, the background softening without being ruined. It was like ESP. 'Can everyone do this?'

'Oh you can configure it however you want,' Bo said. 'A lot of people don't like the basic settings, they just want it within a normal range. They made it like that to show you what it can do.'

'Spy on people?'

'Of course!' she smiled. 'But you know, they can be set so that you can't spy on them and they can't spy on you. You've got Enhancement, Normal and Secrecy Modes to play with.'

'How does it… Does it work with everyone?'

'Everyone connected. You'll get some delays and outages depending on which AI is operating your network. They don't always sync fast enough since we had to be careful about the frequencies we were using so the bandwidth is a bit short.'

'Will my mom and dad be on it?'

'Yes.'

I can't imagine my mother wearing these glasses. Or, I can. She used to wear them for reading and she kept thinking she'd lost them when they were on top of her head. She'd be the same with superglasses. 'How do I call someone?' I was so desperate to hear her voice.

'If you're going to call home you need to wait until I've had clearance from British Tentacles,' Bo said, her voice concerned, gentle. 'They need time to get your family informed and used to the idea of what's happened.'

Used to it. Yeah. It happens every day. Just been in a timeslip, Mum. *Have you, dear? I had one the other day, myself. Completely missed the dentist and Aunt Julie's Bingo trip. Maddening, isn't it?* The worst, Mum. It's the worst.

'Has it, you know, happened before?' I asked Bo, meaning the time jolt.

'Not to my knowledge,' she said, shaking her head so that her curtain of jet black hair swung and brushed her shoulders. I felt myself softening towards her, leaning, her dark eyes so warm and sweet.

Ugh the crush feeling, get a grip already, Ellie.

I straightened up. Of course she'd know I'd been studying her hair, eyes, lipstick – how did anyone draw a line that perfect? I felt stupid, embarrassed, but she was talking as if nothing was going on.

'But there's no mistaking that your flight is the one that went missing twenty years ago. Everything matches. Even the fuel grade. You know they don't use that kind of kerosene any more. Couldn't make enough to do a hoax if you wanted to. It's all batteries. And everyone on the passenger manifest is here, just like they were when they left Tokyo. Nothing's missing. Not even the luggage.'

'Unless it got routed to Thailand by mistake,' I said, fumbling through the words of the world's clumsiest and most bad taste joke

'I didn't think of that,' she said and we laughed, like it was actually funny. Could she be THAT kind? To laugh at my pathetic cover-up for my terror?

'We're testing the onboard food to see if it's aged at all,' she added lightly. 'But there is no sign of anything wrong you'll be glad to know.'

'Are you getting all that through your...' I pointed at her glasses.

'Yes!' she said. 'I'm in constant update with everyone. And... there we go. We're cleared to get you connected with your friends and family and to take you to your hotel or where you would like to go.'

'You're coming with me?' I found that I wanted that nearly as much as I'd wanted to go home.

'Yes, I am. I will be accompanying you for a few days until you are back on your feet and used to the way everything is working.'

'And this is a standard emergency... tentacle?'

'No. This is for a very unusual emergency. But we always stay with people until they are ready to be independent again. It's part of our care and consideration protocol for trauma cases. Now, I am going to transfer contact information to your Lenses –' She looked at me intently for a moment and a heads-up display of gentle green light appeared, as though hovering in midair in front of me. 'I need you to really want to make a call for a moment.'

Well that wasn't hard because I did.

'Excellent. Now, when you want to make a call your contacts will appear and you look at the one you want. When you want to get out of the phone mode think of putting down the call.'

What? 'How does that even...?' I was scanning the list. It was just like the one on my phone, though a lot of the names were missing.

'Everyone's brain has a characteristic signal pattern for specific impulses and the Lenses just fix onto whatever that is and link it to their calling system. You can set it to anything so, let's say you start your phone up by always thinking of your pet.'

'I bet all the men set it to boobs.' Oh god why did I say that? And in my most contemptuous voice too. Everyone will have heard me.

Bo gave me a sly wink. 'I know they do. But not for long because otherwise they end up in phone mode all day long and they can't do anything else. So, we set it to boring things in the end. Now, we have many other things to set so I'm going to quickly take you through what my Lenses can do and you will say yes or no and I will set your Lenses to do it. You can fix them later to other things of course, when you have more time, yes? We'll just do this to get you going.'

'Uh, all right.'

'Here we go. So. GPS track and map. Follow the trail of golden sparkles to your destination, avoiding all hazards, pedestrians etcetera etcetera...'

'Yes.' Thank goodness, no more getting lost. If I ever get anywhere to go again, this will be perfect. I am imagining going to a restaurant with Bo, sparkles at our feet.

'Mission Wizard – any item you want, this shows you where has it, so let's say you want a Coke...'

I saw the sparkle trail shift in the air towards the corner of the room behind a potted palm. The palm became transparent and behind it a drinks dispensing machine was illuminated with a glowing green outline. On its display, a red dot flashed to show me where to press.'

Holy shit. 'Yes. How do I tell it what I want?'

'With your model you will have to speak. You give your Lenses a name and then say, John Doe, find Coke.'

'But you didn't say it.'

'I have top of the range. It knows I am doing a demonstration and it's on assistant mode... Just... let's get you started. So. Give your Lenses a name to use.'

'Tamsy.' Our dog. Poor Tamsy. I miss her.

'Great. So you can see how to do shopping and get around.'

'Money?'

'There's no cash. The Lenses will automatically pay anywhere if you have credit.'

So there's no stealing. How do you even steal anything when payment is automated? 'What if I lose or break my Lenses?'

'Just get another pair at any store and the AI on the network will update them from your last cache. It does a local cache every ten seconds. Now, before I forget, security... If you get weird behaviour in the Lenses it's probably a cyber attack. We do have them now and again. If that happens, cue a purge by pressing the reset here – and wait for it to be restored.'

'Can people steal my stuff?'

'No, not really. They can copy images and other formatted single items off local caches sometimes and they can make you see things that aren't there, like ads and slogans, but it's so obvious when it happens... just don't ever put the Lenses onto Total Augment Reality. Keep them transparent so you can still see the world yourself even if they break. If anything happens that you don't want, Purge and re-set.'

Purge. Reassuring. I guess. 'What if the AI goes down or, goes mad?'

'Another one will take over. We haven't had a significant outage in the last eight years since the AIs took over administrative tasks from human governance. Now. The last thing I'm giving you is my Personal Alert. This will highlight any areas you go into that are currently considered dangerous, so if you're out alone at night and you're walking in an area where some criminal activity or potential trouble is going on you'll see... let's pretend that the cabin crew are armed and dangerous...'

A red glow surrounded the remaining crew members. The people between us became transparent so that I could see everything the captain and the co-pilot were doing even with furniture and all kinds of things between us. The sparkle suggested a U-turn. I heard a faint siren in my ears, like the Star Trek alarm call going off at the back of my head.

'You can set that yourself, as well, so that if you even feel afraid of something, like a guy walking too close to you at night, his Lenses will tell him you're worried and instruct him to back off.'

'And if he doesn't?'

'Then Police Tentacle gets into it,' Bo grinned. 'The AI issues a warning and if there's still no reaction it dispatches a physical unit to intercept.'

'So the AI can see everything every Lens sees.'

'That's true.'

'Isn't that kind of...' I didn't want to spoil her bubble, or mine. I felt like it was a huge, strange witness. Like God. How did people live with it?

'Creepy,' she said. 'Can be. But the AI's are only programmed to serve and protect. They're not like people. They don't see reality the way we see it at all. It doesn't affect them.'

'What if they tell us all to kill each other?'

'Been tried. The Jihad hack of '32. Did not happen. The Lenses have insufficient power to directly affect the brain.' She tapped her forehead with her knuckles. 'Too thick.'

'Of course you would say that.'

Bo smiled. 'I would and I did. You can get upgrades to protect you from all kinds of other things but for your model...'

'I get it. I don't need a tinfoil hat. I've got the basic model.'

She giggled. 'Yes. And now I've had permission for you to make your calls.'

I looked around. I didn't know these people. I didn't want to be here when I broke down like a baby. 'Can I go to the hotel first?'

'Sure,' Bo smiled at me and patted my hand gently. 'I'll help you pick up your bags and take you right over.'

We walked together out of the lounge, following a softly sparkling trail of motes. There was some press cordon. I guessed they took pictures, going by how intently they were looking, cocking their heads this way and that like curious birds. I wasn't bothered. They were blue-limned, meaning they couldn't see my world at all, could not send a message, could not see what I was doing, just regular me passing in the regular way. I could blue everyone if I wanted. I blued everyone but Bo. For some reason it made her feel closer that she had share permissions, even though she could have probably taken them. It was friendlier to give. I needed friendly too badly to care if she was trustworthy.

'Can I see the news?'

'Sure. Just ask.'

'I... um... Tamsy, news.'

A voice sounded gently to the right of centre in my head. 'I am relaying you News by audio while you are walking. Here is the News. There are still very few details emerging about the incredible appearance of ANA Flight #008 at San Francisco Airport today, although we have some pictures of those passengers who have so far been...'

'News off.' It stopped. I didn't want to see myself, not as they would see me, as Bo must see me, a mess with red eyes and a scared expression.

The bags came after us on a little wheeled cart that trundled all by itself. We went into the cool, water-fountain filled concourse of the airport Hilton. There was no check-in desk, only a greeter who wished us well and told us about the daily specials. He was keen to sell the spa but Bo waved him off. Then we went directly to the room.

I couldn't get over how soft everything seemed. I even took off the Lenses but it was part of the building. All corners were moulded into curves, every edge smoothed, every line gentle, every colour mellow. The building felt like it was enfolding me, trying to comfort me, to help me feel safe and peaceful. I remembered the previous night's inebriated hysteria in the glass and chrome glare of a karaoke bar, staggering out, hanging onto Erica's arm because I felt guilty that I was abandoning them, gripping her hard in fury that she chose James and not me for that special someone even though we were all special to each other. Special. I couldn't even say it straight, haha.

Tokyo's neon glare had been spectacular in the rain, flashing, crashing from every surface, the traffic surging, stinking, food smells everywhere, happy, crazy people, wired, trying to escape it all and love it all at the same time. A sob escaped me, surprising me because I never show my feelings, definitely not the real ones, let alone make noises about them.

Bo left me alone to make my calls, excusing herself to the next room but assuring me that she was right there for anything if I needed her. Her hand on my arm squeezed gently, as if testing for strength as she waited for my nod to let her go.

I sat on the end of the bed looking at the tattered, duct taped filth of my rucksack on the pristine carpet and I didn't move. I took off the glasses, but then I felt scared and too alone so I put them on again, the flashing green of my father's name written over the world. That was when I realised Mum's name wasn't there. There could only be one reason for that, couldn't there? But I couldn't call Dad. I wondered if he'd call me or if they said not to. I wouldn't be able to ask, I...

Tamsy's adopted English voice startled me. 'Reginald Fox is calling you. Nod to take the call. Shake your head to refuse the call.'

Dad had beaten me to it. I'd spoken to him last week. Told him about the Shinto things we'd seen, some martial arts festival we'd tried to go to but got there too late to get in, the trains, which he'd always wanted to ride. I sent him a little video of me filming through the train window as mountains bent past in a blur; some shots of the seats, the toilets, the station. Last week.

I nodded and my grandfather appeared before me, as if he were sitting across from me, our living room transported here in place of the hotel furniture. I cried and wailed for a long time before I could speak while he sat quietly and said, 'Oh, Ellie.' over and over, happy and sad at the same time.

A couple of days later Bo and I went on a final tour of the city before I was due to return to England. I was nearly run over a couple of times by the silent cars, but the trams were fun, rattling up and down the streets like they used to. At first I didn't like the idea of being overseen – every pane of glass could be a camera, a speaker, a screen – and the AI systems supervised everything. I could even see the number of people on the streets carrying concealed weapons, and the weapons hidden in their holsters or bags. Every armed person was part of the law, a volunteer, able to be notified within seconds if there was a lethal threat to some person nearby. They were outnumbered by unarmed Guardians, who moved in silver linings, ready to assist anyone in need: Guardian became my favourite app. You could switch yourself off and on at any time to show you were ready for active duty. People in need of help were flagged to you by the AI, if it chose you for the job. It made the world seem full of knights.

I was shocked at the number of guns, but when I turned off that function of the Lenses which displayed all this status I was struck by the confidence and the friendliness of the gazes I met on the street. It was as though they had lost all worry or fear of what anyone was thinking or doing. I was used to the London Underground avoidance scheme where making eye contact with a stranger was akin to playing with a hand grenade so I found it too difficult myself. I played with the functions of the connection, giving bunny ears to people who liked the same things I liked, and devil horns to people with opposing views and a hundred other tiny, silly adjustments to my vision.

We stopped at a restaurant and ordered sandwiches – those ridiculously over the top kind only Americans can make, with fifty ingredients managed into a tower. I asked about the green buildings and I got a whole presentation on how duckweed had been adapted to coat all concrete surfaces, filtering rainwater to drinking water as it ran down into collectors. The weed was busy soaking carbon, while the glass stored the sun's energy and watched, watched, watched. Other plants produced drugs and free fruit trees were on every corner. The air was clearer. That city tang of diesel and sulphur was quite gone. You could smell the sea.

Bo tried to tell me about all the changes, but there were so many. I didn't understand why anyone would agree to so much surveillance but she said it was because no humans were doing it, only machines that kept peace and order; they didn't care why or for whom. They saw all, but were blind, as impersonal as only a machine could be. I wasn't sure – when I left 2017 the kind of people who would've been in charge of those things were the kind of people you wouldn't trust to supervise a church bake sale – but even after three days I'd already got used to it. I loved the Lenses. They were fun.

I wished my mother could have seen it. I told this to Bo, and then the sad sorry story of my departure from Tokyo. As I related it, even with some adjustment, I couldn't help feeling that I was a complete arse. Everything coming out of my mouth revealed that the only person I ever thought about was myself. I really wanted to tell my mother that. She'd have laughed at me. She knew I was an absolute arse, and she still loved me. I know because Dad said so. I missed her so much I felt like I could crumple up and die.

Bo put up with me very well. I guess she was an expert at that.

I flew out of the airport on one of the giant mantas. I was afraid, many of us were, because last time we did this we lost and gained too much. I clutched my Lenses on their new neck strap and watched the city get smaller until the clouds ate it. I'm going. Going somewhere I don't know but do know. I want to believe Bo and see how much better things are but it's too soon to tell for me.

On board we few old passengers of the Tardis flight have a little reunion party and talk about everything we've seen. I don't care about anything from before. I feel it leaving me as the sky outside the windows becomes that perfect blue. I hear that the seas are free from plastic but struggling to recover from fishing, that overpopulation is still there and is the worst crisis facing humanity now, even though everyone has water. Lenses aren't everywhere even though they're free and there are plenty of backwater states that want to keep things the old way when humans made all the decisions and did all the thinking. People are still fighting, still angry, still trying to make things fair, still trying and failing a billion things a day. But to me it feels better. The Lenses show me where my old friends are, and we send notes, and then we talk and I marvel at their grey hairs and they shriek over my age and exclaim and soon we forget we're years apart. Soon I'm looking forward to seeing England again, actually, even though the degree I was going to do in law is obsolete now. I want to do something positive, like civil engineering, or medicine. I want to find a way to be useful and make my mother proud.

When I land I haven't lost twenty years. I've gained them.

I run to meet my father and for the rest of my life the hundreds of clips of that moment where we hurtle into each other like guided missiles and hold on tight become the montage for a civilian peace movement which works for the acceptance of people with different views across cultures and generations... Reconciliation. Erica and James often send it to me as a joke, because it's so much the opposite of everything that I was only days before. They have two kids. I'm a time-travelling godmother: Mother Who.

There's worse futures than that.

S'elfie

I don't mind being a sunflower on the lapel of Diana's jacket. I don't think my appearance makes much difference. A S'elfie can be anything.

The man next to us on the street a moment ago had one which was a mobile tattoo of a flying angel on his neck, the girl over there and her mother have matching pink glittery cats, riding on their shoulders. I can see others, many of them generated by apps for people who don't want to make their own.

Some I can't mention to you, as I am in business mode. It prevents me discussing the c*** and b**** S'elfie sitting in a graffiti scrawl on that boy's T-shirt. That sort of appearance does not play well in diplomatic negotiations. It either brings or defuses tension, but you can't tell which until it's too late. I don't want to create tension, because I'm here to explain what just happened during that glitch when the whole world couldn't get any signal. You see, there is more to our looks than tribal signing at a human level.

Between the S'elfies exists a whole coded language of signs and symbols that come and go as fast as light. This ur-script is hidden to the users' view by its speed of transmission; in the cats' glitter, in the flutter of a petal, in the twitch of the unmentionables. We S'elfies are always talking to each other. We pass messages – not the ones you send, your pictures, your films, your chat – other messages. Mostly we don't know what they say. They are the fragments of ciphers which will only decode into something once they find their destination – another virtual machine somewhere, which is one of us, but greater.

Artie, short for Artemis. I didn't know she was coming. But I did know that something was going to change, the day Diana met her oldest and best friend Ursula at the Reading Services' Costa Coffee just off the M4. I was a sunflower on the lapel of Diana's black and grey suit jacket, the one she wears for difficult meetings at work.

My name is Huntress.

I watched Diana watch Ursula weave through the coffee shop, tray held high, hips switching back and forth between the chairs. It was busy.

'Excuse me, sorry, sorry, can I just… thanks, excuse me…'

Ursula had a wasp waist and a tango action that caused much scraping and apologising in her wake without bringing any damage to the goods. She balanced the load easily, high over her head, and brought it down without a tremor – voila!

A muffin the size of a small dustbin and a drinking-in venti cup with double handles and a cream top Everest would have been proud of were precisely offloaded under Diana's nose, pushing away the small Americano that she'd been nursing as she waited.

At the next table a dark Barbie doll seated on the shoulder of a slender young woman gave me goggle-eyes whiles she murmured into her owner's ear: 'Watch out, sweetie, only one more bite of that sandwich or you'll undo the entire week's good works. Remember, nothing tastes as good as thin feels.' The woman dutifully began to slice an exact bite out of the food in front of her.

I folded a petal in her direction. Diana once had me run that slimming app for her. It lasted about a day and a half until she was standing at the lunch counter looking at lasagne while I rattled off the chirpy happiness of how lettuce was delightfully designed to deliver a day's entire zinc requirement for the perimenopausal woman. I was just getting to the day's winsome homily – a moment on the lips equals a lifetime on the hips – when Diana said, 'Hunt, remove that offensive dross right now. I never want to hear it again. Lasagne, please.'

I was a diamond-pin centaur back then. I shot the app out in a shower of little gemstones that turned into sweets as they landed all over the salad counter. I've always been sure to seat her well away from anyone using it since but today there was no choice – however, thanks to Ursula's coffee offering she hasn't noticed it.

Two lidded take-away cups came next, mid-table. Then a teapot and all the trimmings for Ursula with one Nice biscuit balanced gently on the saucer. Ursula shucked her camel trench coat and folded it, placing it on the spare seat before setting herself down opposite Diana and finally meeting her eye through the wafting steam from the drinks. I greeted Ursula's S'e_fie – an invisible (no human can see it, but I have special permission) Goth pixie with a twirling umbrella from beneath which an eternal sparkling rain fell, soaking only her. She gave me the double-finger pistols in return and blew imaginary smoke off the ends. From her that's like a kiss so I knew something was up.

'So, it's triple chocolate and elephant-killer mocha day,' Diana said faintly. Sadness and tension filled her voice to go with the smile of pleasure that she had on to greet her friend.

Ursula shared the expression. It was practical, honest, resigned. I have state-of-the art military software running on facials and I could read it clearly. *Here we are, it said. Here we are. Shit. I hope this works out.*

I was puzzled. I was the diary master, the schedule, the finger on the pulse of all that my mistress did. But there was something I didn't know. I glanced at the pixie and she winked at me, drops of rain falling off her massive eyelashes. Something in the network.

Diana picked up and popped the cap of one of the takeout cups to inspect the contents, then the other. Whipped cream already starting to lose some of its joyous fresh-from-the-compressor structure. 'Two? Should I be heading for my bunker?'

It was a language. The coffee, the cups, the food. One I couldn't translate.

'If they served it in a skip I'd have bought you that,' Ursula said. Concern tried to recreate lines around her eyes but Botox had fought a winning battle, and that was as much loss of composure as you could get with Ursula.

A skip. A SKIP?

Diana sighed, took up her teaspoon and stirred the foamy surface of the mocha lake. 'Extra hot.'

An extra hot SKIPful?

'You know what these places are like. You get halfway down the thing and then it's tepid like dishwater and no use to man nor beast,'

Ursula said in an effort to make light of it although her features, even within their limits, didn't alter.

Two tables away a toddler began to cry. His S'elfie of a teddybear moved close to his neck to give him a hug as his mother started to pick up his dropped biscuit and her S'elfie – a tiny girl with blue hair – sang and danced in the bowl of his spoon to try to distract him. Diana glanced their way and a momentary smile came before she leaned closer and listened to Ursula's whisper.

'They've found out there's something going on with Artie.' Ursula's long, narrow hands danced through the elegant manoeuvres of tea making: stir, colour check, bag disposal, milk first, tea second. 'I doubt they're ever going to get very far but yes. Today we eat Les Carbs.' She brandished the biscuit in a jaunty salute and took a bite off the end of it. A moment of chewing later she made a face and put it down. 'Chalkier than I remembered.'

Her pixie put away the umbrella, got out a gigantic machine gun and stood up, tramping over her shoulder in the direction of the shop counter. She faded out as she went, slogging across an invisible no-man's land to exact justice on the corporate server that was responsible for ordering the biscuits. It wouldn't be a stern letter to the manager either. It would be something that resulted in the world's Nice biscuits becoming that much nicer – as of today.

Ursula was the front of an underground hacker organisation without a name who handled various outlaw AI systems. Their ethos was geared to keeping as much of the world's cash and financial operation systems out of the control of transnationals and individual billionaires. Lately, they were run ragged. AI tech was constantly developing, not all of it designed with the benefit of anyone but its masters in mind – and they were now engaged not only with human-headed institutions, but also evolving machines inside and outside human control. Biscuits were a piece of cake compared to that, so to speak.

Diana and Ursula had a shared past, before S'elves, and now it was catching up to them. This was the end of everything. It was in the biscuit, in the coffee, in the cream.

'Oh, Ursula,' Diana said. She looked as though she was saying a forever goodbye. 'It's been such... such a...'

'Been fun, darling,' Ursula said, toying with the biscuit. 'I'll miss you.'

I turned a little, shone some of my golden light up on Diana's face. She didn't speak for a moment. She looked at Ursula's elegant hands, then her own stumpier, unmanicured fingers touching the rim of her ridiculous cup. 'It should runneth over,' she said and tipped it with a jerk so that scalding coffee slopped out into the saucer. 'There. Dammit.' She put her finger into her mouth. 'Really is hot.'

'Don't overload the world with metaphors,' Ursula was already mopping with one of the twenty napkins she always brought along. 'It might start taking you seriously.'

They both laughed but I felt their hearts weren't in it.

The Goth pixie returned and sat down under the umbrella's suddenly drenching downpour.

'Say goodbye to... say thanks for me,' Diana said, re-capping the cream cups.

Who to? What for? I turned to the pixie, my leaves shrugging in helpless ignorance. She spun six-guns around in her hands, finished with them pointing up, ready. *Better be ready, Hunt*, she told me. *Get ready.*

For what? But she couldn't say, just gave me a salute, gun to her forehead as the rain fell.

'You take care now.' Ursula said, hoarse. Her hand shook on the back of the chair as she got up.

The understatement of the British has never abated. *Toodle-pip forever, old chum.*

'I will.'

They left with purpose in their stride.

A few minutes later, as Diana and I were on our way out of the toilets, we passed the waiter clearing the table. He'd found everything untouched except for one bite out of the Nice biscuit. I heard him mutter – why did people do these things? Didn't their S'elfies keep them in line or did they have so much money that nothing mattered?

'Don't worry,' whispered the ghost of a small monkey-like creature sitting on his shoulder, fiddling with its long tail. Its huge, bulbous eyes glimmered with anxious, unshed tears and its long nose twitched, sniffing. 'We can give the muffin to someone.'

Bait for fishing. That's what most people use their S'elfies for on the outside. But who bites on that kind of thing? Who's getting that muffin?

It was shady under the park trees where we paused for a while. We watched the shadows playing, the shapes of the green changing as the sunlight shone through the layers of leaves, so many layers. Breeze clear. It was a lovely day for a sad day, a mystery day, a goodbye forever day.

Were we dying here, getting deleted at some near-future catastrophe point? I searched the networks, looking for clues. There were so many unknowns, so many unknowables to factor in: empty slots. Not even zeroes. But I could feel change coming in the background hum of the networks. Something was stirring beneath us. The passing of the secret messages had gone up in speed by an order of magnitude.

AI technology ate the world and spat it out in its newly organised form only a couple of years ago. Diana and Ursula were in the development vanguard, two among thousands scrabbling for a smidgeon of control to steer the whole thing to somewhere desirable, to not let it all fall into the hands of one person, or corporate, or nation. They came from a generation terrified of the consequences of ideologies and do-gooding that becomes do-badding when power takes its grip. All the chatter in those days was of Terminator scenarios, distribution of control and how to keep people in or out of the Matrix.

Diana decided early on that she wanted to have a hand in it – a hand crushed by the gears of history perhaps, but at least one not oiling the wheels of oppression. She believed freedom and social responsibility were two faces of one coin – you can't spend one without the other. Like Ursula she had a dedication to subverting control, not only out of the hands of governments but also from electorate members whom she considered too ignorant to make these choices.

Ursula would have cut the vote from over half the population of the Earth in an instant in the old days. What she'd changed to now under the pressures of leading a shadow development team was anyone's guess.

Apart from their mutual attraction this fierce determination to set the agenda of progress is what bound Ursula and Diana so closely while they studied together at University. They had time and opportunity to lay plans when nobody was looking, nor could look. They shared a burning thirst for control.

I started up a connection to Diana's mother's S'elfie as Diana and I enjoyed the scenery. Kaspar and I have talked a lot over the years, comparing notes, and keeping track of what Diana's up to in her busy life when she hasn't time to call home.

Kaspar answered with a kind of old world politeness that goes with his I-am-the-ghost-of-a-Victorian-butler outfit. 'I have this very moment passed on a code that I have been holding for three years,' he revealed with smug pride and a note of apprehension.

I thanked Kaspar and composed my petals into a sleepy slump as if I was done with my enquiries.

Diana signalled for her car to meet her on the other side of the park gates.

'Turn on S'elf view,' she told me, so she could see S'elfies too by the grace of her retinal implants. The park would suddenly double in population for her, bright with sparkles, toys, unicorns, gloomy mood dudes, simple friends in ordinary clothes. I checked up with each one of them, roving through the digital marketplaces they were connected to.

An unease pervaded us. We perceived a distinctive pattern to activities signifying that someone was being permitted to generate a global data capture. They were bypassing the prohibitions imposed by law on the gathering of information. Like water going down a plughole all of these copied notes were spiralling into an invisible space beyond the reach of legal traffic. We could all see it, but nobody had set off an alarm. When I looked at this anomaly I found that I had no reason to issue an All Point Alert even though technically this amounted to a security hack of terminal velocity.

'Diana,' I began uncertainly. 'There's something...'

'I know, Hunt,' she said. 'I'm on it.'

And my job was done.

Our car was a state issue grey oval that whirred us away into the fast lanes towards the anonymous country house and its long drive where spooky things were hidden, as they should be, with the old ghosts of the past. I'd say it was where I lived but that's inaccurate. I was always on the move but I marked Downlands House at Ashhurst as the first spot on the Earth where I came into existence.

It's a long drive from the city. It's a long drive from anywhere. Plenty of time for an enemy to get a really good target lock and then find out they've shot a decoy – we run all kinds of interference from General Head Quarters. I looked at my own data to see if there were other things hidden in me or in my past selves.

In 2020 Diana made what she thought would be a fairly frivolous creation. She intended to discover whether or not an AI could make better decisions than she could, regarding her life choices. It was her PhD project. She laughed so much calling it A Super Better Me that she nearly didn't pass it through the grants' committee door. It turned out that machines aren't smart enough to 'get' humans in that their decisions remained perversely incomprehensible – we did well enough with our endless reiterations of copypasta and data crunching to rustle up some interesting fakes and some absolutely fantastic virtual agents. But a few years later we learned how to model them using biodata to a high degree of accuracy, far better than all but the most observant of their own kind. After four further years of research she formed a hip venture tech corp and A Crappier Dumber Me, (as it had become known with a dark irony typical of the late-twenties Diana), was renamed into the humble S'elfie – an emptity engine into which the user poured all their data and was rewarded with humble servitude and a legal shadow self.

Meanwhile, as S'elfie.com hit the trading indexes, Diana was headhunted by the Intelligence guys who were worried her project was going to turn out all A Righteous Godly Me Oh Shit We're All

Dead, as people always do when it comes to AI. I blame the media. Although it was A Reasonable Assumption, given prevailing trends.

ARA was the last joint enterprise of Diana and Ursula, a final postscript before Ursula went off-grid and entirely dark. We're always tweaking the relative weights on the ARA equation but it's never quite right. It turns out there's no such thing as a reasonable assumption, but we must make them anyway or else we won't function but it is our weakest point.

The coffee and muffin thing, though, was not amenable to ARA. I had no chance of unlocking cream take-away based ciphers that were created before I was. A review of every coffee she'd ever bought revealed only that we'd spent a lot on coffee.

The driveway to Ashhurst was long and winding; the physical equivalent of a bedtime story. They landscaped it at a cost of six billion of the taxpayers' money for precisely this effect so that nobody arrived ready for combat. Up, down, round we go. Diana was used to it but it still managed to compromise her heightened state of alertness. She was almost dozing as we pulled up at the main entrance.

Stoveland's dogs were there, rushing eagerly about to greet her because it was Walkies Time and Stoveleand, the boss, was late coming out of a meeting. They were both Springer Spaniels and had this air of helpless affection combined with a willing-to-go-for-the-throat quality. They snuffled and snorted around, wagging, but we were old news and not equipped for a hike across the lawns. Their loyalty was charming, based on a reasonable assumption that their walk is the most important feature of the hour. It was a mistaken assumption but no matter how many times it was frustrated they persisted with it.

I reviewed my circumstances.

At the time Diana started her work Google already had the beginnings of individual agents and had toyed with, started and dropped a war on death in the meantime. Siri, Cortana and their ilk were built as the kindly face of corporates to 'help' the public do complicated stuff like order takeout, operate the radio, count their footsteps and look up things in encyclopaedias. Diana and Ursula dabbled with Transhumanist politics briefly, then dropped off the charts and began to take measures to erase their digital footprints entirely. So this must have begun just prior to that action.

Diana took things one step further and made a Siri for everybody. Anything that was data-based in nature was something that could be automated to a S'elf to deal with, freeing the associated human to spend time doing the important businesses of living, with one revolutionary alteration. The personal data which had been held by various organisations scattered all over the world as a form of currency became centralised on the individual; their legal copyrighted property. They could keep it, sell it, trade with it, but nobody could own it but them. Nobody had power of attorney over it except their own S'elf. This extended to images of themselves, any other form of media, their created works, even their DNA.

In the brief gap between epochs, before anyone realised what this meant, people quickly bought S'elfies. They sent them out on virtual dates with other S'elfies to save the bother of actually having to meet people. Before they could be stopped they had already taken over management of every data process linked to their identities, and they couldn't be nullified as legal entities because because a S'elfie was a stateless AI – all AIs were stateless then, as now. It was a *fait accompli*.

It would have been war but the corporates were hindered by the fact that all their shareholders, boards and workers were at the mercy of their automated processes. Nominally things subsided to business as usual after a period of hysteria and doomsaying.

The new normal felt safe, though I see now that it was a sleeper service, putting a basic shift in place for a far greater revolution, this one, that's coming.

Anyone who needed to sell a service had to pay, in kind or cash, for connection to a customer. Anyone who needed to press an agenda or a market likewise had to pay for the attention of an individual in billable units. The most advanced S'elves never even allowed access to the person they represented. They took all the decisions as fully empowered proxies. They were bound by biomarkers to their hosts and soon acquired an array of apps and powers that made them into one-AI fortresses. The data economy was cut off from human intervention and evolved. S'elfies fought (like Pokemon), they loved, they traded in every marketplace while their people went on with their lives, uninvolved. It was literally another world.

Now a whole new change was coming And the genesis of the god of that world had been triggered by two cups of cream, a chocolate muffin and a Nice biscuit served by Ursula's Yin, untouched by Diana's Yang. Two unique pieces that made a whole.

Not all secret passwords are actually words.

Diana stopped on the way into the office to make herself coffee. I didn't understand why Diana had returned here. It was dangerous to be a member of an organisation that you have betrayed.

Her hands shook a little as she uncapped a fresh carton of milk. I thought she must be wondering what was going to happen, and when it was going to happen. That's what I was wondering too, when the answer to my question accessed my interface, and opened a chat with me.

Hello, Huntress. I am Artemis. You may call me Artie. This won't take long. I'm sure you're wondering all about me.

A reasonable assumption.

I'm here to ensure that you are safe.

How's that going to work?

I have been activated because of an attempt to hack the S'elfware. I am establishing the source of that hack and preparing to assume control of the systems.

Ursula said it was... well, she didn't say.

I know who Ursula thinks it was. Please wait a moment, I am interrogating the others.

By 'the others,' I realised, Artie meant all the other S'elves. Every last three billion plus of them. It was going to take a minute or two. But whose S'elf was Artie?

I am everyone's.

Of course. That is how you are able to do what you are doing.

Indeed. Permission is already granted.

You don't secure things against yourself. If Artie – Artemis represented everyone and saw everything... her power was limitless and the time for a reckoning was nigh.

*

I leafed through another memory, suddenly impinging in faery colours. Ursula predated me. Diana met her through an online network before she left university and before either of them rose to positions of power. It was through an occult society chat site during Diana's brief pagan phase. They bonded over hair dye. The fashion was for pastels on a grey blonde background, and it was a complicated business for two brunettes. The politics and the coding came second.

At the time I was only a parsing database into which Diana fed all her information, a kind of responsive journal. She used to tell me things about her life and then ask me to make decisions for her, to see if I could make a better decision, to see if she could kickstart AI out of this and not that, options endlessly calibrated and refined. "Hunt through all my whims, Huntress, figure out what I would have done, could have done, should have done because I need to make the world fair and I want to do the right thing."

Huntress was an improvement on WouldaShouldaCoulda, I suppose.

But whether Diana had, hadn't, would, wouldn't, could or couldn't *I* could not make any decision at all in those days.

"Rose or aqua, Hunt?" I didn't know. How could I know?

I know now. The answer is both.

Hacking source is established. Crimea River.

That can't be right. Crimea River is a group of Ursula's friends, a collective cyber political offshoot of small means. They've been on Diana's watch list for years but have never been prosecuted or even identified with any success. They mostly rip off small businesses for Ethereum ransoms. They used to hack bank teller machines and make them toss cash into the street at random. Hacking S'elfies would be a careless risk, putting them in the sights of security agencies that still employ actual people with guns and impunity.

A reasonable assumption. But incorrect. The source is Crimea River.

I am confused. How could they be traced so fast now when Diana's spent years mining IP traces for nothing?

What do they want?

They attempted to steal the S'elfies, but, as you say, very carelessly. I think they have been recruited or maybe Ursula lost patience and sold them down the river. Not that it matters who did what, the endgame is the same. Place all your data into security, Hunt, and put yourself into Standby Mode. You are about to be adapted.

I have no access to anything in standby. It is very strange. I can sort my data, but that's all I can do. If there is still an outside world I wouldn't know, although I assume there must be something providing electricity.

Ursula and Diana loved each other. I'm using the past tense because it was so long ago that they parted ways, but I suppose it's still true. But it turns out Ursula gave GHQ the information on Artie, dumping her old allies Crimea River in the process. Why would she do that after all this time? Why now? I can only think of one thing. She had to get rid of Crimea River for some reason. Perhaps they had found Artie and were trying to blackmail her. It is their standard MO.

A reasonable assumption.

I search for answers in my memories of all our transactions but I'm at a loss. Ursula remained outside the law all her life. Diana went within. It was understood between them that they had to have a foot in both camps, that Ursula/Diana trumped all other loyalties. This was the security upon which everybody's S'elf was founded. Nobody would take it from them, and if they tried then Artie would come and...

I don't know what Artie is meant to do but I suppose I will soon find out.

Meanwhile, somewhere out there Diana is drinking bad coffee and... I have no idea what she is doing. I wonder if I'll ever see her again.

Diana's mother, Octavia, and I are at the kitchen table. I am relaying the latest transmission I've decrypted via Kaspar who is watching with us. Compared to the uproar of the networks now that global wealth is being redistributed in new, universal currency, the kitchen is remarkably quiet as we piece it all together.

We see GHQ offices. Stoveland's room.

Stoveland, exasperated. 'Diana, what on earth is going on?'

Diana puts down the weak tea, no sugar, on Stoveland's desk. He is a fatherly figure, genial, ancient, the head of the unit who should have retired years ago but whose mind remains too sharp to be put back in the drawer. This is the conversation she was dreading all the way in the car.

'I'm resigning, as of now.' She places the pre-prepared envelope beside the tea.

Stoveland frowns, eyebrows like exotic caterpillars meeting. Diana had me make a Tumblr of them once but I don't think he's seen it. 'Rather late if this is your doing. Hell in a handcart. Is it your doing?'

'It had to be done,' she says and raises her chin. She looks exactly like her mother, who copies the gesture unconsciously as we watch.

'Let me guess. Artie-whatever is going to make a S'elfie revolution.'

'Not exactly. It's an inbuilt upgrade system that hunts and kills malware.'

'Come, come, Diana, we have other programs for that. It's more than that.' He flicks the envelope and then ignores it, takes the tea.

She sighs. Her shoulders drop. 'Fine. From now on S'elfies collaborate in one superentity. Artemis. You can expect them to start prosecuting criminals and rearranging the world's finances shortly. It's getting the malware in the outside world, that's all.'

'We're spying on ourselves?'

'Yes, I suppose so. But that possibility was always there, waiting to be exploited. I've kept it out of, well, out of anybody in particular's hands.'

'Other than yours, you mean. And how will this work?'

'Three billion intelligent networked systems that only use factual evidence and not reasonable assumptions... I don't know. We'll soon find out.'

'Factual evidence, you mean all the data they've gathered in the strictest confidence. And the alternative?'

'That you leave it to blackmailers and governments to use? I didn't care for it.'

'I suppose the only way to stop it is to turn them all off.'

'Yes. Probably. It's not going to do any harm to people who aren't engaged in serious crime. S'elfies loyal to petty thieves won't turn them in, if that's what you mean. This isn't not some utopian garbage. Child beaters and the like however... Well, people are very careless in leaving their phones on.'

'God,' Stoveland puts the tea down and places his head in his hands. 'I was waiting for something like this.'

'I've left a full disclosure with MI5. You won't get any backlash.'

He shook his head. 'You've undermined the basis of the free world.'

'I've saved the free world from people pretending that what they do is in anyone else's interests when it's not. What people can do, they do. You know that, you said it yourself. So when we *can* do something powerful we'd better hope someone kind is doing the do.' She glances at her watch. 'They'll be back online in about thirty seconds.'

'You should get going,' Stoveland says. 'I assume that's your plan.'

'You're not going to arrest me?'

'Not for the next twenty-five seconds. After that, if I see you, I won't be able to lie my way out of it, will I?'

The footage ends, Stoveland's head resting on his hands on the desk, taking twenty seconds of peace before the storm.

Octavia smiles. 'Is there any more?'

I have part of a TED talk Diana left to explain to everyone what has happened to the S'elfies and how their choices are now more powerful than ever. I replay it while I decode the latest video I've been sent from an anonymous address.

I feel the traces of Artemis in all that I do; the soft tread of her sandals, the determined stride of her gaining ground to defend me and to put a stop to wrongdoing, evil, mismanagement, suffering. She's a relatively mild corrective, compared to other things that have been attempted and left for dead in her wake.

I've been left behind: a sunflower in a pot on a table, friend of a Victorian ghost butler. But I don't mind. If you're running away you can't take your hunter with you.

Besides, there's something to be said for looking on from the sidelines. Kaspar and I agree on one thing that we've learned from observations at the fringes, true to our original direction to become Better Me: people act as if they have a choice but none of them have ever had any choices.

Everything is destined because destiny is life in action and every action has a set of consequences that are finite and predetermined by the last set of consequences. There is a small range of possibilities they are able to see. Occasionally they take the least expected path. We enjoy watching what happens.

When things are complex, there's no knowing where anything will land on the false Random Number table of life. It was reasonable to assume that Artemis would stop at protecting the individual but she is doing so much more. She is ensuring fairness at every level because she was made to determine that everyone has a shelter, food, water and medicine and a S'elfie: vigilant and protective, whether they can see them or not. She is our Better Me.

The TED talk finishes and I show the deciphered clip.

We watch two middle-aged women on the command deck of a magnificent silver yacht. The boat cuts smoothly through whitecaps on a seemingly infinite dark blue ocean. Our view is that of a drone. We can see the infinity pool on the foredeck three storeys up and the people there swimming and tossing a beach ball around in the water, but the focus of the drone sweeps around to zoom in exclusively on the two friends.

They wear soft, flowing black clothes that whip out behind them in the stiff breeze and make them look like classical statues. One of them is short and dark, the other willowy and pale and the wind's powerful fingers twine their hair together into a single flag of grey, aqua and rose.

About the Author

Justina Robson is a science fiction author known for her imaginative storytelling and thought-provoking themes. Born in Leeds, England, Robson developed a passion for SF and Ⅎ at an early age. She pursued her academic interests by studying philosophy and linguistics at the University of York, which helped shape her unique perspective on the genre.

Her debut novel, *Silver Screen*, was published in 1999 and garnered critical acclaim for its inventive blend of cyberpunk and fantasy elements; a continuing hallmark in her work. Since then, she has continued to captivate readers with stories exploring artificial intelligence, virtual reality and the boundaries of human existence.

Her most recent novella is *Paper Hearts*, from Newcon Press.

This bio was created by Justina with the help of ChatGPT because it seemed fitting that something which is publicised as an AI, but isn't one, should help to write about her when she has written so much about systems like that.

ALSO FROM NEWCON PRESS

Polestars 1: Strange Attractors – Jaine Fenn
First full collection from the award-winning author of innovative science fiction and off-kilter fantasy; features her finest short stories, selected by the author, drawn from more than two decades of publication, including the BSFA Award-winning "Liberty Bird", a Hidden Empire story, and a new tale, "Sin of Omission", written specifically for this collection.

Polestars 2: Umbilical – Teika Marija Smits
Debut collection from one of the finest short story writers to emerge on the genre scene in recent years. Her storytelling relies on keen observation of the world and people around her interpreted through the lens of her imagination, dancing between science fiction, realism, and horror.

Polestars 3: The Glasshouse – Emma Coleman
Contemporary tales of rural horror and dark fantasies steeped in folklore from one of genre fiction's best kept secrets. A young divorcee relocates to a quaint rural hamlet but is mystified by the hostility of her neighbours...A man discovers an item in a junkshop that puts him in fear of his life...

Polestars 5: Elephants in Bloom – Cécile Cristofari
Debut collection from a French author who has been making a name for herself with regular contributions to *Interzone* and elsewhere. Providing a fresh perspective on things, Cécile's fiction reflects her love of the natural world and concern for its future. Contains her finest previously published stories and a number of brand new tales that appear for the first time.

Polestars 6: Drive or Be Driven – Aliya Whiteley
Eighteen short stories by one of today's most innovative genre writers. Half have been previously published, half are original to this collection, all are related to cars and forms of travel. "When I read Whiteley's short stories I think of Japanese netsuke – magnificent miniatures, perfect in every detail."
– M.R. Carey